CHASING SHADOWS

CHASING SHADOWS

STEVEN SMITH

As the Crow
Flies Publishing

First published by As the Crow Flies Publishing 2021
https://authorstevensmith.co.uk/

Copyright © 2021 by Steven Smith

ISBN: 978-1-8381434-0-4
First edition

Typesetting and cover design by Jen Parker, Fuzzy Flamingo
www.fuzzyflamingo.co.uk

This is for all the dreamers and adventurers in search of their own little piece of magic in the world.

"Books are a uniquely portable magic."
Stephen King

ONE

"Oi! Stop there! Get back here boy!"

A grubby little boy, no more than eight years of age, tore around a corner, bursting out into the marketplace, thronged with people browsing amongst the stalls. His battered leather boots, the soles patched with tatty cardboard, slapped the ground, vainly seeking purchase. Peering over his shoulder, he tripped over his frayed long coat riddled with holes, about ten sizes too big for him, sprawling into a farmer's stall. Curses rang out as soil-coated produce scattered across the damp cobbles. Crates and trestles splintered, a large sliver of wood gouging a rough wound beneath the boy's left eye. Feeling warm dampness, he swiped at his cheek, a pale hand coming away slick with blood.

Scrambling to his feet amidst the wreckage and debris of the stall, the boy made a break for the gates back out to the warren of streets that make up the beating heart of Murkvale, before the guards carried him off to The Island. Nobody – man, woman or child – ever wanted to find themselves on The Island. The ruling classes would have the people believe it was a centre of re-education and

1

reformation for those who had strayed from the path of civility. Many knew it to be a place of darkness, torment and isolation.

With the gates in sight, he picked up his pace until an imposing figure of a man decked out in all black with a long trench coat, glistening in the rain, filled the passageway. Unlike the city guards tailing him, this man said nothing. He merely stared at the onrushing boy, raising his hand, holding the biggest pistol he had ever seen. All six chambers were loaded, and the gaping maw of the long barrel seemed to be drawing him in. He was certain the man would not pull the heavy trigger, but staring into the black maw of the six-shooter, he was not prepared to risk it.

A sudden commotion drew the eye of the dark figure, just long enough for the boy to dive down a side alley. He cursed under his breath, realising it was leading him away from the only exit from the market. The pursuing guards had crashed through a crowd of shoppers, scattering people and stall tables about the marketplace. By the time the man turned back he saw the boy disappear around a sharp right bend in the alley and took off in pursuit. He fired a hasty shot down the alleyway, sparking off the wall as it ricocheted around the bend, coming dangerously close to its mark. The whining noise of the bullet echoed unpleasantly around him. As the boy barrelled down to a three-way divergence in the alley, a curt voice barked at him.

"Up here!"

Shaken by his near-miss, he looked around the narrow passage until he spotted a mud-smeared thin arm reaching down from the wall. He scrambled up the wall, snatching at the proffered hand. The two bodies tumbled into a heap on the cobbles at the foot of the wall, that same slender, grimy hand clamping firmly over the boy's mouth. Struggling against the surprisingly strong grip was futile, his grunts only earned a brief hushing from the unseen figure behind him. The sound of heavy boots slapping against the damp cobbles grew to a crescendo in the alley. They suddenly paused slightly further down the passageway at a junction.

Curses filled the narrow, walled-in space as the head of the guards, normally so calm and composed, lost his cool and, with it, lost his target. The sound of stumbling, weary footsteps entered the passage, pausing for a moment. The figure still with a hand over the boy's mouth stretched up, peering over the wall to see the anger and rage in the face of the senior guard, his eyes burning into the two hapless officers.

"Find him!"

With that, the senior officer stalked back out of the alley, barging through his subordinates, leaving them to scurry away in vain pursuit. Eventually, the strong, slender arms around the boy loosened, the hand finally released from his mouth. He collapsed against the wall, peering at his rescuer – a girl, close in age to himself. She was striking in her silence. Long black hair, shaved on the right side, worn in a tight ponytail over her right shoulder. As she lifted her aviator goggles, he couldn't help but notice her intense steely-grey eyes. No words were said, but the look she gave him spoke volumes, clearly unimpressed by his brash, noisy way of carrying himself.

"You're not one for the art of subtlety, are you?" It was the first complete sentence spoken by the mysterious girl.

The boy proffered a hand, accepted in the coldest of fashions.

"Crow. Edison Crow. Pleased to make your acquaintance." He flashed his most disarming smile, filled with a warmth and confidence that didn't entirely reach his eyes.

With a single shake of his hand, the girl offered, "Selah."

"Selah…?"

"Just Selah. You need not worry beyond that."

"Well, 'Just Selah', your assistance here has been greatly appreciated. Should you wish to benefit from my skills and protection, you are free to partner with myself henceforth!" Crow proclaimed. Selah had not seen such a swagger on a scruffy street rat, certainly not one of their age.

A snort of derision caused his beaming grin to falter momentarily.

"As I see it, you need my help far more than I yours."

"I am plenty capable of carrying myself, dear Selah, but I see no reason our blossoming partnership cannot deliver mutual benefits."

The faintest upturn of the corners of Selah's mouth hinted at a smile, the closest to a show of emotion he had seen from her yet.

"Let's go, Edison Crow. Even those guards will manage to find us eventually if we sit here all day."

Sneaking through the narrow back streets, leading away from the bustling market, Selah and Edison made for the busy thoroughfares thronged with people rushing about their daily business.

"Stick with me, young Selah, and we will go far! We shall be famous! From the farthest reaches of the Coal Islands through to the largest cities and onwards to the mighty metropolis of Copper Lakes!"

"Mighty confident for a street dweller…" Selah opined with a roll of her eyes.

"A street dweller I may well be, but I have grand plans!"

Crow snatched a loaf of bread from the bakery window as they walked past, feigning nonchalance as he did so.

"Oi! You two! Get back here with that! GUARDS!"

The large six-shooter fired again, the boom echoing around the streets, drawing cries of fear and shock from bystanders. With a furrowed brow and a tightness in her jaw, Selah shot a look in Crow's direction before she took off towards the outskirts of the city, Edison not far behind.

TWO

PRESENT DAY

The stirring wind snapped his waxed leather long coat around his legs as Crow maintained a precarious grip on the coarse rope ladder. Only his left arm supported him, looped through the fraying rungs. The only sounds, barely audible over the wind rushing through the deep, fog-shrouded cavern, were the whipping sound of the leather, the creaking of the rope ladder and the occasional hiss of hydrogen from the long, sleek pontoons holding his airship aloft. Fighting against the swaying ladder, he lifted a tarnished brass spyglass to his eye, sighting his quarry through the smudged lens and dense fog.

Gas lamps over the door burned with a murky corona of yellow. The bronzed dome, usually a gleaming beacon in the golden wash of the sun, was nothing more than an inky blot through the fog. As Reuben brought the ship around, Crow could see the lights burning bright through the glass roof sitting high above the ballroom of the Clawridge Gorge town hall. A whistle from below told him that Selah was in position at the front doors, ready to make an entrance. As the ship drifted into place, Crow pocketed his spyglass and descended the rope ladder to the roof below.

Crow gave his own whistle before he opened the access port in the glass roof. In the ballroom below, shouts rang out as Selah kicked her way through the ornately carved wooden doors and threw smoke bombs ahead of her. As the thick smoke filled the room, Crow slid down the access ladder, his thick-soled black boots striking the wooden floor with a thud, tarnished silver buckles softly jingling before silence enveloped the room. He strode toward the centre, drawing his trusty shooter; eight rotating cylinders making for a quick-firing long gauge pistol. A dark wood handle, with copper metalwork overlay, and silver filigree inlays along the oiled black barrel made for an imposing, yet ornate weapon.

Straight armed, he raised the gun above his head, firing a buckshot round into the air, entirely forgetting about the glass roof. The boom left a ringing in his ears, and those of all in the room, closely followed by the shattered shards of glass tinkling upon the polished wood floor. Crow, his composure falling only momentarily through the shock of the rain of glass falling around him, cast a wide smile around the room through the dissipating smoke. Confident and self-assured, Crow stood before them in his finest attire. His trousers freshly pressed, black with pinstriping tucked into his leather boots. The silver buckles were tarnished, he was never able to polish them the way they used to look. He wore a now-customary cream button-down shirt under his favourite maroon waistcoat with black detailing. He finished his look with black top hat and big, round aviator goggles. Edison Crow's look was nothing if not theatrical.

"Ladies and gentlemen! Tonight, I ask your forgiveness

for our rude interruption to your proceedings! Please allow me to introduce my good friend Selah, and I, your humble host for the moment, am Captain Edison Crow!"

He spun a slow circle, taking in rapt attention of the patrons gathered in the ballroom, as Selah herded them into a corner, aided by her double-barrelled shotgun. The double doors opened as four crew members of the airship Arcos strode in with lengths of rope and sacks.

"Now, we all know the purpose of tonight's festivities is to raise much-needed funds for some wonderful cause or another, dear to all of our hearts, I am sure! My crew and I are merely asking for some of that financial aid. As recovering street children ourselves, Selah and I are seeking your support in our continued recovery. If you would be so kind as to deposit any items of value, jewellery and money into the sacks our associates will be bringing around, then please form a crowd in the centre of the room, thank you!"

The rough, hessian sacks were brought around, as the good and wealthy of Clawridge Gorge donated their valuables, coerced by a pair of men with rusty cutlasses in hand. As their targets shuffled to the middle of the ballroom, the remaining crew bound them tightly with ropes, completing this eventful interlude to their evening.

"We thank you profusely for your unprecedented generosity, and would like you to know how much you helped a wonderful cause! It will help change lives, and for that, you have our eternal gratitude."

Stepping forward, Crow sought out the mayor in the bound crowd, and delicately removed his ceremonial chains. In their place, he pinned his trademark business card – a dark crow in flight – to his robes. The crew left the room with sacks filled with valuables, leaving only Crow and Selah behind.

"Before we bid you good evening, please allow me to praise your wonderful cooperation here. Please enjoy the remainder of your wondrous event."

While Crow delivered the most theatrical, deep bow to his 'audience', Selah had silently crossed the vast room to the double doors, looking back with an almost imperceptible roll of her grey eyes. With his act complete, the flamboyant captain turned on his heel and strode with confidence that belied his humble beginnings, out of the town hall.

Arcos had landed on the lawns in front of the town hall. A chorus of shots echoed out as guards stormed from the shadows of the many streets that all converged at the focal point of the sprawling town. Without pause, Crow and Selah broke into a sprint, leaping for the rope ladder as the crew pulled Arcos into a steep climb, hoping to avoid major damage from the deafening cacophony of rifles lighting up the dark in a vain attempt to stop them. Shot and bullets peppered the vast wooden hull of the battleship, the metal framing pocked and dented with impacts. A lucky round struck the lifting rudder on the rear of the port side pontoon, leaving Arcos listing heavily. Soldiers flooded the gardens, eager to stop the fleeing bandit crew, taking up positions just as Arcos rose clear of the city walls and disappeared into the mists of the gorge.

THREE

The captain's quarters aboard Arcos were dimly lit at best, deep shadows pooling in the farthest corners of the room. The stuttering yellow glow of candles provided a meagre light by which the trio sat about the map table, were counting the takings from the night's escapades. Crow, Selah and the ship's purser, Thaddeus S. Robinson, set to work dividing the wares out into jewellery, money and any other valuables, ready to be documented and locked below decks in the vast secure cargo storage, behind thick iron gates. The safes could only ever be opened by three keys, one held by Crow, one by Selah and one by the purser.

Following their trip to Clawridge Gorge, Arcos had taken some minor damage. A lucky hit from the late-arriving soldiers damaged the port pontoon rudder, making for a tense, unsteady trip out of town, and a nervy flight through the narrow twists and turns of the gorge. Reuben came with Arcos when Edison succeeded the previous captain, a stubborn, intimidating hulk of a man by the name of Rohgar. He knew every inch of the ship and how everything worked, making him the most qualified to pilot it. He was no stranger to flying the ship in less-than-optimal conditions since Crow's stewardship. This was one of the hardest flights he had made but safely saw the ship through to an outpost settlement at the end of the gorge.

On arrival, Selah had Reuben organise the rest of the crew to seek out fuel, hydrogen, food and water, as well as everything needed to patch the rudder and holes along the hull of the ship. They had been fortunate that the port and starboard hydrogen pontoons and their propellers had completely avoided damage.

The ship was silent, save for the occasional hiss of gas flowing around the pontoons and the creaking of the deck as the airship settled at a makeshift berth. Selah sorted through a smorgasbord of items looking for value. Hip flasks, purse pistols and even gold false teeth had been given in fear.

"Ugggh! I know they're gold but why do people insist on giving us their false teeth?"

The purser typed and cranked away on his old adding machine, totting up all the different coins, of which so many had been collected in the raid. He barely acknowledged his colleagues, lost deep in concentration.

Crow was in his element, appraising every piece of jewellery through his loupe that was always in his jacket pocket.

"Maybe your menacing scowl scared them into handing over everything they had," Crow mumbled as he studied a chunky diamond necklace. "Nice… very nice!"

"Maybe if you could skip the act a bit more often, I wouldn't be so menacing. Having to listen to you carrying on every job is enough to drive anyone mad!"

Crow put his loupe back in his pocket and turned his megawatt smile on Selah.

"Why, my dear Selah, do you not like my polite, gentlemanly ways?"

"Not so gentlemanly when you point your pistol at elderly aristocrats and politicians, Edison."

"Oh, that? Mere persuasion to help people arrive at the correct conclusion."

Selah snorted with derision, returning her attention to valuing the evening's haul. A quiet hush fell over everyone, lost in their work. The only sound was the clink of coins and jewellery and trinkets landing in piles on the oak table, and the creaking of the ships' timber and rigging. Crow paused, seemingly paralysed all of a sudden. He tilted his head about, a look of stark concentration on his face.

"Something the matter, Captain?"

"Hush, Thaddeus!"

"What troubles you, Sir?"

"I said hush!"

Selah looked confused. Then concerned as an unsettling sound played at the edge of her hearing.

"I hear it too, Crow."

"Did any of the crew remain aboard? I was certain Reuben took everybody ashore to prepare for maintenance."

"I did a sweep of the main decks, galley and mess before I came here. Arcos is a ghost ship, Crow." Selah's voice betrayed a hint of concern, if not quite fear.

"Right now, that is precisely what worries me."

"Don't be so stupid, Crow, ghosts are the stuff of superstition!"

A strange susurration filled the room. It started almost imperceptibly, barely audible. It seemed to rise, a faint hum increasing to a buzzing sound. If Crow didn't know better, he might have thought a swarm had descended around Arcos.

"Look, outside!" barked Crow.

Selah turned to look over her shoulder in the direction of the round portholes set in the wooden double doors leading out to the main deck. Two indistinct figures were peering in. They appeared as shadows, fuzzy, vibrating almost. It was impossible to make out any details other than they were small. Two piercing yellow-white points stared blankly inside from where their eyes must be. As quickly as they seemed to appear, the two mysterious figures disappeared. Crow and Selah bolted for the door and out onto the deck. They came to a sudden halt, stunned and motionless by the sight before them. The two blurs stood at the mid-deck, still too indistinct to make out any real details. The buzzing sound rose to a deafening crescendo as more figures appeared with unsettling speed. They lined the port and starboard sides of the deck, with one – clearly their leader – on the tip of the bow cannon. As suddenly as they appeared, they all flickered and blurred before disappearing.

"What the ever-loving fuck were they?"

"That might be the first sensible thing you've said in months, Crow."

The ageing purser shuffled out of the cabin and sidled up between Crow and Selah, looking from one to the other. The pair continued to stare at the nothingness on the deck.

"Sometimes I wonder if there is something not entirely right with you two," he grumbled, as he shuffled down below decks to his cabin.

"I think I need a drink," opined Crow.

"You are getting good at this sensible talk all of a sudden."

Crow stalked back to his quarters in search of something strong to help make sense of what he had seen, Selah not far behind him.

FOUR

"What the hell was that, Selah?"

Crow stared up at the ceiling, a crystal tumbler in one hand and a matching decanter of thirty-year-old single malt in the other, keeping him topped up. He drained his glass in one quick movement.

"I've never seen anything like it. It was… unsettling. That noise, those… things, people, I don't know what."

"Yeah, I don't know either. If they were people, I would say they were children, pretty young too."

"There's no way they were people, Crow. Their movement… it's as if they jumped from one space to another without moving. And why couldn't we see them clearly? I don't like it."

Selah finished her drink, snatched the decanter from Crow and poured herself another generous measure of the earthy amber drink. Crow was brought out of his thoughts by this, thinking Selah must be truly rattled. She rarely finished one small measure, let alone more. He would know, he always finished her forgotten drinks – no sense in wasting fine whiskey. The pair sat in awkward silence, desperately hoping they wouldn't hear that buzzing again.

They both jumped as the doors crashed open, forced

15

inwards by stormy gales and a squall of rain. A large figure stood in the doorway, a shadow against the glow of the lanterns outside. For the briefest moment, Crow and Selah's eyes widened with a spark of terror, before Reuben strode in. He forced the doors shut against the battering winds. The pair settled back in their seats uneasily, Crow listening to his racing heartbeat, finally beginning to slow after the sudden shock. They remained jumpy after their earlier encounter.

"We got all we need to fix up Arcos, Captain, but this bastard weather is goin' to slow us up, no mistake. I'd wager no chance of us getting away tonight, but if the storm blows itself out overnight, we can patch her up and be gone at first light. Robinson and the galley boys are sortin' some provisions for everyone before we hunker down for the night."

"I would much prefer it if we could be on our way this evening. What chance of the repairs being carried out this evening, Reuben?"

"No can do, Captain. It's too blustery out there to get men out on the sides of the hull to fix that rudder. And no way you wanna be trying to hold her steady short one rudder in this storm. Here, did you hear that funny noise earlier? Like a plague o' some kind came over the village then seemed to head this way. Not heard a thing like it before!"

"Did you see anything when you heard the noise?" Selah wasn't sure how she hoped he would answer, but she couldn't look at Reuben as she waited.

"See? There was nothin' to see! It was dark as anythin'

out there, all you could see were shadows slippin' through the darkness. That aside, it were just the weird buzzin' sound."

Crow shared a look of concern with Selah. Only brief, but enough that Reuben noticed something.

"What is it? Did you see somethin' out there?"

"Now is not the time for concern and fear, Reuben, it was nothing, I am sure. I suspect it was merely the product of overactive minds after the exertions of earlier. I think we all need to get a few hours' rest if we are to rise with the sun to ready Arcos for the off."

He rose from his seat, a reassuring hand placed between Reuben's broad shoulders and gently steered him through the doors of the cabin. He dropped back into his chair, massaging his aching temples, eyes shut.

"Why did you keep that from him, Crow? We should all be on the lookout. Who knows what that was!"

"Selah, while Reuben may be learned enough to think critically, the men who look to him for guidance aren't. If he passes the story on and it is even slightly misconstrued, well that would not do with such superstitious men as those in our fine ship's crew."

The sun cast a faint, watery light through thick clouds as it crept over the wetlands to the south of the gorge. The heavy storms of the previous night had calmed down, just occasional gusts of wind and intermittent bursts of rain remained, and the sun managed to filter through the cloud enough for the crew of Arcos to begin working on the repairs. Reuben rose before the sun had even peeked above the distant horizon, assessing the damage to the ship by torchlight. Selah and Crow emerged on deck, as Reuben supervised five of the crew. They scrambled their way across the support struts, securing the portside pontoon to the rugged hull of Arcos. Ropes were precariously secured to large brass eyelets fixed to the metal skin. The crew attached themselves and descended to the underside, inspecting the rudder before setting to work on makeshift repairs.

"Captain. Selah. The men should have the rudder sorted by noon. Maybe sooner, but it's still a little blustery up there."

"Let me know as soon as we are ready to go, I want to cast off as soon as possible."

Reuben acknowledged this and excused himself. Crow leant upon the railing running down the starboard side of the ship, staring out over the little settlement, the last one before the vast wetlands spreading towards the metropolises of the Northeast.

"What a dive, Selah. The people here know it. They didn't even bother to name the place."

Selah stood next to him in silence; she knew when he grew melancholy like this that it was better to stay quiet, let him ride it out. Leaning over the railing, she saw Reuben hoisting lengths of timber into place as he and the crew worked to replace planks riddled with bullets. She pondered over what happened last night. None of it made sense. As a child, she and Crow had always told and listened to stories of monsters and creatures and things that go bump in the night. But those were just stories children told to forget how grim life on the streets could be. What she had seen last night, though, that was no story. It was no folktale or superstition told to keep people in line. She looked out across the plains, wishing they were somewhere else, anywhere. For once in her life, she longed for the bustle of a city, the safety and anonymity of the crowds. To put the unease behind them.

FIVE

Much to the annoyance of Crow, the repairs took significantly longer than predicted. The hull was patched up in no time but the damage to the rudder was more significant than any of the crew realised. As noon drew closer, Reuben entered the cabin to break the news to Crow. He had known Crow for so long he didn't need to knock. Selah and Crow were bent over the charts, plotting out their next journey.

"Ahhh, Reuben, just the man! Come over here, let us discuss the route ahead of us before we set off."

"I need to talk to you about that, Captain. There's a problem with the rudder. We got significant damage to the substructure that runs inside the pontoon that needs fixin'. We got what we need to do a job, but we need to vent the hydrogen in the pontoons so the lads can get in and fix it up. Then we need to dock her up somewhere a little more civilised to fix her proper."

"How long are we looking at, Reuben? When can we be airborne?"

"We gotta leak the hydrogen out so it's safe for the men, then we gotta see the state inside there, fix it and refill the old girl again. If we weigh anchor before dark, I'll wager it was a miracle."

Crow's jaw clenched, his hands on the desk bunched into fists, knuckles turning white.

"Perhaps overseeing the work in the interests of expediency would be prudent, Reuben," Selah offered.

"Yes, Miss. I'll see it done as soon as possible."

The aluminium-clad pontoons of Arcos – one of the few remaining Explorator Cargo class airships still in service – began to fill with hydrogen as the late afternoon sun turned a fiery orange, slowly beginning its inexorable descent below the horizon. The continual hiss was punctuated with a creaking sound as the mighty airship gained buoyancy. The crew hurried about the deck, checking gauges and making sure pressure release valves were operational, loading additional canisters of hydrogen for their long journey over the wetlands, refuelling the old steam engines – forever prone to belching clouds of smoke and leaking oil – and ensuring the hold was stocked with sufficient provisions. There would be no settlement to drop anchor at for several days once they took off – and though nobody spoke of it, no one wanted to have to land in the wetlands to scavenge food. There were far bigger and far worse things than themselves out scavenging for a meal in the darkness.

The sun, now almost fully below the horizon, was a riot of colours; the deepest oranges and reds, purple, violet,

21

indigo through to the inkiest of black further to the east. As darkness swallowed them, Arcos gently lifted from her ramshackle berth at the unnamed settlement on the edge of one of the most inhospitable places in Auridia. Up close, the sound of instructions shouted by the crew could just about be made out over the rumble of motors throttling up, and the sound of many copper rotors biting into the air for purchase. From further afield, the vast airship seemed to rise into the darkening sky as peacefully and effortlessly as a feather caught on the wind.

Standing at the helm, Edison looked out over the wetlands. A vast ten-spoke wheel, made of ebony trimmed in polished brass, took centre stage. Though Crow was captain of this grand airship, in truth there was far too much to flying this marvel of engineering than one man alone could do. Reuben supervised four men responsible for ensuring the motors ran with a precision that belied their noisy operation. Selah stood at his side, silently watching, always ready – poised like a coiled spring. The airship was outfitted with six navigator and lookout posts – one each front and rear of the port and starboard pontoons, and two more front and rear of the main deck, positioned close to the main cannons. There were half a dozen cannons on either side, along with guns fore and aft and a mighty, large-calibre machine gun at the bow. It seemed well-defended but, in truth, if Arcos came upon raiders, or worse – gunships of the High Commission – she would rely on her slight speed and manoeuvrability advantage to survive.

Crow stared straight ahead, not that he could see anything beyond the bow cannon, adjusting levers to pull

Arcos into a steep climb, propellers spinning furiously to lift the vast vessel into the air.

"Are you sure cutting through the wetlands is wise, Crow?" Selah glanced at him, a look of concern etching her face. "We could loop through the west, using the larger towns for cover and skirt around the gorge. We would hit the cities in a week and a half, two at the worst, and we could stock up as we go."

"I understand your concern, and believe me I feel it myself. But I... I can't. Whatever that was last night, and I hope it was a bad dream we shared, though I doubt it, I can't. The wetlands are always a risk, but in three days we will be safely docked in something resembling civilisation. The bustle of people, the clank and clatter of machinery, the oily smells and sooty smog thick in the air – it is safety, security."

"I've never known you to call the bigger cities 'safety or security' – especially not when you've got a job in mind. And I know you have something planned."

"You know me well, Selah, too well I wonder on occasion," he mused with a wry half-smile. "As circumstances have it, yes I do have something in mind, a nice little job to put recent events behind us."

Selah gave a wry smile. "I would not expect anything less from you."

⚙⚙⚙

Crow stood watch all night as the crew rotated in shifts at their posts. They had not seen the ground since they took flight late the previous evening. A whistle pierced the nighttime silence from the lookout post at the rear of the airship. It came from the watch post on the starboard pontoon. The lookout had sighted something. Up until now, the only signs of life had been the sounds of wild beasts in the fog – the thumping footsteps of large sabre tusks. The blood-curdling howl of the canivulpines. The earth-shattering growl of the ursanids – an enormous bear-like beast that hunted for sport as much as for food. But this was something else. A stuttering, rumbling mechanical sound.

Reuben and Selah raced to the rear of the ship, telegoggles over their eyes, lenses clicking into place, zooming in and out, hoping to spot the source of the noise. A squat, bulbous airship lifted above the mist, rear and starboard of Arcos. It was a mess – cobbled together from pieces of junk, scraps of wood and metal salvaged from scrap sites and cannibalised from other airships.

"RAIDERS!" The shout rang out loud and clear as the ugly craft tried to catch them out.

Reuben wrenched the wheel hard left, turning the airship in a tight arc as the pursuing raider craft lumbered past, incapable of such a tight manoeuvre. There were several clunks punctuating the air, barely audible through the air that rushed past Arcos.

"Grappling hooks!" A shout rang out from one of the crewmen.

Savage yells filled the air as raiders launched themselves from the side of their ship. They propelled through the air, swinging in long arcs towards Arcos.

"They're boarding us!" Selah pointed out the figures whizzing recklessly through the air towards them.

"I can bloody well see that, Selah! Man the cannons and ready machine guns!"

Selah started directing the crew ready to defend their airship with all they had. Reuben maintained a visual on the attackers, helping direct Edison. The boom of mortars rang out as the raiders attempted an assault on the bigger ship. Shouts rang out as a small party of raiders hauled themselves over the railing.

Much like their airship, they were a ragtag bunch with whatever tattered clothing they had managed to scavenge over the years. There was nothing theatrical about them, no pretence about them. Just aggression that was driven by a desire to plunder anything of worth. They were a rough bunch that rushed in all directions, stunning the crew with their sudden pace. Only a few carried guns, though they weren't trained or used to using them. Wild bullets flew about, piercing the wooden deck, cutting rigging and ricocheting all over.

A deckhand was caught off guard as a screaming, dirt-covered raider dashed him. She leapt through the air, an unseen blade in her hand. It was pitted and rusty, but still slashed through his shoulder. Screaming with searing pain, the deckhand threw her malnourished body overboard. She shrieked with rage as she descended into the mist. The crew regrouped, fighting against the vicious assault, soon overpowering the small boarding party. Thankfully only minor injuries had been sustained in the short, ugly fight.

"Take her down!" Crow commanded. Reuben vented

the pontoon, causing Arcos to dive in sharp descent into the fog.

"Are you insane, Crow? I can't see past mid decks, let alone see what is coming ahead! The forests must be nearby, you'll wreck us in the trees!" Selah raged at what seemed to be pure insanity.

"That would be a vastly better demise, my dear, than anything we would experience if those cretins take us! Besides, unless you can come up with a better suggestion then I think that the time for common sense is long past."

The heavy machine guns at the rear of the ship tore out into the night, sporadic cannon fire erupted from the sides in a bid to dissuade the raiders. There were several screams, ragged and trailing as raiders were dislodged from ropes. Crow steered the ship left and right amongst the towering trees, praying for all his worth they wouldn't hit one.

More screams and then someone called out, "There goes the last of the…"

The words were cut off as an almighty boom echoed through the forest, sending winged beasts spiralling into the air. A blossoming orange glow spread somewhere to their port side. Whether the crew had struck it out of the air, or it had come upon a tree, nobody knew, but Crow was not a man to look a gift horse in the mouth. Pulling Arcos into a gentle climb above the swirling fog, he relinquished the helm to Reuben.

"Nobody wakes me. I need to sleep." And with that, the captain descended the steps and disappeared into his cabin.

SIX

Arcos was hit hard in the skirmish. Crow had taken a big risk taking them down into the forests, but it had paid off. They outran the raiders, though not without damage. The propulsion pontoon mounted to the keel was almost completely demolished. All three propellers were gone, broken beyond use and the wooden skin was shredded, leaking oil and fuel. A stray mortar from the raider ship had torn the starboard pontoon fin away, leaving a ragged, snaggle-toothed piece jutting downwards.

The crew managed to wrestle the damaged vessel above the fog and pointed her back in the direction of civilisation. Losing propellers meant the ship had to limp its way across the wetlands. Damage to the pontoon played havoc on altitude, meaning they were only a little clear of the thick blanket of fog obscuring the ground below, and the damaged fin kept pulling the airship to port. Reuben, Selah and Crow took turns piloting through the wetlands. The journey took far longer than it should have, a week and a half, following the damages. Fuel and supplies began to run short; nerves were frayed. The slightest sounds, especially in the dark of night, had the whole crew on edge. Lookouts maintained a vigil the whole time, an unusual scenario aboard Arcos.

As the sun cast an amber glow over the vast wetlands, ten days after they set off from the end of Clawridge Gorge, the enormous smokestacks of Coalrock Creek thrust forth into the sky, belching thick, cloying clouds of black smoke, came into view. The lookouts at the front of the airship and the tip of the port and starboard pontoons blew hard on their whistles, an ear-splitting sound pierced the air. All eyes turned forward, Selah and Reuben rushed on deck from their cabins, to stand beside Crow. His tarnished, dented old brass spyglass held to his eye, he focused on the skyline of chimneys. Selah and Reuben operated their more modern telegoggles. Cheers rippled through the crew all over the ship as word spread that landfall was only a matter of hours away now.

After everything that had happened on what should have been a shortcut through the wetlands, the slow, limping cruise to the maintenance dock, high above the city, seemed agonisingly slow. It took Crow, Reuben and Selah all of their skills to wrestle Arcos to a high enough altitude that she could be met and aided to a berth by the dock's tug airships. With Arcos secured at the dock, the crew scrambled up and down the gangplanks assessing the damages and organising repairs. Galley crew set out to restock the supplies to refill the hold. Reuben organised the engineers aboard to start draining the pontoons of hydrogen for the second time in a fortnight. This was becoming a costly habit for Crow.

Having been all but confined to quarters by the lack of civilisation at the small settlement on the edge of the wetlands, Selah and Crow took their chance to head down into the town. Signing the relevant paperwork at the dock office, they rode a rickety, rusted lift down from the docking pads to the town below. The greasy, fraying steel cable creaked and groaned the whole way down, drawing uneasy looks from the two old friends. They rode on in silence, taking in the sights of the sooty city busy at work in the early morning light.

As the lift descended through the smog of the industrial city, the golden sunlight took on a decidedly murky hue, the sun itself no more than a fuzzy disc of brownish-yellow through the cloying haze. Selah coughed into her hands, the air so thick and chemical-filled it made her eyes sting. Regaining her composure, she stood to find a disturbing visage where Crow's face should have been. He had produced a respirator mask from his bag. Large, smoked orange lenses set into a cracked black leather mask gave him an insectoid appearance. Two large filtration canisters, one either side of his mouth, drew air in, straining out the soup of toxins. An exhalation tube exiting at the mouth of the mask was coiled around in front, not unlike the proboscis of a fly. Selah glowered at him, a sullen look upon her face, knowing he would be smirking under that damned mask. Right arm outstretched, he handed her a mask. She snatched it out of his hand, pulling it over her head.

"Bastard."

Walking through the streets, the smog hung high above them like a ceiling. The air wasn't so bad at ground level, but as Crow and Selah weren't used to the conditions, they kept their masks in place. Unfortunately, it marked them as outsiders to the insular inhabitants of the small city. The ground rumbled underfoot with the heavy vibrations of refineries and heavy processing plants that made up the industrial life of Coalrock Creek. White wisps of steam billowed up from metal grates set into the pavement, leaving behind a permanent humidity. The outsiders drew nervous glances from the locals, but most carried on their business, eager to avoid them.

"Selah, we need more munitions. If we encounter an armed response like we were greeted by in Clawridge, I'd rather be ready."

"I thought we were scavengers of honour, Edison? Do no harm and all of that?"

"We are, my dear, we are. But you can be sure if some paid brigand with an inflated sense of self-worth fires a single shot towards my person, I will happily, and forcibly, dissuade them from repeating any such course of action."

"An eye for an eye…"

"A crude summarisation, but somewhat accurate."

"What do you propose?"

Crow strode on in silence, snagging a loaf of bread from a street seller's stall, tearing it in half to share with his friend. He seemed to be pondering this notion as they reached the road that crossed the creek. Pausing on the bridge, he leant on the railing, staring at the water below. The creek flowed sluggishly through the city, so viscous it might be molasses. It slurped and sucked as it oozed around the bridge supports. Crow looked back to the city. He could barely make out the docking pads through the steam and smog.

"There will be an armoury up there. At the very least a store. Once Reuben has the ship fit to fly, I say we take as much as we can gather up under the cover of night before we make good our escape."

"And you think this will work?"

"When have my plans ever failed?"

Selah failed to contain a sarcastic snort of laughter.

"They may not have failed – yet – but we've come pretty close to absolute failure, Crow."

"Well, there we go then. Come, Selah – we have a meeting we are rather late for."

Narrow and dingy, the confined alley between two vast buildings muffled the noise of the city, enshrouding Crow and Selah in a claustrophobic silence. Though the sun was setting, even at its zenith its light would struggle to reach the alley, the cloying smog of hundreds of chimneys blotting it out. It probably wouldn't want to stray into this part of town even if it could; a great many of the soot-streaked workers avoided the alleys with a studied determination. It seemed as though the narrow street swallowed most of the noise from the routes beyond, and the only inhabitants besides worryingly well-fed, long-clawed things with beady red eyes and a distinct lack of fear, were not the sort of people outsiders or locals wanted to meet.

A nondescript door was set into a vast steel wall, many of its rivets missing. Crow stepped forward, mustering all the confidence he could, and struck the door with his balled fist. Five sharp, clanging thumps echoed back and forth through the alley. Nothing. No sound or sign of life. As he started banging against the door once more, the wall started to vibrate with the grinding of gears, a long hiss of steam as the motor groaned to life sprayed hot vapour over the visitors.

The pair passed through the doorway and, as it clanged shut behind them, they removed their respirator masks. The single bulb in the hallway hung precariously from a frayed wire. It swung in the breeze from their entrance, flickered and buzzed in its mount.

"Through here!" A disembodied voice hailed them from the back room, gruff from years spent working the coal pits on the edge of town. Picking a path through the small room around the stacks of wooden shipping crates, they worked their way to a larger, yet more cramped back room. Curses rang out as something crashed to the floor, numerous unseen somethings clinking and rolling off in all directions. Crow led Selah through the unlit room, between the canyons of boxes to the source of colourful language, mutterings and noise.

As they rounded the last stack of crates a small, rotund figure rounded on them. He gave Crow and Selah a fright, his working goggles making his eyes seem disproportionately large, the mounted torches blinding them.

"Crow!" he grouched. "You're late!"

"Cornelius, my good man! Please accept my apologies for the brief delay!" he beamed the most charming smile he could muster.

"Brief delay? Hah! You shoulda been here and gone seven days past! I could 'ave 'ad the High Commission crawlin' all over my arse, thanks to you two!" He jabbed Crow in the chest with a fat, grease-stained finger.

"But you are still here, unmolested by the Commission, Cornelius, so calm yourself. Remember, I am doing you a favour here. Where is the stock?"

He looked around the storeroom, eyebrows rising comically.

"Right here, lad. Everythin' in this room will be carted to the dock later this evenin' so you and your crew best be ready, it's gotta be in the air tonight."

"When have I ever let you down, Cornelius?" Unconvinced about how the old man would respond, Crow forged onwards, leaving no opening for a retort. "And the payment?"

"Never a social visit with you, is it? Business, business, business. As agreed, I've had my half payment upfront. You'll receive your thousand shruckles on delivery."

"A thousand? We agreed to four thousand!"

"And you're a week late, had to lower the price so we keep the customer. Deal with it, Crow!"

Crow growled with anger, uncharacteristically losing his composure for a moment.

"Fine, tonight then."

With that, he pushed past Selah and stormed out, leaving her to hurry after him.

SEVEN

as lanterns stuttered and flickered in the smog-filled twilight. The bustle around the loading docks was at its peak as delivery craft flew in and out and shuttles ferried people back from the pits out on the Coal Islands, out in the coastal estuary of the Creek. Cornelius hobbled out of the gloaming, leaning heavily on the cane he held in his right hand. Behind him came eight street children, faces streaked with soot, pushing over-stacked trolleys piled high with the wooden crates Crow and Selah had meandered through back in Cornelius' ramshackle unit.

"Wheel 'em in the lift, kids!"

"Cornelius, this looks a lot more than the original agreement…"

"You show up a week late, there's more stock to be delivered. No need to worry about old Cornelius, though, my payment'll be delivered once you complete the job."

A big, charming grin spread across Crow's face, and immediately Selah knew something was afoot.

"I suppose that sounds reasonable enough. Though I don't particularly want or need The High Commission Inspectorate poking around in my hold, and I am most sure

35

you and your business associate don't want these crates opened before delivery?"

"Between us, Crow, the contents may be of a somewhat ill-defined provenance, best they stay unchecked, yes."

"In that case, if you could just sign here and this will be all any Inspector needs to see to satisfy the legitimacy of my cargo."

"What's this now? You never had me sign anything before."

"Quite right, my fine fellow, but I have never burdened myself with such a risky amount of cargo. This mere scrap of paper, when signed, will allow unfettered passage, free from confiscation. Best they remain unchecked, yes?"

Cornelius eyed the rogue before him suspiciously but relented under Crow's unflappable charm. He laid it atop a rough, splintered crate and produced a gold pen with inlays of highly polished shell from an inside pocket of his long coat with a flourish. Cornelius snatched it out of his hand with a scowl, unscrewed the lid and scratched his moniker onto the document in the hand of one unaccustomed to writing. Before he could read the document any further, Crow secreted it into his coat so quickly it appeared to vanish, the pen not too far behind it. He grasped Cornelius' right hand in both of his, shaking vigorously.

"It has been a pleasure doing business with you once more, my dear friend! Now, we must prepare to embark on our journey to deliver these fine wares!"

And with that, Crow turned on his heel and strode into the lift, Selah close behind. They left Reuben at ground level to oversee the loading of the cargo.

"What crazy scheme was that, Edison?"

"No schemes here, Selah. Just business," he exclaimed with a grin.

"What did you have Cornelius sign?"

Crow reached inside his coat and passed her the document. It was folded in such a way that nothing more than the signature line was visible. She unfolded it, scanning along the lines of practised penmanship of her old friend. A mischievous smile, brief and small, flickered over her face.

"You devious bastard. I cannot believe you convinced him to sign over his pay for the extra cargo!"

"I cannot be held accountable should a man not check what he signs his mark upon before doing so. I am merely redistributing the finances to those doing the heavy work!"

With that, they headed up the gangplank and back to Crow's quarters to prepare for their daring evening raid.

Reuben's efficiency was something Crow spotted early on. He neither pushed back against him nor deferred to him instantly when Crow took over Arcos from its previous owner. Reuben was reliable and dedicated. He committed himself to the crew and gave his everything to protect them and ensure Arcos ran smoothly and efficiently. Under Crow he had eventually earned more respect and more responsibility – his thoughts valued, his knowledge irreplaceable. He often ran the helm, freeing Crow and Selah to conduct other business, safe in the knowledge that everything would continue to run smoothly. At least, as smoothly as anything can run on a ship of rogues involved in less than legitimate activities.

In just over an hour, Reuben had seen that the entire stock of crates containing who-knew-what was hoisted up to the docking pads and then secured in the hold below decks. The cargo hold was filled wall to wall with crates. With the loading complete, Reuben seamlessly transitioned into final preparations for departure. Having landed at a purpose-built docking facility, everything he needed was readily available. Fuel and provisions taken on, the crew took the chance to give Arcos a mechanical once over.

In the captain's quarters, Crow and Selah sat at the vast, hardwood table. A crude plan was drawn before them, a rough overview of the upper docking area. As the crew had gone about their work, they had all been tasked with getting a feel for the layout of the place. The dock had eight pads, three were occupied including their own. The administration room closed at night; everything was manned at ground level after hours. The armoury was on the far side of the facility but was left unattended. In a city whose focus was coal mining, there wasn't a need for much in the way of an armoury or an armed force either.

"This should be a nice, easy job. We take a small group, no more than six of us. Have Reuben ready Arcos to leave as soon as the last of us is on board."

"Never say anything will be easy. We always have a way of making the simplest task difficult."

"But what could be easier, Selah? No guards, no staff, no interference. You crack the locks for us, we get in, clear out and we'll be long gone before anyone notices a thing in the morning."

Night enshrouded the docking area in a blanket of inky black. Only the landing lanterns glowing red and green and the soft yellow glow of lanterns on the gangplanks of the few airships at berth pierced the darkness. Reuben held his post at the helm, the engines at their lowest idle in case a speedy departure was called for. Crow and Selah had gathered four of their most spry crew for what looked set to be a straightforward job. Selah moved quickly and quietly across the docking platform, picking her way past crates, hoses and machinery left lying around by the dock crew at the end of the day. Reaching the armoury, she produced a small leather roll of picks and tools and set about unlocking the sliding door in the side of the hut. The faintest of whistles drifted through the darkness, and with that Crow led the small party out to the armoury.

As the crew arrived behind Selah, she was removing the last of three surprisingly fiddly padlocks. The security measures seemed somewhat over the top for a small-town docking pad armoury. If they had a single, rusted old lock on them, that was a lot in many other cases. She quickly disregarded them, giving them no further thought. The crew dragged the large door open, everyone flinching as the rusted wheels squealed briefly in protest at being opened for the first time in what seemed like forever. With the door open, everyone paused, statue-still and completely silent, seeking any sign that their presence had been noticed. Nothing. The night remained still and quiet. Had they been less wrapped up in the job, they may have considered it abnormally quiet – the city below, though much quieter without the clanking of machinery, the hubbub of crowds, the hiss of steam, never truly slept.

"Okay – get in, load what you can on the trolleys and get it back to Arcos, quick and quiet, men. Guns, munitions, cannon shells, mortars. Let's stock up," Crow ordered his men, keeping his voice to a barely-audible whisper.

He and Selah stood upon crates by the door, overseeing the men working through the racking efficiently. Barely ten minutes had passed and the crew had already picked a healthy supply of weapons. That didn't stop Crow getting twitchy, he wanted to be gone as soon as possible. As the men and women of his crew started to wheel heavily-laden trolleys back to the ship, he jumped off his crate and began dumping bullets and shot into an old, beaten bag slung over his shoulder. Selah followed suit until something made her pause.

"Crow, stop!" she hissed.

He stopped, turning his head to one side.

"The lift, it's coming back up."

"Fuck! Those damnable nightmen must be coming up for a walk around. Get back to Arcos. Go!"

No longer concerned with making any noise, the two broke into a fevered sprint back through obstacle-filled darkness, many of which sought to trip a dangling foot, sprain an ankle. They realised all of the lifts were grinding their way up from the ground. Something wasn't right.

They rounded the dockmaster's office, Arcos came into view, a blazing light in the dark. The noise grew as Reuben throttled the engines up, someone on deck had noticed a problem. As the lifts arrived at the docking platform, it became clear it wasn't nightmen Crow and Selah needed to worry about. A small army of men appeared. All were dressed in dark flowing robes, heavy hoods pulled low over masked faces. Blood-red gloves and military boots polished. Some bore pistols, some swords, others carried staffs aflame at either end. Metal pauldrons bore the dark blue on black insignia of the Commission finished with gold detailing – a serpentine beast with five heads, the mighty hydra – making them instantly recognisable. Inquisitors of the High Commission.

"Run, Selah, get on the fucking ship!"

The silence of the night was torn asunder, the sound of dozens of running boots, the roar of gunfire filling the air. Arcos started an ascent from the pad as shouts rang out, a rope ladder dropped down the side of the hull. Something was thrown at the pair sprinting for the edge of the platform, exploding in a fireball as they leapt into empty air, their legs pistoning for every extra inch they could manage, fingers stretching out to snag the rungs of the ladder. In a mad scramble, Selah and Crow climbed from opposite sides, face to face, sharing a startled look of fear until they hauled themselves through the boarding hatch before the crew slammed it shut.

"Why the fuck are High Commission Inquisitors after us, Crow? What is going on?" Selah yelled at Edison, her characteristic composure snapping.

41

"I know as much as you! I need to get topside." And with that, he was making his way up the stairs at a run.

Deafening explosions rang out as black powder barrels were launched at the dock platform, their flashes blinding the Inquisitors as Reuben powered up and away.

"Douse the lanterns!" Crow bellowed at his crew, all growing dark on deck.

The propellers at the front of the three vast hydrogen-filled pontoons span so fast they became a blur as the vast airship powered out and away from the city, looping back around the outskirts, hoping to mask their direction. Pulling a sturdy iron lever, an audible hiss gained in volume as he flooded the pontoons with hydrogen, lifting the ship high above. Far below, six vast black gunships drifted slowly above the city, searchlights strobing back and forth in search of Arcos.

"Captain, with respect – the fuck were that? Worst I thought some o' the staff may come to check the docks. That were the High Commission!"

Selah pierced him with a fiery glare, seeking answers. Thankfully, the rest of his fifty-strong crew were busy ensuring the ship ran smoothly.

"How the fuck am I supposed to know? We've committed worse crimes than tonight, and the High Commission has never batted an eyelid. What is going on now?"

As Arcos flew through the night, Crow, Selah and Reuben stared out into the inky black, lost in their thoughts.

EIGHT

The escape from the Coal Islands was pleasantly uneventful, having lost the High Commission back in Coalrock Creek. The journey to Rookhaven, a hub of illicit goods and services available for the right price, would take Arcos through a series of canyons. It was easy to lose your way in the canyons, which made them the perfect location for such a town. They were crisscrossed with a network of vast, unending railways connecting some of the larger settlements. These were notorious for attracting the attention of smugglers and rogues alike.

As the sun began to stain the sky murky orange, Arcos flew silently above one of these lines. Rounding a curve in the canyon, a lookout approached the helm breathlessly.

"Captain! We sighted a train below!"

"Unsurprising really, when you consider we are following one of the main lines back to Copper Lakes."

"But Captain, this one's a bullion train. And, well, it's got High Commission insignia on its sides!"

Crow, a surprised look upon his face, strode purposefully to the large glass window, taking out his spyglass to inspect the train. A hulking black locomotive pulled it, six huge smokestacks belching thick black smoke into the canyon.

Eight cars made up the train, each one potentially packed with gold bullion. High Commission bullion always sells in Rookhaven. The final car was there for protection – two guards and a Gatling gun facing backwards. Between the insignia and the guns, little else was usually needed to dissuade would-be gold thieves. Crow had too much confidence to be put off, though.

"Reuben, can you bring Arcos in from above? We cannot be seen by the guards. I need you to hold in place so a boarding party can drop down between the last bullion wagon and the guard car."

"Aye Captain. Get yer boardin' party set, I'll have to drop in fast and get outta here or they'll spot us. You'll be down in five."

"Selah, let's get the crew together and ready the ropes."

Ten ropes dropped over the sides of the airship as Reuben swooped down over the train. A boarding party made up of eight of his longest-serving men and women slid down the ropes, closely followed by Crow and Selah. On landing, two of the crew set to work uncoupling the guard car without alerting the two men inside. With the couplings separated, the car began to slow. The confused guards ran to the door, realising too late what had happened, shouting at the top of their lungs. Their voices were drowned out by the clacking of the steel wheels on the tracks and the huffing and puffing of the engine echoing off the canyon walls. Half the crew made their way along the carriage roofs, while the remainder cleared through the train, loading the bars of gold into their bags.

The crew on the roof were heading down the train when shouting and gunfire rang out behind them. They dashed back, dropping down to find their crewmates struggling with four Standard Bearers – the standing army of the High Commission. One of the lads was lying in a heap on the floor, a ragged bullet hole through his chest. There was no getting up from that. A scrappy, aggressive fight was underway. The narrow walkways within the carriage left little room for weapons but kicks and punches rained down from all quarters. The fight turned dirty, eyes were gouged, and cheap punches were thrown in desperation by the Standard Bearers. Their professional training was all but forgotten as they found themselves overwhelmed and outnumbered. Crow's boarding party managed to wrestle weapons from the Standard Bearers, and eventually overpowered them. The crew quickly set about tying them up in the now-emptied last carriage of the train. Crow sent two of the crew to the engine to tie up the driver.

"Crow, you can't tie up the driver!"

"If the rest of the people on this train are anything to go by, he will be High Commission. We've lost a man here, I will not risk anyone else. The train will stop when the coal burns out or the water tank empties. By then we will be long gone."

"I don't like this. Why is the High Commission suddenly so visibly active? What the fuck are they planning?"

"I don't know, but this gold will be a massive blow to

them. Get as much loaded up as you can and we'll get out of here."

☼☼☼

The boarding party gathered in the rear carriage of the speeding train as Arcos descended into position. The dead crewman was hoisted aboard, and the remaining boarders scrambled up the ropes. Reuben pulled up and away, leaving the train to sail on through the canyon, leaving a black trail of smoke in its wake.

The purser rubbed his hands greedily down in the hold.

"My, oh my! This unimaginable bounty will be worth the Commissioner's ransom!"

Crow, Selah and Reuben said nothing, lost in their thoughts.

"I'd wager back in Rookhaven you'll see tens of thousands of shruckles, especially to the right buyer. You'll have plenty of ready cash from this fortuitous, opportunistic job."

"Shut up, Thaddeus! Do you think the bloody money matters? Arlo is gone!"

Silence came over the cargo hold. Everyone in the dim space was rattled. He seldom lost his characteristic cool and composure. Certainly not to this degree. He and Selah had been each other's shadow for twenty-seven years. Reuben had been with them for eighteen. While most crews see churn over the years, Arlo had served under Crow for twelve years – one of his longest-serving crewmates. Crow had plucked him off the streets, taking him from a life of starvation and destitution, and gave him a life of adventure and exploration. Arlo was like a brother.

Arlo idolised the captain. Edison never played favourites amongst his crew, but Arlo ensured he was indispensable to any of Crow's crews. Other than Selah, Arlo was as good as family to him. He stalked out of the hold, leaving Selah and Thaddeus in uncomfortable silence.

"Don't take it personally, Thad, the captain was fond of Arlo, we all were. Lock this all up and get some rest."

With that, she walked solemnly back above decks.

He liked it up in the observation room. It was the highest point on Arcos, glass windows all the way around affording continuous views. It wasn't a large room and, between missions, it was always empty. Crow always found it a peaceful space where he could watch the world drift by, and see his crew scurrying around on deck keeping the vast airship running smoothly. His eyes were puffy and red. Whether it was the whiskey or the tears that he could not stem, he wasn't sure, though if asked he'd blame the alcohol. He slumped in the chair, staring out ahead. Selah opened the hatch and climbed in, the wind roaring through the opening before she slammed it shut. Edison swiped at his eyes with the sleeve of his shirt.

She set herself down on the remaining seat, taking the bottle off Crow. She briefly looked at him the way a mother might an errant child, before softening and taking a long swig. She grimaced slightly as the whiskey burned on its way down her throat. She leant forward, elbows on knees, forearms hanging down, gaze to the floor.

"The High Commission hasn't been this active since they made their power grab. Something's up."

"No shit. It's a bloody mess. What were they doing up on the docking platform in Coalrock Creek? That wasn't normal. And they never have guards on their bullion trains."

"I don't like it, Crow, we need to get some answers."

For a moment, the captain was silent, hunched forward in his seat, eyes shut. Selah wondered if he had passed out. Suddenly he spoke, not moving as he did.

"We'll dock in Rookhaven by nightfall. I think we need to stop a while, dig for some answers."

He stood up unsteadily, swaying side to side.

"I need to lay down. Rest before we arrive. You should too."

Selah nodded and watched his slow, ungainly descent down the ladder.

❁❁❁

As dusk took hold of the world, Arcos glided over the railway tracks heading towards Copper Lakes. The slow-moving High Commission train could still be seen as it continued its journey to the capital, a black smudge of smoke blotting the sky in its wake. Crow was awoken by a sound from his nightmares. A faint hum, growing, becoming something almost tangible. A buzzing sound that seemed to emanate from everywhere and nowhere. A cold sweat slicked his body, pupils widened in fear. He clasped his hands around his ears, though that failed to drown out the awful noise. He burst out of his cabin, wearing only his rough cotton trousers that he wore to bed, looking around. The canyon walls were shrouded from sight, Arcos enveloped in an ominous fog. It was almost impossible to discern if it was dawn or dusk, day or night through the clouds.

Out on deck, the crew had gathered, looking all around them, terror etched on their faces. Though crewmen on airships knew their superstitions were just that, superstitions, at this moment in time it felt to the crew of Arcos that their superstitions had been made real. Crow sprinted up the steps to the helm. Reuben was staring ahead, eyes wide, struck mute. He looked toward the front of the ship. A shadowy figure stood on the bow cannon. It seemed to be vibrating, indistinct in detail with the same horrific, glowing yellow-white discs of light for eyes that Crow and Selah had seen previously. Selah arrived unceremoniously in a fluster at Crow's side. More figures appeared on the port and starboard sides of the airship, perched on the railings. Not one of them moved. They vibrated and shifted, like a blurred image on the periphery of vision.

"W-w-w-w-what the fuck?" Reuben stammered, struggling to comprehend what he saw before him.

Selah and Crow said nothing, just looked fearfully from one shadowy figure to the next. In a flash, so fast it was imperceptible to the human eye, the figures turned in the direction of Crow. Their awful eyes seemed to burn through his soul. As one they seemed to scream. A horrible noise, not unlike the screeching of nails on a blackboard, though higher, louder. But through this scream, it seemed like one long, drawn-out word was being shrieked into the night sky.

Crow.

And with that, the figures were gone in a blurred flash, taking the nightmarish buzzing with them.

NINE

Panic began to wash over Arcos. The crew had seen something they had only heard about in tales amongst other airship crews. They all looked to the helm in fear, seeking guidance. Murmurs rippled through the crowd. Only the briefest of snippets broke through the noise.

Shadow wraiths.

Crow looked around the assembled crew slowly, before looking at Reuben and Selah.

"Did they say 'shadow wraiths'? What does that even mean?"

"Captain, it's those things what came in wi' the mist. Tales tell of 'em being bad omens – a symbol of ill-fortune to those who encounter them."

"Shadow wraiths, an increase in High Commission incursions. I don't buy it, something is going on."

"You may very well be right, Selah. I am not one for coincidences, and it seems these two things are suddenly appearing so close together.

"Crow, I've known you long enough to know you are cooking up some kind of plan in that head of yours. What do we do?"

"We have to get to Rookhaven. Look around, talk to people, see what we can find out about recent events. The High Commission. These shadow wraiths. Someone somewhere has to know something. Reuben – I need you to help get the crew onside. At least get them settled enough to make it to Rookhaven."

"Aye Captain."

"Selah – we need to talk to everyone if we must, we have to know what is going on. Both of you see me down in my quarters in an hour."

Crow was dressed, though somewhat differently to his usual formal, flamboyant attire. Selah had been wondering if something had changed in her friend, but this confirmed her concerns. Black boots up to the knee, sturdy and practical. Lightweight leather trousers, patches covering tears, and a loose tunic completed the look. On his desk lay a quilted leather cuirass – brown trimmed with black leather and gold piping. A pair of rapier thin swords with polished black stone handles inlaid with gold, set in scabbards, two thick leather bandoliers, and a large holster on a belt were laid out. A hook screwed into a ceiling timber held a heavy dark grey cloak, lined with a luxurious dark red material. While Crow may be eschewing style for practicality, he would never go for completely plain materials.

He didn't look up as the door shut. Selah and Reuben walked over to find the table scattered with a map and papers. Books lay scattered around the floor. Documents about the High Commission, a map of Copper Lakes, newspapers.

"I've been looking through reports and documents to see what's going on. The High Commission has been more present lately. They-they-they-they-they've, uhhhh, they've been cropping up in towns and cities all over."

He scrabbled around the table looking for some papers.

"Crow, they show up in towns and cities where they have interests, where they have High Commission halls. There's nothing unusual there."

"Aha! Yes, but what concerns do they have in ahhhh, in mining towns, fishing villages, industrial cities? There are no High Commission halls, no companies in their pay, nothing! But this last year, their presence has grown. Inquisitors roaming the streets, Scribes in libraries and museums filled with nothingness. They were seen on the edge of the wetlands, the settlement where we saw them! The shadow wraiths!"

"Are you sure? This sounds like a massive leap, seeing connections that aren't there."

Reuben had remained silent, looking through some of the loose papers on the desk.

"Captain, what's this? Reports of street kids, orphans disappearin'?"

"Ah, yes! That's what I was looking for, good find, Reuben! Now, check the dates against the details of High Commission appearances. They coincide. Here it is! Right, look at this! Sightings of shadow wraiths. They happen around the same time. I don't like it. Something looks like it joins these three happenings together. We need to look into it."

"You sure? We got nothin' certain on any of this. Do we wanna be upsettin' those High Commission types?"

Crow paused for a moment, looking down at his documents. He took a deep breath, thinking about everything he had come across.

"I think you may both be right. We need to be cautious. If it is a coincidence, much as I doubt that, we need not attract more attention. Carelessness will have the Commissioner looking our way. Not what we want. Reuben, I need to calm the crew, see to normal running once we dock. Rookhaven is what we need right now – maintenance, resupply, rest."

"Aye, Captain, I'll see to it."

Excused, Reuben left the cabin and returned to the helm to oversee the remainder of the passage through the canyons to Rookhaven.

"Edison, we need to think about this very carefully. If you are right – and I am not saying you are – then this is big."

"Oh, I know that, believe me. I've been looking into it since we encountered the High Commission down in Coalrock Creek. Something was off there, why did they have such a heavily armed force there of all places? It serves no vital purpose to the High Commission."

"It's a coal mining town, Crow, maybe it is strategic for them."

A frown furrowed the tanned brow of the captain. He shook his head lightly.

"No, Selah, that makes no sense. The High Commission hole up in their ivory towers in Copper Lakes.

They own Copper Lakes. They have The Pits, Black Rock and Cauldwell Caverns all close by. Why would they have somewhere at least a day's flying away so heavily guarded? It's too risky for them to ferry the coal by train from there, and by air would require a lot of airships or longer flights to carry the load. Something is up."

Selah lapsed into a pensive silence, turning ideas over in her mind. She had always had a quieter, more contemplative nature than Edison – it's why they always worked so well together. She broke the silence, though the expression on her face seemed distant.

"Do you remember when we met, Crow?"

"Why yes, I do – I rescued you from a life of poverty and despair, starting you out on a path of excitement and adventure! Ahhh, such wonderful memories," Crow mused wistfully.

She punched his arm, not entirely playfully. "I'm serious, Crow. And for the record, I recall it was me doing the saving. Those city guards that were chasing you. There was something about them." Selah frowned, the memories slowly coming back to her. She hadn't really had cause to dwell on that time very often.

"You are not wrong there. Something lacking. They couldn't catch Edison Crow!"

"Stop being an arse for one moment, will you? City guards were all polish and little substance. More for show than anything. I don't know about you, but they held little fear for me. More often than not, they'd not even try to chase down street kids. Not worth their while."

"You are not wrong there. I have lost count of the

number of times I went out of my way to goad and antagonise them. A few yelled expletives was all I ever got. It was rare, if ever, that one of them considered taking after me."

"Exactly. But those bastards that went after us. They didn't fit the bill. Where was the polished metal armour? Where were the feathered plumes in their helmets? Ceremonial swords, capes, whistles – all missing. They were all in black. Nothing flashy or pretentious, just cold and clinical. Little to no armour. And that brute that fired on you with that pistol. No city guards I've ever encountered used those. He had some sort of insignia on the shoulders of that coat, too."

"You don't think the High Commission was up to something, even then, do you?"

"I don't know, Crow, it was twenty-seven years ago. All I know is city guards only made a token effort to chase street kids. They knew we were starving, desperate and they knew we would do anything to make a clean getaway. Those men chasing you, untrained though they seemed, were certainly something more than just city guards. I think we have to consider the notion that the High Commission has slowly been building their power, slow enough that the people haven't noticed."

"Shit. I think you are right, Selah. But why? They always pitched themselves on being 'of the people, for the people'. Bullshit. We need to find out what's going on."

"What do you suggest then, Edison?"

"I think we need to tread lightly. First, we need to go about business in town, preferably unnoticed. I need to deliver Cornelius' cargo, and if we can offload the bullion later tonight, then we can start to dig a little deeper."

"And, of course, you fully intend to ensure Cornelius receives his money in full?"

"Selah, he signed control over to us. We are merely redistributing the wealth to those far more in need. Besides, it will aid us in our good cause!"

"And what, might I ask, is our good cause?"

"Once we've got to the bottom of whatever the hell is going on, then I'll be able to answer you that."

Crow stood up and strode to his desk. He looped the bandoliers across his chest, the belt around his waist, ensuring the scabbards and holster sat right. Taking the cloak off the hook, he swept it around his shoulders with flair, affixing an ornate clasp – two crows in flight – of polished silver to hold it around his neck. Crow pulled the hood up, covering his eyes. He took the leather gauntlets from the desk and headed for the door. Turning to Selah, a determined look on his face, he said: "Let's go."

TEN

Rookhaven came into view as the canyon passage opened out into a wide basin, where numerous rocky gorges converged. The city of rogues sat at the hub of the confluence, shrouded by the mist and spray from the waterfalls that formed a ring between the mouths of the canyons. The city was formed of shacks and shanties, buildings and warehouses and homes and bars made from scraps of metal and the wreckages of unprepared and unsuspecting airships. These were no scrapyard constructions, however. This was a town with a purpose, with a design. On the outskirts of the city were the black-market traders, wheeling and dealing in small-time contraband – ammunition, banned texts, illicit liquors – the kind of thing any rogue worth his salt needs to ply his trade. Head inwards, through a maze of tight, narrow alleyways and a series of more legitimate traders and domiciles. In the very centre, a tall structure thrust above the city – a boxy base construction, administrative rooms, with an octagonal tower leading to a squat round upper floor extending out beyond the base, overlooking all below it. Here the defacto city leader resides, Maxwell Gladstone – a man with ideas above his means and social station, but a man worth keeping onside, nonetheless. Eateries and bars surround the residence. All streets seem to lead to the residence at the hub, as did money and information – not too dissimilar to a spider's web.

Arcos silently cruised to berth at one the docking pads fringing Rookhaven, Reuben expertly shutting down the motors on the vast ship, knowing it would drift to a halt in place. Once secured, the deck of the ship was a hive of activity. Standing above the cargo hatch, Captain Crow observed Cornelius' crates being hoisted from the bowels of Arcos and loaded onto wagons waiting on the dock. The crew worked efficiently, all wagons loaded in half an hour, horses straining at their reins. Selah took a seat in the lead wagon and headed to the warehouse district. Crow watched the small caravan of five horse-drawn wagons draw past him, hoisting himself up into the last as it came past. The risk of attack was slim, but Crow was naturally predisposed to being suspicious, especially with the concerning levels of High Commission presence.

The owner of the warehouse slowly raised himself out of his chair, eyeing the caravan of wagons with suspicion. Crow hopped down and bounced jauntily over with his most charming smile.

"Hello, good sir! Please accept my sincerest apologies for the delay in delivering this cargo on behalf of Cornelius in Coalrock Creek. He also includes the next shipment for expediency."

"Where's the old crook? He normally comes along on 'is deliveries."

"He saw my delivering the cargo as an opportunity to prepare future business opportunities. I will also be collecting the payment on his behalf."

"Now that sounds off. No way Cornelius would miss the chance to get some cash straight in his pocket."

Producing the signed document from a pocket in the quilted leather cuirass bearing Cornelius' scrawl, Crow turned up the charm.

"Ahhh, dear fellow! He has signed this document to ensure the payments are released into my possession such that they not be risked via postal service. He also advised that, as a gesture of goodwill, the fee will be reduced by two thousand shruckles!"

The warehouse owner stopped in his tracks, eyes narrowed with suspicion. He turned to face Crow.

"You sure you didn't fake tha' there bit o' paper? Cornelius has never let his shruckles be taken by nobody. An' I'd wager it'd be a cold day in Hell before he gave a discount on the price of business!"

"Surely as a business associate, you would recognise his signature?"

"Yar... that's true. Pass that paper."

He raised a pair of scuffed half-moon reading spectacles from his chest where they hung on their tarnished chain and perched them on his bulbous nose. His lips moved noiselessly as he read through the document.

"Looks to me like Cornelius has tidied up his scrawlin' hand," the warehouse owner said over his spectacles with a mischievous look on his face. Crow maintained his poise, though he was beginning to feel a sense of trepidation.

"But, jus' as you say, the old man says here to hand over the payment, less a discount of two thousand fer late delivery, to you. And despite him never bein' one to write much, this here's his signature, make no mistake. Have your crew get the crates inside, lets you an' me go to my office to talk business."

Tobacco smoke left the small, dimly lit room hazy. The anaemic sunlight struggled to penetrate windows coated with decades of grime. A single hanging lantern over the desk did little to dispel the shadows, though that could be considered a blessing. The old man was bent over a small floor safe, poorly hidden under a stained, cigarette-singed rug, turning the dial this way and that. He mumbled under his laboured breath as he recalled the combination, just audible enough that Crow committed it to memory in case he fancied a future visit. He cautiously took a seat in a once-plush wingback, replete with a collection of mystery stains so vast in number the original colour was impossible to discern. The chair creaked in protest, old broken springs digging into his back. The bustle of the streets was dulled to a murmur only just on the edge of hearing, the occasional clattering and slamming of wooden crates being stacked in the warehouse.

The warehouse owner, who Crow realised had not deigned to proffer his name in greeting his guest, straightened as much as he was capable, an audible grunt accompanying the strenuous act. He turned, heaving three large sacks of gold and silver coins onto the ancient desk, years of use scarred into its wooden surface. Returning to the safe, a small wooden box was carefully lifted out. He slumped back into his chair, replacing his old smoking pipe between stained teeth as he rekindled the embers in the bowl, adding a meagre pinch of fresh tobacco leaf before taking a deep pull on the pipe. He slid the cracked lid off the wooden box, filled with far more notes than the man's appearance would have anyone believe.

"The extra shipment would've netted old Cornelius eight thousand shruckles. After his concession tha' leaves six as my debt to you, Captain."

The old man thumbed notes off a large roll. As he went to hand over the notes, Crow held his right hand out expectantly. The man paused, a thoughtful look crossing his face.

"Though this need not be the conclusion of our dealings, if my meanin' be clear?"

Edison eyed the notes, tantalisingly close to hand.

"What have you in mind, sir?"

He paused, waving the signed letter from Cornelius in Crow's direction. "How shrewd you are, lad. Sharp. I'll not mention to Cornelius what's happened here, but I admire your ingenuity. Quite impressive. Take this," he slid a bag of coins towards Crow, handing him the notes. Crow eyed the bag suspiciously.

"An extra two thousand fer your troubles."

"Forgive me for asking, but what precisely would this be buying?"

"Absolutely nothin'. No expectations on you or yer crew. Consider it, hmm, well an investment in yer business. And should we have the opportunity to do business again, well, you just see that it happens."

"I think we have an accord, my good man. I look forward to future business ventures."

Removing his pipe, the old man spat in his palm and proffered it to Crow. Accepting the handshake, he had never been so happy to have his thick leather gauntlets on.

⚙⚙⚙

Crow wiped the palm of his gloved hand with an old rag he found on his way out of the warehouse. He looked around the bustling street for Selah. She was perched upon a stack of crates outside a small storefront selling black market products. In Rookhaven, you could purchase anything for the right price, as long as you asked no questions. She didn't look up as he approached, carrying on cleaning and reassembling her revolver.

"You took your time. Was it worth it?"

"Six thousand from Cornelius' shipment – not bad at all for a simple cargo run."

"Not exactly life-changing, though."

"No, perhaps not. Though this bag of coins to the tune of two thousand shruckles is another nice bonus."

"Two thousand? Why?"

"Future work for the warehouse owner."

She raised her eyebrows.

"And you fully intend to honour this deal?"

63

"Who knows. Maybe this is the day Captain Edison Crow turns over a new leaf, takes the straight and narrow path."

Selah snorted in surprise and disbelief at the words Crow spoke.

"Yeah, I suppose you are right, Selah. I am a creature of habit, so why would I change the habit of a lifetime?"

She rolled her eyes at him, barely concealing the trace of a smile.

"If you're quite finished patting yourself on the back, Captain, we still need to see what we can dig up on the High Commission, and see if anyone knows what these blasted shadow wraiths are."

ELEVEN

The hooded figures of Selah and Crow blended into the crowds of Rookhaven that flowed through the streets as one. In a town filled with villains, scoundrels and rogues, conversation was easy, but information carried a price. If you pressed the wrong person that may well be your life. The chatter gave nothing away. There was only one place in town where they would find out anything of worth. A grimy, run-down public house close to the centre, The Sinkhole.

They settled into their seats at a rickety old table in the darkest corner of the pub. From their position, the door was in their line of sight – they didn't want to be approached unexpectedly. A small donation to the barman ensured an exchange of information. No matter how guarded or careful the clientele, barmen were deemed of no threat, which made them a great source of information from inebriated customers drinking to fill a void within. The information so far had been meagre and uninformative. Crow felt his stomach sink, anticipating their investment was likely going to fail.

Rain began to fall in the late afternoon, turning the already-bleak town darker and more intimidating. The wind howled through the maze of streets, rattling doors and shutters. The door swung open, banging against the wall, caught by the wind. A small man soaked through made straight for the bar, a haunted expression etched on his face. Three others followed, presumably his crew, sharing the same look, terror leaving them on edge. Whiskeys were knocked back, the barman attempting to engage them in conversation.

"Shadow wraiths. We saw 'em. They surrounded our airship."

Crow and Selah could not hide their shock. They hadn't realised the wraiths were presenting more frequently. Something was going on, and they needed to get to the bottom of it. Crow strode to the bar, standing beside the group, Selah on the other side. He signalled the barman.

"Another round, please."

He turned to the group, their attention turned towards the captain now. The barman poured and distributed the amber liquid, glinting in the light of the gas lamps, even through the smudged glass of the tumblers.

"We've seen the shadow wraiths, too. Twice. I had heard of the superstitions but never truly believed they were real."

"You seen 'em too? Where?"

"Aboard my airship. Both times. And on both occasions, soon after conducting 'business' and going about our way."

The rest of the bar had gone silent, listening to what was being discussed. Airship crew had a list of superstitions naval seamen would covet, but for most, they were never realised.

"We finished a job. Snatch and grab in a lil' warehouse in a cavern settlement in the canyon. Job were as smooth as you like. Easiest three hundred shruckles we done! As we thought we were away, the noise. The buzzin'. It were awful."

The little man must have been their captain. Probably the crew of a small airship, picking the scraps of jobs that can be found on the back roads.

"That noise is the stuff of nightmares. Did you see anything?"

A woman, she looked fairly young, dirt smeared over her face, spoke up.

"Things. Creatures. Like people. Small, I think. Hard t'say. They weren't clear. Like blurry or somethin'. Yellow glowin' eyes. Never seen anythin' like it. Never want to see their like again, neither."

She slugged back her whiskey, drinking to forget. A lone figure at a table, a sunken, lost look to his eye, coughed.

"I seen 'em. Was just countin' out our takin's from a job. Surrounded my home. The way they look is enough to give a man terrors. It ain't right. The buzzing, though, I can't sleep for fear of hearin' it just as I slip to the edge of sleep."

He went silent again. Stared down at the now-empty tumbler in his hands. The pub grew melancholy, every patron lost in troubling thoughts. It would seem most of them had seen something recently. The notion troubled Crow. Though the sightings weren't unique to his crew, they were on the rise.

Another man piped up, emboldened by drink.

"Bah! Shadow wraiths my arse! Superstitions of washed up, drunken crewmen. We should be worrying more about the High Commission."

Crow's head snapped toward the man who had spoken. "What do you mean about the High Commission?"

"Those bastards with the robes been nosin' around towns lately. Just last week they were here pokin' their noses into people's business. Folks round here don't like familiar faces gettin' too friendly. Outsiders, 'specially ones wi' authority and power, are less welcome."

"What were they looking for?"

"Dunno. Didn't talk. Spent two days just lurkin' down by the docking station. After that, they marched down to Gladstone's. Spent an afternoon and evening there before gettin' outta Dodge."

Crow looked over at Selah, a concerned look playing over his face.

"What in the fuck did the High Commission want with an overblown fool like Gladstone? This is not good."

Without another word, Crow made for the door, drawing his hood up over his head. Selah followed out into the late afternoon.

Crow was on a roll. Thoughts and ideas tumbled out of his mouth, a stream of consciousness that Selah knew better than to disrupt. When an obsession of any kind wrapped its claws around Crow, he had to work through it. Some of his best ideas had come from this process. And many of his worst.

STEVEN SMITH

"So, the shadow wraiths, a crewman's superstition until recently, are appearing all over. And it's not just us that have seen them. Seems like they appear somehow following heists, big or small. Maybe we need to look into those. What ties the jobs together?"

Was that possible? Selah was starting to turn Crow's mad ramblings over in her head as he spouted them. But on this occasion, was he on to something? Could the appearance of shadow wraiths be connected to the heist jobs of crews?

"And then there's the High Commission. What are they looking to gain? They've no reason to be in Coalrock Creek – it makes no sense. Or any of the other sightings. Too close to the other two events to be a coincidence."

He meandered through the streets, back towards the dock, much as his mind meandered from one thought to the next.

"Selah, the High Commission has to be involved somehow. They are up to something, I just haven't figured out what yet."

"Are you sure? That's not an accusation you want to be throwing around lightly. It might come back to haunt you. To haunt *us*."

Crow strode onward in silence, a look of deep concentration over his shadowed face.

"You're right. I think we need to keep these thoughts to ourselves, for now at least. We need to work this out. Until we have anything concrete to go on, anyway."

"Good idea. But even if we do find evidence, can we be sure people will listen? And can we be sure the

Commissioner won't seek to silence us?"

"Oh, I know he will. He won't stand for us shouting heresies as he will claim they are. But we have to be resolute. Sure of our convictions. I will understand should you, Reuben or anyone else for that matter not want to involve yourselves in the mess I know this will bring. If we find anything against the High Commission, it will bring the spotlight firmly upon me."

"Us, Crow. There is no you, or I, and I suspect Reuben and the crew will feel the same. We aren't going to leave you alone to tackle this. You'll only get yourself killed."

The narrow streets of Rookhaven began to widen, the open expanse of metal grilles that formed the docking pad came into view. Dusk began to fall, the cooler air and the mist of the waterfalls surrounding town left a damp sheen on the leather of Crow's cuirass. Water droplets beaded on the thick material of his cloak as he strode purposefully towards the long, rough gangplank leading into the mid-deck of Arcos.

As the misty sky darkened, young lamplighters ran across the dock area, shimmying up the tall lamp poles to light the gas lanterns, casting a murky yellow light through the haze.

TWELVE

In the early evening gloaming, Crow sat at his ornate desk in his quarters. Two lanterns on either side of his desk cast a pallid glow over him. He was hunched over maps and books, furiously scrawling notes and thoughts. The only sounds were the mutterings and ramblings of a man puzzling his way through a troubling problem. Selah sat at the large oak table in the centre of the room, discussing the possibilities with Reuben. While the whole situation sounded like the biggest of conspiracy theories, even without much evidence, it seemed like Crow may have been on to something.

"Captain. Here, look at this." Reuben continued looking down at what was in front of him. A newspaper article from the morning after the raid on the town hall in Clawridge Gorge. The crew of the Arcos rarely – if ever – looked at newspapers, knowing there was a chance their antics would feature. It never paid to be too cocky, newspaper sellers were likely to spot a face seen in ink on paper.

"Murder??" Crow roared. "What murder? Nobody was hurt! Bound and gagged, yes, but nobody was murdered! Not like Arlo! They murdered him, killed him like he was nothing!"

Selah peered over Edison's shoulder at the full front-page image of herself and her childhood friend under a banner crying out 'WANTED FOR SERIAL MURDER'. This was not good. An official High Commission resolution calling for the capture or death of Crow, his crew and their ship.

"I was right! The High Commission is involved! It says here that Inquisitors *'engaged the notorious Captain and his crew in a violent firefight, suffering the loss of five brave soldiers. Upon securing the grand ballroom of the town hall, Inquisitors entered to inspect the crime scene. Within, a group of respected members of the town were discovered bound and gagged, stripped of all valuables, each with a single point-blank bullet wound to the forehead. The Mayor suffered a similar fate. Crow's calling card – a white card with a stylised black crow – was secured to his chest, held in place with a thin knife through his heart.'* That's utter bullshit! None of that happened! A few potshots aimed towards city guards, aimed to scare, never to hit! What the fuck??"

Reuben went pale. The article troubled him.

"Cap'n. Tha's not true, is it? You'd not take a life unless they threatened yours?"

Selah rounded on the large man, snapping, "Don't be so bloody stupid, Reuben! Crow is harmless, you know that almost as well as I! This is High Commission propaganda at its finest."

Crow riffled through other newspapers. Similar reports about heists by other enterprising airmen featured. Violent robberies, heated skirmishes with Inquisitors, callous murders for what seemed to be minor takings.

"Look – the High Commission is involved. They claim

to have appeared at the sites of all the heists we heard about in the pub earlier. Appeared at the sites of shadow wraith appearances. We've got a connection, slight though it is right now."

"We need more, though, Edison. As it stands, the Commissioner will have no problem denouncing this. He'll wind up his propaganda machine, decry you as a heretic trying to save his hide. You'll be hunted. He'll stop at nothing to silence us. An unfortunate accident over sea, Arcos downed with all souls lost. Or more likely, a noble battle led by the Inquisitors to defeat the vile and murderous Captain Edison Crow. This is something, but we need more. You know who we need to speak to."

Crow sighed heavily, standing to pour himself three fingers of his strongest whiskey.

"I know, Selah, I knew we would. He'd be the only person who could help take the bullion off our hands, anyway. That's a life-debt of its own. But we need his help or we're not going to get out of this one. Reuben, go see Robinson. Tell the old miser to put all the bullion in satchels, bring one back to me and let me know how many we have. Selah, we need to go and pay a visit to Gladstone tonight."

⚙⚙⚙

Selah walked through from her quarters, across the map room from Crow's own space. Leather greaves tucked into thick boots, a quilted leather cuirass over a lightweight chainmail under layer, thick pauldrons of rich brown leather with metal detailing, gauntlets and heavy black hooded cloak held in place with a scarf offered her an element of anonymity, armour and freedom of movement. Never a fan of firepower – too messy, too unreliable – Selah carried a long hardwood staff with ornate and deadly metal caps on either end in her right hand. Reuben returned to the captain's quarters with a battered old brown leather satchel. The bag weighed heavy slung over his shoulder. The chunky, solid weight of the bullion dug into his hip, reminding him of the burden presented by their pursuit of the truth. The risks were high. Crow pulled the shoulder strap tight, snugging the satchel in close before putting his cloak over the cuirass, ensuring it covered the bag.

"How many other bags like this one?"

"Thirteen more like this one. One more, a third filled or so."

"Good. Ensure they're secured. Let's go, Selah."

Even with gas lanterns dotted sporadically in the streets of Rookhaven, the city was marred with pockets of deep shadow. The thronging crowds filling the streets were no less dense by night than they were by day. The smell of burnt coal hung in the air, the hiss of steam pipes and pressure valves and the clanging of machinery provided a constant background to the furtive, murmured conversation – deals being struck, information bartered, plans shared – of the crowds in the town. The two figures in dark cloaks, hoods covering their faces, blended with the crowd. They dodged and weaved and sidestepped their way ever closer to the hub of the town with practised grace, a choreographed dance of sorts. Rounding a corner, the pub came into view. The glow from within was inviting, as though it were calling him inside for a drink. Every time the door opened, joyous voices spilt out with laughter and drunken songs. The strains of a piano drifted out on the night air.

Across the lane, the imposing wall of Gladstone's property was broken by watchtowers. Hired henchmen kept watch on the immediate area, and two guards stood either side of the door. Crow and Selah approached the door, where the guards blocked their path.

"We need to see Mister Gladstone. Immediately."

"No chance, pal. You ain't just gonna stroll in 'ere demandin' to see the boss man."

"I have a feeling he is going to want to see us."

Both Crow and Selah removed their hoods. He opened his satchel, revealing the bullion. He pulled a bar out and waved it in front of his face. The guard's eyes widened at the sight of the gold bar, before looking closely at the hooded man before him.

"Edison Crow?" the guard asked incredulously.

"Pleasure to make your acquaintance. Now let us up to see Mister Gladstone, please."

The smaller guard seemed a little quicker on the uptake and disappeared behind the door. A lift could be heard ascending to the top of the tower. The wait, though likely no more than a few minutes, felt excruciatingly long to Crow. The bell in the box in the guard room rang. The guard opened the door, ushering Crow and Selah through to a holding room. A long hiss from somewhere above them was followed by a loud mechanical clanking as gears meshed together, lowering the lift back to the ground floor to a backdrop of creaks and squeals. It clanged to a stop, the door slid open, rusted metal screeching in protest.

The small guard beckoned them in.

"Mr Gladstone is waiting for you in the penthouse. Please, this way. May I carry your bag for you?" A hand outstretched toward Crow.

"Thank you, no. I believe I will keep a hold of it myself." He pulled his cloak back over the satchel, placing a hand over it protectively.

The door closed and the lift began its precarious, rickety ascent to the top of the tower. At the top, the entire car shuddered to a jerking halt, an ominously loud clanging sound heralding its arrival. With an effort, the guard dragged the door open as its tortured squeal of protest faded away. The penthouse apartment was something special, and not just by the standards of Rookhaven. Plush velvet curtains in the richest of blues were embroidered with a glittering gold thread in floral designs. A deep-pile burgundy rug sat in the centre of the floor, with an antique table sitting atop it. Large wingback chairs were positioned around the table. Candles glinted and shot rainbow sparkles around the room from a vast crystal chandelier hung from the ceiling.

A large man, dressed in a red-quilted smoking jacket and a wide-brimmed hat with a large feather in the band, stood at a drinks cabinet. He was pouring three tumblers of vintage whiskey from a cut-glass decanter. Placing them on a sterling silver tea tray, the eccentric figure turned to greet his guests.

"Welcome! Welcome! The esteemed Captain Edison Crow, I presume?" He walked across the room, placing the tray on the table. He extended an arm in a warm greeting.

"Mister Gladstone, thank you for seeing us on such short notice." Crow shook the gentleman's hand with confidence.

"Please, call me Maxwell. And you must be Selah, the faithful sidekick to the good captain here." He removed his hat and bent at the waist in a theatrical bow.

Selah inhaled deeply through her nose. Her pupils narrowed to pinpoints, lips pinched tight, fists balled at her sides. Crow knew what was coming, but he needed Gladstone on his side. He interjected before Selah had the chance.

"Partner, Mister Gladstone. Selah is my equal in all areas of the business we conduct."

Gladstone raised his eyebrows in acknowledgement. Wordlessly, Selah bowed her head slightly in silent, frosty greeting. Gladstone took a seat in one of the plump wingback chairs, indicating to his visitors that they should do the same. Leaning forward, he slid two tumblers towards his guests, before picking up his own and settling himself back into the chair.

"Now I imagine this is not a social call, much as I welcome the opportunity to meet enterprising entrepreneurs on their way up in a relaxed atmosphere. What business might I help you with, Captain?"

"Thank you, Mister Gladstone... Maxwell. There

are a couple of bits of business we would like to discuss with you. Firstly, we have a proposition, a sale if you will."

Crow unclasped the silver cloak pin, laying his cloak over the back of his chair. He opened his satchel and placed a stack of bricks on the table. Maxwell's eyes widened; he saw nothing in the room but the shining yellow bricks before him.

"Is that satchel full? More of the same?" He licked his lips involuntarily, his innate greed consuming him. His beady little eyes could not stray from the bullion.

"Aye, Maxwell, a full satchel. I have another thirteen in my possession, a further one is a third full. All contain this same bullion."

That tore Maxwell's attention away from the shiny yellow bricks, if only briefly.

"More than fourteen satchels of bullion…" He turned one of the bricks over in his hand, revealing the Commissioner's seal stamped into the precious metal.

"So, the reports were right. You held up the High Commission train. You killed all those Commission foot soldiers."

"That is a fabrication. Yes, we held up the train, relieved them of their cargo. The guard train we disconnected and left behind with two men inside. The rest of the guards were knocked out and restrained, as was the driver. We left everyone alive. That is more than can be said for one of our men! The High Commission did not attempt to announce themselves or to arrest us. They shot to kill. And in that they succeeded, young Arlo stood no chance."

Crow lapsed into his melancholy state, staring at the floor.

"Arlo had been with us for many a mission. Many a year. The captain was fond of him. May I ask, Mister Gladstone, would you consider a purchase of these bricks of gold?" Selah took over from Edison.

"If you speak the truth with the number of satchels in your possession then there is a lot of worth there. To the right person, close to fifty thousand shruckles. But this will be tough to move with the seal on them. I'll have to melt them down, have them reformed and restamped just to be able to move them. Ten thousand."

"We lost a good man getting this gold! That is far too low. Respectfully we cannot take such an offer."

"I can offer you fifteen."

Edison Crow snapped out of his malaise.

"That is a disrespect to Arlo. That is not good enough. Thirty-five. And you will have the remaining satchels before the night is over."

"Twenty and I'll take it all off you now, Captain."

"Twenty-eight thousand shruckles AND your assistance on a more pressing matter. Or I walk. I'd rather not, we need your help. But not so much that I will sell myself short, Mister Gladstone."

Gladstone frowned, deeply furrowing his brow. Only after a protracted silence did he speak again.

"We have an accord, Captain Crow."

Shaking hands, Crow replaced the bricks of gold into the satchel. He rose from the chair and set his cloak about his shoulders, fastening the clasp.

"Head to the docks in one hour. We shall meet aboard my ship, Arcos. Bring the agreed payment. Leave your men on the dock."

With that, he and Selah entered the lift, the small guard dragging the door shut with a squeal of rusted bearings. Amidst steam hissing, a loud clanging announced their descent.

THIRTEEN

Even in the dead of night, the streets of Rookhaven thronged with life. Gas lanterns cast a weak, watery yellow light that diffused through the mist cast off by the waterfalls. The rogue town was permanently damp due to its location. In winter, the mist was a biting cold that coated any exposed skin, soaking through clothing and chilling to the bone. In the summer, the air hung thick in the streets – sticky, humid and oppressive, even in the most shadowed of alleys and passageways. No matter the time of day, the streets bustled with energy; scoundrels, rogues, smugglers and criminals of all kinds plied their ill-gotten gains at all hours, and illegitimate traders happily welcomed them. The soundtrack of the city was made up of the scuff of boots on cobbles, the hiss of steam, the whomp of propellers carving into the air, the murmur of furtive conversation and the incessant background roar of waterfalls.

A deck boy on Arcos rapped his knuckles upon the door of Crow's quarters.

"Come in!"

The young boy entered the cabin and approached him at his desk with youthful confidence.

"Captain, a man's on the dock, says he's to see you immediately!"

"Thank you, Micah. Are there two men with him? One short, one tall?"

"Yes, Captain, how did you know?" Micah looked up in wonder and awe as though Crow were some sort of god.

Crow stood, rounding the desk and tousled the boy's hair.

"A good captain always knows what's going on. Thank you, Micah, you may go. I will see to him." Crow retrieved a hexagonal silver coin from a pocket in his cuirass. He danced it back and forth over the knuckles of his right hand before flicking it through the air towards Micah. The boy deftly snatched it as it flew towards him. He promptly sprinted out of the cabin, slamming the door behind him.

Crow returned to his chair, checking a pocket watch. He picked up an inkwell and pen and continued writing in his leather-bound journal.

"Are you not going to welcome Gladstone aboard, Edison?" Selah arched an eyebrow.

"My dear Selah, you know how I feel about early arrivals."

"Much the same as you feel about tardiness."

"Correct! I arrive exactly when I intend to, it is nothing less than a courtesy. And in that vein, I expect my guests to do the same. At twenty minutes early he is keen. I shall allow him to calm down a while before we greet him."

"CROW!"

Edison pulled out his pocket watch again. An intricate silver chain attached it to the inside of his pocket. The watch was not overly large, round with a snap cover. The gleaming silver cover, expertly carved by a master craftsman, bore an intricately detailed depiction of a crow in flight. The carving was oiled, stark black discoloured the indentations making the crow appear alive. The minute hand put the time at just a few moments before the hour. He snapped the cover shut and pocketed the watch. As Crow rose from his desk, he pulled his cloak from the hook and clasped it around his shoulders. Bandoliers in place, swords in their scabbards and belt buckled, the captain pulled his hood over his head and strode towards the door, ready to greet his guest.

"Come, Selah, I think we have left Mister Gladstone waiting long enough."

Outside his cabin, a small cadre of the crew waited – ten of the best men and women aboard the impressive airship. Crow strode toward the gangplank, Selah kept pace just off his left shoulder. The crew formed up behind them as they marched down to the dockside to meet Maxwell Gladstone.

"You bastard! How dare you come to me for help then leave me standing here like some commoner!"

"What a pleasure to see you again Mister Gladstone. I am so pleased you made it at the agreed time!" He spread his arms welcomingly, a disarming grin spread across his face, though not quite reaching his eyes. "Please, join us in my cabin where we can conduct our business in private. This way, if you will."

Crow turned on his heel and returned up the gangplank, Selah close behind. The leader of Rookhaven followed grudgingly, escorted by five of the crew. The remaining men and women moved to block access to the airship for Gladstone's guards.

"You're to wait here. Captain's orders." Five hands rested upon pistols tied at the hip, enough to discourage further argument.

Crow led the party up the plank and across the deck, entering his cabin. Without a second look, he made for the vast oak map table that occupied much of the open space in the cabin, removing his cloak and draping it over the back of a chair.

"Please, take a seat, Maxwell. Can I offer you a drink? Brandy perhaps?"

Gladstone scowled with anger at Crow but grunted acceptance. Crow took three glasses and an old bottle from the cupboard, pouring out the drinks. Setting them down, he took a seat next to Selah and across from Gladstone. The two men eyeballed one another – one with contempt, the other with a confidence that belied the nerves he felt inside.

"Cut the bullshit, *Captain*. Why am I here? Don't waste my time."

"Please bear with me, my colleagues are making the necessary final arrangements for our meeting and will join us forthwith."

An uneasy silence fell upon the cabin, only broken when Maxwell Gladstone dragged his brandy slowly across the scarred surface of the old table. He maintained eye contact with Crow, daring him to castigate him, searching for an excuse to verbally spar with the man across the table. The unpleasant atmosphere was broken by the less than subtle entrance of Reuben, carrying satchels of bullion, three younger shipmates struggling in behind with the remainder. With a heavy cacophony of thuds, the satchels were dropped upon the table, sloshing brandy over maps in their wake.

"As previously discussed, Maxwell – fourteen full satchels. A further one that is one third filled."

With greedy eyes, Maxwell Gladstone eyed the bulging satchels. He stood up, pulling one across the table towards him.

"May I, Captain?"

Crow tilted his head in acquiescence and spread his hands. "By all means."

He slowly unbuckled the satchel, lifting the flap. Peering into the opening, his pupils dilated, taking in the sight. He whistled in surprise.

"And every bag is the same?"

"Correct. Pure High Commission stamped bullion. Feel free to check it all."

Being of a covetous mindset, Gladstone did just that. Over the next half hour, every individual brick was removed, counted and replaced in their satchel. Finally, he sat back down heavily in the chair, smiling with satisfaction.

"Well, you weren't wrong, Edison. That's a hell of a lot of gold. But it is well worth it for that much bullion."

"I may be a criminal and rogue, Maxwell, but my word is my honour."

"As is mine, Edison. My men on the dock have your money. Twenty-eight thousand shruckles all ready to go."

"You'll not mind if I have one of my men bring the bag up here to be counted?"

"I welcome it, Captain."

Crow turned to one of the deck boys and beckoned him over.

"I want you to head dockside and have Jeremima bring the bag up to me. Reuben, I want you to go and get Thaddeus up here as quick as you can, please."

With a curt nod, Crow dismissed Reuben and the deck boys, leaving the trio in the cabin as they set about their tasks.

⚙⚙⚙

Thaddeus finished counting the money. All twenty-eight thousand accounted for, counted twice, with Reuben counting over his shoulder. He turned to Crow, looking over the rim of his spectacles, and nodded.

"Excellent, thank you, Robinson. Selah, please go with them both and ensure it is locked away securely." He handed her his key. Wordlessly, she departed the cabin with Reuben and Thaddeus. As the door shut, Maxwell returned his attention to Crow.

"So, what is it you need my assistance with, Edison?"

"The murders of the High Commission Inquisitors are only the start of something brewing. I think the Commissioner is at the heart of it all, but we need to prove it. I need eyes watching for us."

"What do you mean 'only the start', Crow?"

"How long have you been here, Maxwell? Pulling the strings and hearing every piece of news or gossip, sitting in your tower at the beating heart of Rookhaven?"

"Going on for sixteen years now, I'd wager. Where's this meandering talk leading, Crow?"

"So, you must see lots of airships, large and small, pass through town, hear lots of talk. I trust you have heard of the shadow wraiths?"

"Of course, I've heard these tales. The tales of drunks and the superstitious. Nothing more than the fabrications of the less educated minds."

"If I had met you a month ago, I might have agreed. But I know different now. The shadow wraiths exist. We've seen them."

"Come now, Crow, I did not expect you to believe that kind of bilge."

"Hear me out, Gladstone. We've seen them twice. I don't believe them to be anything supernatural or otherworldly, but there is something strange going on."

"What exactly did you see? Who else saw them?"

"The first sighting was Selah and me. We saw them while we were docked at a small settlement on the edge of the Wetlands. They appeared after we had committed a heist in Clawridge Gorge. Our hostages turned up dead, a single bullet wound to the head. According to reports, a battalion of Inquisitors arrived in town as we made our escape. We encountered no High Commission resistance, just a few pockets of City Guards."

"The first? You've seen them more? That doesn't sound

like it fits with the stories. I hear you see them once and are marked for death."

"We saw them again, in greater numbers. The whole crew saw them. After we raided the High Commission bullion train, we took a circuitous route through the canyon in case we were tailed. A mist swallowed the canyon, it was all we could do to see the walls in time to navigate. The ship was surrounded by a dreadful buzzing, a sound that seems to herald their arrival. Then they were everywhere – on the deck railings, pontoons, the turrets and towers and even the observation tower."

Maxwell leant forward in his seat as Selah returned, now fully invested in what he was saying.

"What happened, Crow? Did they say or do anything? What did they look like?"

Selah interjected, picking up the story from her old friend. "Horrid. Vaguely humanoid, but indistinct, unclear. Almost as if they were shadows, vibrating so fast as to blur their features. Small, almost childlike in stature. Their eyes – two large yellow discs of glowing light burning through the mist. But that noise, haunting."

Maxwell slumped back in his chair, a sigh of disbelief escaping him. He indicated that another brandy would be in order. Crow poured another round, handing them out to his company. Silence enveloped the room, everyone lost in their thoughts.

"Crow, these are troubling tales but two sightings, well, it's not exactly concrete proof." Gladstone sounded unsure of himself as he spoke. It almost seemed like he was beginning to doubt his own strongly held beliefs.

He drained his brandy in one long swig. The melancholy silence was broken by the return of Reuben. He took a seat around the table.

"We aren't the only ones to have seen them, Mister Gladstone."

The town leader looked up with surprise, addressing Selah.

"Can you be sure? It could just be rumours. We all know how small tales are blown out of all proportion when shared from crew to crew, town to town."

"Before we met with you, we visited the tavern across from your residence. Some crews recounted sightings of both High Commission forces and shadow wraiths. In each case, the sightings of both came close together, and followed heists both large and small."

"The High Commission *and* the shadow wraiths are appearing in the same vicinity, soon after crimes are committed? Crow, I doubted what you were telling me. I thought you had been taken by the ramblings of superstition. I was wrong. There's got to be a connection, but I don't see it as yet. We need to find it."

Crow stood, pacing the cabin in thought before returning to the old oak table. He leant forward, palms down on the surface.

"This is where you come in, Mister Gladstone. A man of great resources and means like you must have contacts across the land."

"True, Crow – I have access to men and materials all over. How can I help?"

"My crew and I need to make for Copper Lakes. It's

where the High Commission stronghold is. If there are answers to be found, I think we'll find them there."

"And you need airships. Men. Money perhaps."

"That may well be needed before long if you'll help. But first, we need information. I need to know if the link is correct. Can you arrange some heists in different locations? The target and value are of little consequence or concern. I need a crew watching the area – to see what happens after the heist. We need to prove the connection."

Maxwell Gladstone paused, thinking the proposition over.

"Aye, Captain. You'll have my support. I will set the wheels in motion immediately. Can you send for one of my men to be escorted here? We cannot delay."

Reuben left the cabin to see to it personally.

"I'll need to refuel, rearm and refit Arcos and its crew for our arrival in Copper Lakes. On the balance of the information we've seen, I fear this mission may turn bloody very quickly, though I dearly hope not. I've seen more loss recently than I care to see."

"Black River. It would be the perfect staging ground. Pretty small as towns go, really, but it has everything you will need – including additional men, should that be required. I have contacts there, I can prepare them for your arrival."

"Very good. Thank you, Maxwell, I fear we are going to need all the help we can get if we are to unravel this troubling mystery. I suspect this is going to be difficult and highly dangerous, I hate to ask more of you, but if you can rally support here it could very well help abate the coming storm."

"What would you ask of me, Edison? I shall try to assist as best I can."

"We will need ears and eyes on the ground. Much as I entrust my life to my crew, if we are to go toe to toe with the High Commission, we few will never be enough. If there is any chance you can provide men and vessels, we stand a chance. But we need to be subtle. Airships – big and small. Cargo vessels, gunships, personal craft. We need to flood the city, airships scattered at all docks, men on the ground. They need to be in place before I arrive."

"I'll see what arrangements I can make for you. When do you aim to be there?"

"If we depart for Black River at first light, we can be there by midday. The rest of tomorrow and all of the day after should suffice to prepare my crew and Arcos. We will fly for Copper Lakes the following dawn. A days' flight should see us arrive by dusk. We'll spend two days gathering as much information and insider knowledge as possible. Day three, we will strike. I'll have a finalised plan before we leave Black River, which I will ensure is dispatched to you immediately."

"That's a big ask, Crow. But a lot of people in Rookhaven and beyond owe a lot of favours – perks of my position, I suppose. It's one hell of a favour and many people in my position would ensure you were indebted to them for a long spell. I may just call in the occasional favour from time to time, but I'll see to it. I'll leave word at the postal facility in Black River."

Gladstone pushed his chair back and stood. The enormity of the task ahead of them was not lost on anyone in the room. Crow walked to the door of the cabin with the town leader, offering a firm handshake in thanks.

"I wish you well, Captain. I wish us all well, I fear we may need it."

"Thank you, Maxwell. I will send word soon."

Maxwell Gladstone cast a sombre look at those assembled before departing to make arrangements. Crow strode back to the table where Reuben and Selah were busy discussing options, poring over charts and maps.

"Reuben, please set the crew to work preparing the ship, we have an early departure. If you can trust them without your eye over them, return here. There is much to discuss before daylight if we are to go after High Commissioner Anvil."

FOURTEEN

The Commissioner was a secretive figure. Rarely did he make public appearances, and when he did it was to serve his own devices – keeping the masses in check and bent to his will. Though not a religious institution, the High Commission wielded power through punishment and reward in equal measure, much like any faith. Commissioner Mordecai Anvil was revered by his most ardent followers with the fervour often only offered to deities of the highest order. A gentleman of a high society background, Mordecai Anvil formed the High Commission over fifty years ago as an alternative political group to galvanise the people around. Many had become so disillusioned with the tired battle cries to support the working class, raise the poorest out of poverty or to protect the wealth and power of those at the top.

The High Commission promised to redress the balance. To oversee all facets of everyday life. To rule with fairness in all matters, maintaining balance and order in all things. Support grew rapidly, and their ranks grew exponentially as the organisation became unstoppable. In under a decade, the High Commission had swept every seat in the Copper Lakes assembly election. The change was swift, with satisfaction across the city growing to previously unseen levels over the next two years, allowing them to abolish other parties, ensuring they would remain the only ruling party in the city-state. The once-thriving democracy with twelve core parties vying to win control of the Chamber. The party ruling the Chamber made and upheld the laws and governed Copper Lakes. Elections took place triannually, mandated by the founding parties. It ensured the people would hold accountable those in power, re-electing those who performed well or electing a new party to undo the damage caused by the previous party.

The charisma that the younger Mordecai Anvil oozed charmed the people. They had never encountered a visionary with such bold plans and ideas to revitalise their city. Copper Lakes had always been the unofficial capital of the region, but Mordecai promised to cement their status. The High Commission swept the election in a landslide victory – an unprecedented eighty-seven per cent of the electorate cast their ballots in favour of the new party. The remaining eleven parties slunk off to the shadows to lick their grievous wounds and plot their campaigns for the next round of elections three years away. Staggering reforms took place in the first year of the three-year reign of the High Commission. Industrial output rose sharply, as did wealth and employment. More people than ever before had roles in the hot, smog-belching factories, the bustling workshops and the ever-running power plants that churned away on the outskirts of the city. More residents than at any time in the history of Copper Lakes were working and able to sustain their own families.

The Commissioner opened the historically secretive city-state, welcoming all and sundry to visit the now vibrant city, bringing tourism inside the old city walls. An influx of visitors brought outside wealth, helping to rejuvenate and revitalise the city. Copper Lakes developed a highly-rated local cuisine, museums sprang up all over, theatres and opera houses, stunning green parks everywhere. With it came an improved infrastructure – wide tree-lined boulevards filled with colour all year round traversed by the hissing, clanging trolleybuses, and state of the art air docks formed a halo around the outside of the city accommodating long-distance airships and smaller commuter shuttles. A maze of suspended rails crisscrossed the sky, conveying hanging carriages around the city in clouds of steam.

In twelve short months, the city of Copper Lakes flourished and prospered. So much so that more coal supplies were required to keep the shining jewel of modern civilisation running. Mordecai Anvil used his youthful charm and exuberance to win over nearby mining settlements. Swiftly they found themselves incorporated as outlying suburbs of the city-state, enjoying a portion of the wealth in return for sending their black gold into the growing metropolis. Towards the centre of the city was its namesake – the twin Copper Lakes, so-called for the colour of the water caused by the unique sediment on the lake beds, and the way the sunlight hits the water. One lake sat like a reservoir above the other, held back by a natural rock wall. Both lakes were fronted by sprawling properties of the wealthy, enormous mansions with lush green gardens and wooden docks extending out into the clear water.

Built into the rock face between the twin lakes was an enormous contraption of steam pipes and cogs and gears. Water from the top lake fed boilers to continuously provide the steam to power an unimaginably vast clock face. The enormous hands mark the inexorable passage of time in a cacophony of clangs and whirs from cogs, gears and flywheels forming the clock assembly. Beneath the clock face, protruding from an ornate wheelhouse was a vast, churning water wheel connected to turbines generating power. Water constantly flowed down through a wide channel in the rock face with a constant roar, fuelling the boilers and turning the wheel generating power. Through the mist of water droplets, the sun created rainbows in the air. With such an enormous piece of engineering, Mordecai Anvil had created a spectacular attraction that drew visitors all the time. The introduction of power turbines also made Copper Lakes the first city with an electrical supply.

The High Commission, and Commissioner Anvil, had won over the hearts and minds of a city. His upgrades to industry, travel, commerce and infrastructure cemented his place as a man of grand plans and great means. He turned his reforms to policy, the largest of which was law and order. Historically retribution for crimes had been swift and bloody – gruesome capital punishments were doled out for crimes great and small. Fraud and embezzlement were rife, allowing the rich to get richer and the poor to become poorer. With the rise of the High Commission, crime was punished far more proportionally. Capital punishment was saved for only the gravest of crimes. A lot of smaller crimes went unpunished, Commissioner Anvil seeing these as a simple means of redistributing the wealth. The resurrection of the once-languishing city of Copper Lakes was incredible, more so for such a turnaround in a year.

The city guards, once an independent force whose sole purpose was to uphold the law and protect the people of Copper Lakes – the rich and the poor, politician or factory worker – were incorporated into the High Commission by the end of the year. Little seemed to change. Outwardly their uniforms were almost identical, though newer. Leather coats went from a stock brown colour common in towns and cities everywhere to the inkiest of blacks. Upon the upper bicep on either arm, the dark blue emblem of the High Commission left nobody in any doubt who employed the guards. For the most part, they continued to serve in much the same way they always had done, swiftly and with a firm hand. But over time it became apparent that those they pursued with vigour and those they let go were less decided by matters of a legal process, and more by High Commission decree.

Such a rise, like a phoenix from the flames, drew covetous eyes from across the land. With the success of the city-state, the most corrupt were driven out, and neighbouring towns and cities grew envious. Civic leaders took umbrage with the rise of the young upstart, Mordecai Anvil. Dissent and dissatisfaction ran rife through neighbouring towns, black High Commission flags bearing their blue sigil were waved in streets and squares – a direct challenge to other rulers. Word began to spread of leaders coming together, clandestine meetings held with the beaten parties of Copper

Lakes. Plots were hashed out in an attempt to overthrow the Commissioner. One plot made an effort at a coup, though it was ultimately doomed from the outset. It seemed the wily Commissioner had eyes and ears everywhere. So sure were the co-conspirators that their number was trustworthy and dependable, yet somehow the entire plot was known to the High Commission.

Their meeting place was stormed in the early hours of the morning. Standard Bearers kicked doors off their hinges at all points of entry. They swarmed in, swords, staffs and in a few cases even guns drawn, and levelled at the conspirators. Meeting in the city seemed the sensible step to allow the expeditious enactment of their plans. Fortunately for Mordecai Anvil, this also meant he had full legal jurisdiction over a most heinous crime. Fourteen men and women involved in the botched assassination were arrested by the Commissioner's police force an hour before they were due to put their plan into action. They were shackled, wrist and ankle, and marched through the city streets. Word had spread, crowds of residents thronged the roads, four or five deep in some places. The solemn procession wound its way to the newly constructed grand Commission Hall, where the co-conspirators were held in grim cells below the ground level.

The clamour of the outraged citizens was immense. Even behind the thickest of brick and concrete walls and two floors below street level, the angry shouts and jeers filtered down to the prisoners. The minute slot windows high up in the walls of their cells admitted dishwater-grey light and a view of steep walls rising two storeys above them. Wrought iron railings thankfully held back the baying crowds desperate for blood, but did nothing to give the incarcerated any sense of hope or belief that clemency would come their way. The most senior High Justice of the Laws within the High Commission was called to preside over the trial. Politicians looked on with grave concern that this would be a kangaroo court, the judgement passed with the opening statements barely completed.

High Commissioner Mordecai Anvil appeared only as a witness when called, and made no public appearances or statements, while the trial process lasted nearly two months. It seemed the legal process was being given the due respect it commanded. Unfortunately for the accused, the duration did not reflect the direction the trial was taking. Fourteen competing legal representatives spent their time trying to lay blame at the feet of the other conspirators, rather than presenting any beneficial evidence. Though the trial went on far longer than any observer could have imagined, the verdict shocked nobody. Guilty. All accused were found entirely guilty for their parts in orchestrating an assassination on the High Commissioner. For such a grievous crime only one punishment was viable. All were exiled from the city, banished. They were to be escorted on an airship to the heart of the inhospitable Wetlands where they would be abandoned to survive or die trying in a harsh and desolate landscape. In all likelihood, those pampered politicians and one-time members of high society would not live long once left.

The verdict was announced to a capacity crowd at the courthouse, the noise was deafening. The newspapers in Copper Lakes and the surrounding towns and cities were awash with the news of the foiled plot, all seeded and embellished by the propaganda department of the High Commission. It swept the people into a frenzy, the sentiment towards the accused was one of utter outrage, the desire to see justice served grew by the day. When the court announcer burst through the huge, polished cherry wood doors, sending them crashing into the marble-walled facade of the courthouse, the protesting masses fell silent. Unfurling an official scroll signed by the High Justice herself, the announcer delivered the full statement of charges and verdict in a deep baritone. The joyous roar that arose was unimaginable, the frenzied masses delirious that justice was served on the would-be killers of their beloved High Commissioner.

A week later, on the eve of the conspirators being flown out to the Wetlands, Commissioner Mordecai Anvil took to the radio to address his people about the failed plot. He expressed great sadness that those from outside the city and the opposing leaders in Copper Lakes' political system would feel the need to consider such an awful act against a fellow man of the people. He expressed an impassioned promise that he would see the city steered right through troubling times, to balance the scales of justice. This stirred the people further in their love for their Commissioner and the High Commission. Peaceful protests saw calls for the city to be rid of elected officials, handing permanent rulership to Commissioner Anvil. With a degree of measured solemnity, the Commissioner enacted a law abolishing the political structure in Copper Lakes, leaving only the High Commission to draw up and pass all laws and practices. In barely a year and a half, he had seized complete control over Copper Lakes.

By the end of his second year in power, High Commissioner Anvil had neighbouring towns and cities seeking incorporation into Copper Lakes. Seeing the city-state as his flagship blueprint for society, he was reluctant to expand it or damage what he had built. At the beginning of his third year, the wily leader stood upon the steps of the Commission Hall and addressed his people in a rare State Address. The speech was broadcast on radio, where people in neighbouring and distant locations could hear the High Commissioner's proclamation. He announced plans to revitalise society with a new nation – the United Republic of the High Commission. It was open to all regions prepared to exist under their flag. With promises of wealth and prosperity, if they aligned themselves as part of the United Republic of the High Commission, many of the neighbouring towns and villages ousted their mayors and politicians, flying the black flag with the High Commission sigil.

Over the coming years, the Republic grew in size and wealth. Enclaves that held out, wanting to remain independent, suffered. They withered; poverty sank its diseased claws into the jugular. Without the investment from the High Commission and its immense connections, trade evaporated. With nobody to trade with, vast amounts of crops died, gone to waste as once-fertile fields went to seed. The larger enclaves became hotbeds of dissent and a constantly simmering anger. Ousted leaders, bitter over their loss of power, came together in the hope of cementing a form of opposition to the High Commission. Enclaves coalesced in the ghost towns, small settlements coming together with their disenfranchised neighbours in the hope that a coup would succeed. The rebel enclaves were spread so sporadically across the growing Republic that communication was difficult, and a unified leadership was nigh on impossible in any meaningful capacity.

High Commissioner Anvil allowed these settlements to exist for decades, wallowing in their self-pity, their threat so negligible it wasn't of concern. Besides, it looked better that he should show compassion rather than ruling with an iron fist. It suited his plans that he be considered benevolent and tolerant of other views in the eyes of his followers. Until they acted on their dissent and bitter resentment, he would abide. As the decade drew to a close, the United Republic of the High Commission had trebled in size. Vast networks of roads, waterways and rail systems radiated outwards like the spokes of a wheel from the capital of Copper Lakes at its hub. Anvil's reforms to ensure farm produce and mined resources were purchased for guaranteed rates was a huge boost to the economy of the United Republic.

Farmers, miners and other resource producers, for the first time in history, had a stable income, allowing them to prosper and partake of the strong economy they helped create. As more and more of the producers aligned themselves under the High Commission flag, the dissident enclaves suffered further, falling ever deeper into poverty. They became nothing more than scavengers, drinking water from puddles or collecting the condensation from caves and derelict buildings. Food was scarce. They foraged for what little they could find in the way of edible plant life and no creature was deemed too disgusting to be consumed when times were tough. Things became desperate for the dissident factions.

Some of the larger or bolder or downright most desperate factions took action; better than waiting in vain for communications of organised attacks. Under the cover of darkness, raids on mines were carried out. Some were far too audacious to work, picking those with the most valuable resources and the highest security. Some succeeded in scavenging dynamite and blasting caps, fuse wire and ignitors. A small number of storage facilities were targeted, destroyed in the face of detonating explosives, smaller farm holdings set ablaze around the Republic. A few unfortunate souls lost their lives in these tragic attacks, causing outrage throughout the thriving nation. Though a blow to the High Commission, such uncoordinated attacks did little to disrupt its expansion. This, however, did not prevent a swift and powerful show of force against these crimes.

These events offered Mordecai Anvil the opportunity to reveal his reformed militarised law keepers. No longer were laws and ordinances policed by the civic guards of years past. Now a more imposing and threatening organisation ensured compliance in all areas of day-to-day life in the Republic, bringing security and safety to the people. The Cabal emerged from the shadows to put down any slight rumblings of dissent. The disenfranchised were sent to re-education camps while the hardliners involved in the destruction of property and loss of life were tracked down. Cabal Inquisitors used the most state-of-the-art investigative techniques to pinpoint where the hardline dissidents were hiding out. Standard Bearers – an armed force tasked with direct peacekeeping and crime prevention – were sent to make arrests. Their appearance was enough to make the most hardened criminals take pause. Their uniform was all black. Heavy boots were polished to a high shine. Heavy leather robes were worn over the top, bearing the blue High Commission emblem prominently on their backs. Large hoods pulled low over their eyes, their faces were hidden behind masks – partly for safety, largely for appearance. They carried a wide array of weapons from heavy handguns, swords and long staffs with sharpened blades on either end. The sight of a troop of Cabal Standard Bearers was one that single-handedly reduced crime to almost zero.

After countless failed attempts on the High Commissioner's life over the decades, he became ever more reclusive. His decrees were always made a matter of public record, displayed on Commission Hall noticeboards and published in The Commission – the approved newspaper across the Republic. Occasional radio broadcasts were made, but never from an open or publicly attended venue, only ever from the sprawling residence of the Commissioner, Sunrise House. Mordecai Anvil was the first High Commissioner, so was afforded the right to name the official residence. With no great amount of modesty, he named the house after his somewhat arrogant belief that his rule was the dawning of a wondrous age for his growing nation. His paranoia grew as his life came under threat, even though most of the threats never materialised. He delegated public events to the lower order High Commission. Inquisitors and Standard Bearers became a common sight around the Republic and often beyond, in a bid to maintain power. Meanwhile, rumours spread about the health of the High Commissioner – that he was already long dead, and the Commission was guided by an unseen person behind the scenes. One thing that was never debated was the power the High Commission held and the immense militarised force ready to do its bidding at a moment's notice.

FIFTEEN

dison entered the working space of his quarters, shutting the door to his cabin. The open space was unusually packed with silent figures. He cast his gaze over all assembled before he strode to the head of the worn oak table with a confidence he did not feel inside. He took his place alongside Selah. The table was littered with documents, papers, maps, charts and reports. Anything and everything they had managed to scrounge up from paid-off sources around Rookhaven. Often mission planning was conducted by Captain Crow with Selah on hand to help moderate his more brash ideas. If air travel through riskier regions were needed, then Reuben would also be present. But those missions revolved around relieving the wealthy of their wealth, redistributing antiquities from large organisations or smuggling goods of a less than legitimate provenance under the radar. This evening, however, the table was surrounded by ten of the longest-serving crew members. Those who Crow trusted, who had worked with him for years, those who had shown their unwavering loyalty. If they were to take down Commissioner Anvil, they were going to need all the help they could get.

Never had Crow or any on his crew considered

undertaking a task of this scale. An unwritten rule of every smuggler, wheeler, dealer or rogue of all forms was that the High Commission was to be avoided at all costs. Often little to no action was ever taken by the High Commission unless the crimes committed were too grievous or violent. Though never publicly admitted, the Commissioner viewed a modicum of crime to be healthy in maintaining a balanced, cohesive society. He believed in neither a utopian nor dystopian system. He had no desire to create a paradise or hell on earth for his citizens. Balance in all things. Order from chaos. These things pleased him. A balance between poverty and wealth, crime and security, the haves and have nots. Balancing the scales was something that brought an inner calm to the secretive head of the High Commission.

But the High Commission had escalated of late. Nothing made sense. Platoons of Standard Bearers appearing where they were not expected, putting pressure on smuggler towns, insinuating themselves into the everyday machinations of people and places not under the direct rule of the Commissioner. Their tactics had escalated. They had always been about subduing and containing a suspect at all costs rather than resorting to unnecessary violence. Now they were shooting on sight, even in instances of the most trivial of crimes. Edison Crow thought back to something Selah had mentioned before, about the city guards that chased them as children. Those were no regular guards with average training, commonly found patrolling the streets of most hamlets, villages, towns or cities. They were shot at as children stealing food. They were fired upon for theft as adults. The Standard Bearers had been becoming more aggressive and less tolerant. The order sought by the Commissioner evolved into control.

The Inquisitors were vastly more troubling. Before the last decade and a half, they had only been seen infrequently. They were wildly intimidating, not least because they were only ever dispatched to the worst of situations. Where Inquisitors were found, nothing good ever followed. They never spoke, and conducted their business with a meticulousness that was unnerving. They had been sighted more and more throughout the last decade, almost coinciding with an increasing silence from the already somewhat reclusive Commissioner Mordecai Anvil. The thriving economy continued to thrive, but more so under an increasingly militarised state.

Much was discussed amongst the crew, thoughts and ideas shared back and forth in the hope of coming across the perfect solution to their predicament – the means to remove Mordecai Anvil from his seat, wherever he may be hiding. Voices raised as it became clear there was to be no ideal solution immediately available. Frustrations overran, friendships and loyalties were momentarily forgotten in the flaming heat of impassioned discussion.

"ENOUGH!" Though well-spoken when charming people around to his way of thinking, his voice could drop the heaviest of silences when the moment called for it.

"Enough. We aren't getting anywhere like this. We cannot make any rash decisions. If we do, make no mistake, we will not see another sunrise. We need the link between the shadow wraiths and the High Commission proved before we act."

"The Captain is right. We need to tail Gladstone's bait crews as subtly as we can. The Commission will be looking for Arcos, especially after the bullion train in the canyon." Selah always managed to get people on side, something about her, a quiet seriousness that spoke far more than any words she spoke.

He paused for a moment, allowing Selah's words to sink in. The crew assembled around him had grown silent, contemplative. The only sounds, the gentle creaking of the thick timber planks of the vast airship as it bobbed at anchor, rising and falling gently, much as a ship docked at anchor on a gentle tide.

"We cannot enter Copper Lakes with Arcos. I imagine every Inquisitor, Standard Bearer and High Commission member has our description if not a picture. They *will* have my picture, likely Selah's too. And this airship's not exactly subtle. Fast, manoeuvrable and well-armed yes, but she'll stand out even in the city."

"But Captain – she'll stick out even more at a small port on the outskirts of the city limits."

"Correct, Fi, and thank you for volunteering yourself for a task." A mischievous smile briefly played across Crow's face. "I need you to get maps of the area surrounding the city. If you can get them before we leave Rookhaven, so much the better."

"Do we not already have all the maps we need?" A puzzled look furrowed Fi's brow.

Selah seemed to have caught Crow's train of thought even as it left the station. "We have many city and ordinance maps here, Fi, but nothing geographical. If I know the captain, he wants maps of the forests, hills, valleys, mountains, lakes and caves in the area. When you get the maps, see if you can get any tips – we need somewhere big enough to hide Arcos from prying eyes."

Edison Crow nodded with satisfaction. "I knew there was a reason I kept you around, my dear Selah." Even in times of tension, Crow managed to lighten the mood with a castaway comment. Selah glared daggers at him before rolling her eyes with just the merest hint of a smile turning the corners of her mouth upwards. Before the captain could make another jibe at her expense, Selah carried on.

"Eliza, Rose – go with Fi, we are going to need all the tips we can get – the more diverse the better. If no single scoundrel knows exactly where we hid Arcos, it will slow down the Commission if they come looking for us."

The three young women stood from their seats and, donning their cloaks, left the cabin in search of maps down in the warren of illicit wheelers and dealers down in Rookhaven.

"Booker, Mycroft, Abel – don't get too comfortable, I've got a job for you as well. And you please, Reuben."

"Captain." Reuben stood, grabbing his cloak before Crow had even given him his orders.

"Even if we hide Arcos, I suspect she won't stay out of the fray for very long. We need contacts in and around Black River. Reliable, trustworthy as much as possible. I want her fitted with extra weaponry, and she'll need her armour strengthening. We need a shipyard where we can anchor and have the work carried out. Reuben, it needs to be done in the day and a half we have there. We cannot stay any longer."

"Aye Captain. We'll see to it."

"Thank you, Reuben. Go and see Maxwell Gladstone, he may be able to help with this one, or at least point you right."

Without hesitation, the men departed. Only Crow, Selah and four of the crew remained.

"This last job is going to be a little more difficult, particularly here in Rookhaven. We need to arm ourselves. The usual big-bore handguns, shotguns, longswords, they won't work. We need to be inconspicuous, subtle. Whatever our people carry has to be more than enough to defend or attack if it comes down to it. BUT – nothing big, showy or ostentatious. We need to be able to conceal everything, and that includes ammunition. I need everyone to be light on their feet and able to move when things go sideways."

"*If* things go sideways, Crow." It unnerved everyone to hear Selah being the voice of optimism in the face of Crow's saturnine statement.

"I applaud and appreciate your attempt at optimism, Selah. However, I must remain realistic for a change. This is not a simple raid that I somehow manage to escape unscathed from all the time. There is a very real chance that this could go very badly very fast. I will speak to the crew before we leave Black River, it is only fair they have a chance to leave."

"No one will leave. You've given them all, *us all,* a chance to get out of the slums." Hester had been running with Crow and Selah for a long time, more than twenty years. Their worlds collided when Crow and Selah were working their earliest jobs, knocking off small stores and post offices. Like them, she had been a child of the streets. She was the voice of reason amongst the crew. If she got wind of even the slightest threat of dissent or dissatisfaction towards her captain, it was often her who turned the tide and kept all in line. She was also the voice of the crew, understanding their sentiments and articulating them in a way Crow never failed to grasp. She always knew which way the wind blew when it came to the one hundred and fifty-odd crew aboard Arcos.

"Thank you, Hester, but I feel I still must allow them a choice. This is my battle, and nothing like we have ever taken on. Now, we must prepare. See what you can find here, black market, second-hand, brand new. We have the coin to buy it, but barter or trade if we can. Selah, we need to make ready our plans for arrival at Black River. First, though, send word ahead of our arrival – we need smaller vessels, something to get us to Copper Lakes unnoticed."

ᴏSIXTEEN

Edison was up well into the twilight hours as the sun began to lighten the horizon from inky black to a rich, deep purple. The crew worked late preparing Arcos so that it could cast off at first light, making the journey to Black River. Those dispatched the evening before to carry out their assigned tasks scurried around the maze of streets and alleyways in Rookhaven, seeking the cargo Crow had requested, seeking information to assist them on their travels. Eliza, Fi and Rose had returned barely two hours ago, just as the busy captain was considering a short spell of rest in his bunk. He rubbed his tired, strained eyes and stood ready to douse the oil lanterns as the doors to his cabin burst open, the three women entering with excited energy.

"Captain, the maps!" Eliza brandished a rolled chart in his direction, the other two carrying similar rolls. They dropped them on top of the table, weighing the corners down with whatever they could get their hands on – whiskey tumblers, inkwells, and even a dagger.

Crow perked up again seeing the geographical charts. He moved around the table with a twinkle in his eye. He almost barged Eliza, Fi and Rose out of his way as he scanned the charts laid out before him. Each had various markings and annotations scrawled about them. A range of clearings, caves and outcroppings were marked as possible locations to hide Arcos.

"This is great! Once we arrive in Black River, we can acquire a smaller vessel or two, see which of the locations works."

Fi spoke up. "How did the others get on?"

"As well as I hoped, Fi. The hold is loaded with crates of weapons and lightweight armour. Arrangements have been made through Mister Gladstone for a ship refit. I haven't seen Selah, but trust her to have arranged for smaller vessels to get us into Copper Lakes."

"And the crew?"

"I will address them tomorrow once we are underway. Now, get some rest – things are going to be a little busy before long."

Ropes, now untied from the mooring posts of the dock, lay neatly coiled like sisal serpents at rest. Crew scurried about the main deck preparing Arcos for departure. The vast pontoon-like tanks either side and below the airship echoed a slow, continuous hissing sound as the hydrogen from the storage tanks filled them, slowly raising the vast vessel into the early, indigo sky. As final preparations were made, and Arcos drifted up and away from the dock, the mammoth coal-fired steam engines hissed to life. Enormous propellers began to spin, slowly at first. Their vast blades sliced through the air with ease as they picked up speed. A loud whirring hum filled the air as the blades caught purchase and began to drag the hulking airship smoothly through the early morning sky.

Trailing a plume of steam from its funnels, Reuben piloted it into the brightening dawn, flanked by Selah and Hester. The captain, having pored over maps and charts long into the early hours of the morning, was asleep in his cabin, where Selah intended to leave him unless it was necessary. Hester was looking out over the deck, overseeing crew as they assembled and maintained the cache of newly acquired weapons, ensuring their readiness. She had no doubt they would be necessary and would be much needed and well used in Copper Lakes. Selah appeared distant, staring out over the reddening sky as if the sun were painting an omen of things to come. Reuben cast a glance her way, his eyes pinched with concern.

"Everything okay, Miss Selah?"

"You can drop the formality, Reuben. We've known each other long enough." A tense smile crept over her face.

"Old habits, I suppose. Now, enough skirtin' the question. I've known ye' long enough to know somethin's on yer mind. Best not let it fester, you'll be needing clarity by the time yer boots hit the ground in Copper Lakes."

Selah sighed wearily, feeling the weight of what was to come firmly upon her. She couldn't place a finger on it, but something filled her with unease. Everything was wrong, and she feared things were apt to get worse for them before they got better.

"I'm filled with dread, Reuben."

"I am sure there will be a reasonable explanation once we're done in Copper Lakes, very few supernatural things end up being so."

"That's not what I mean, Reuben. I cannot explain it, but something about what we are heading into concerns me. I feel like we are wading out into a storm."

Reuben grew silent and thoughtful at this. He maintained a watchful gaze on the skies around him, guiding the airship on its course. Hester had departed to assist the crew below decks. Checking his pocket watch, he corrected their heading with the slightest turn of the large ship wheel.

"Captain Crow will see us through. He's a good man, even if a bit overconfident at times."

"That's a part of what troubles me, though, Reuben. This time he doesn't seem in the least bit confident. He seems worried like he expects that he won't get through this one. He's talking of offering the crew the chance to disembark at Black River if they don't want to risk it. It isn't like him."

"Bugger that! There's no way in hell a single man or woman on this here ship is gonna leave 'im! He's always pulled fer all of us, so we're all gonna pull fer him on this one!"

"You know that as well as I, Reuben. Hester told him as much, in her blunt way. You saw everyone gathered last night, they all know the crew inside and out. Not one of them voiced concern. For Edison to be so concerned in the face of overwhelming support, well, frankly that scares me."

"Sure it isn't just the jitters? It is a big job, plenty big enough to make anyone a mite twitchy, Selah. And with everythin' what went down in the wetlands, the shadow wraiths, those High Commission bastards, would you blame him?"

She let out a long weary sigh. "I know, I know. But this just feels different. He was up all night as far as I can tell, poring over his charts, scribbling notes, planning everything. We know he is meticulous when it comes to planning, but this was something else, Reuben. Fevered. Frantic. Hardly anything ever seems to trouble him. Something is now, though. I can't tell if it's Copper Lakes, the High Commission, or what. I hope all will be well, but I fear we are heading into a storm."

Selah and Reuben grew quiet, listening to the hustle and bustle around them as they flew on. Towards what, though, neither knew.

Crow gasped, startled awake by another night terror. They had become frequent visitors when he closed his eyes, tormenting him most nights since they had first encountered the shadow wraiths. He shuddered upright stiffly, bathed in sweat. His hair matted to his brow, the bedsheet twisted and tangled about his legs. His breath, ragged and uneven, tore from his throat, and in his terror, Crow could feel his pulse pounding at his temples. This night terror was the worst he had experienced lately. He had never felt a fear reach its cold, sharp talons into his heart. As his mind quelled the terror screaming through his mind and his breathing slowed down, he took a pause, realising Arcos was already in motion. He should be at the helm.

He doused himself with ice-cold water, washing the fear away. He needed answers, needed a resolution. And most of all, he needed a full night of rest once this was all over. He pulled on his leather trousers, long boots, belt and bandolier, tunic, leather cuirass and finally the heavy cloak. Fastening it with his clasp, he pulled the hood over his head and solemnly strode out onto the deck, heading for the helm. Selah and Reuben turned as his footsteps thudded up the steps.

"How long have we been underway?"

"About an hour, Edison. We didn't want to wake you. Did you sleep at all?"

He was gazing out toward the horizon, a distant and troubled look etched upon his face. He appeared distracted, haunted by something.

"Crow?" Selah touched his arm with concern, causing him to jump.

"Hmm? What? Oh! Yes! Sleep, hmmm, yes a bit, I suppose."

"What's wrong, Crow? I know when you aren't telling me something."

"Oh no, nothing. Just, errrm, bad dream, you know? Nothing much."

Selah dragged him away from Reuben and Hester. She knew him well enough that she could always see when he lied. They had supported each other through so much and for so long now that they were two halves of a whole.

Edison rarely ever had nightmares. For one to have left him as distracted as this one had was troubling.

"Come on, Crow, talk."

He would not make eye contact with her. Selah took his shoulders firmly in her hands and shook him roughly.

"Don't shut us out, Crow. What we are going into now, this is too big for you to manage alone. And if we are all coming with you, well you can't hide *anything* from us! You've said it yourself more than once – you are worried that what we are planning to do is risky, if not outright deadly. You worry that it is so dangerous our crew deserve the chance to leave Arcos if they so wish. If you truly believe it to be as bleak as that you need to be honest about everything. I know nightmares aren't something that trouble you, so what did bother you last night, Edison?"

Crow went silent again, a frown crowding in on his brow with all the ferocity of an incoming storm. A long, defeated sigh escaped him, knowing that everything Selah was saying was right.

"You're right. It was more than a nightmare. More like a night terror. Even though I knew it to be a terror, it shook me. I expected it again and yet the shock and horror still hit me like a hammer blow. It was awful."

"Are you saying this has happened before last night, Edison?"

"Well, I didn't say that…"

"So, are you saying I'm wrong? That I've misjudged you? That I don't know you as well as I thought?"

"No, you're right. And I need to be open, full disclosure. I've been getting them most nights."

"Most nights? Since when – this week?"

"Since Clawridge Gorge. I've been seeing things in my sleep every night since we first saw the shadow wraiths. Each night I see more, and more."

"What are you seeing?"

Selah looked at Crow, the concern radiating from her was palpable.

"To begin with, nothing too much. I am standing at the helm, just me. No other crew is anywhere to be seen. Not you. Not Reuben. Nobody. Then the buzzing, that awful sound surrounds me. With a flicker, they appear. All around, on the railings, on the bow cannon, everywhere – just as we have seen them previously."

"To begin with? That means things are evolving, correct?"

He sighed deeply. It seemed to Crow that sighing was something that he was doing far too often right now. Things were weighing heavily upon his shoulders, making him doubt his abilities. He had many doubts in his life, and yet he never doubted himself. Until now. He began doubting himself, his skills, he doubted his ability to protect his crew and deliver them safely through whatever trials lay ahead of them. After a long moment, Crow turned to look at Selah – looked her deeply and honestly in the eye before he spoke.

"He is there. At least, I think it's a he. You know, their, well, their leader. To begin with, he wasn't. Then he stood upon the bow cannon, like when we have seen him, seen them. More recently he has been moving closer, further down the deck, drawing closer. Never speaking. Though as nights progressed and the nightmares continued, they started acknowledging me. Turning those hideous yellowish orbs upon me. Staring at me. Through me. Until last night. He spoke. 'We are family. We are one.' That is what he said. Pointing directly at my chest. 'We are family. We are one.' I couldn't see a mouth, but I felt his voice. Their voice. Some kind of shared voice, as if they are all connected. But the voice never touched my ear. It manifested in my head, never having been truly spoken."

"Shit, Crow, what does that even mean? It sounds pretty ominous. And why are they directing things at you? I know it's only a dream, but it is beyond eerie."

Crow slumped forward, his elbows on the wooden railing surrounding the raised wheelhouse, staring out at the gathering clouds starting to blot out the horizon. His right hand reached up to rub the pale, twisted knot of a scar beneath his right eye, an injury he sustained all those years ago on the day he first met Selah. An action he replicated subconsciously when he was deeply stressed, an action he hardly realised he was doing, yet one that Selah noticed immediately.

"I don't know, Selah, I don't. I am not even certain it was just a dream. It is one thing to suffer a nightmare for a night or two after some sort of trauma-inducing event. That is a given, the brain trying to process and reconcile that which it has encountered in our lucid, waking moments. This I am not so sure about. Are those shadow wraiths more like the myths we have all heard? I am beginning to fear they may hold some form of ability. To communicate as one, much like some form of symbiotic being. Channelling their abilities together into a pooled consciousness that doubles to amplify their thoughts."

"Edison, surely you are not saying what I think you are? Do you realise that sounds insane?"

"I wonder if through shared consciousness and an amplifying effect due to the mass of linked minds if they are capable of projecting thoughts, ideas, messages. Perhaps what ails me are not mere night terrors, but a message of some form or other."

"Edison, I don't need to tell you that that thought does not make things any less troubling. I don't doubt you, but think about this: if that is the case, why you? I've seen them, Reuben, hell the rest of the crew – we all have. Why are they only conversing with you? And their message – 'We are family. We are one.' I don't think I want to know what that means."

"Nor I, dear Selah, nor I."

The entire crew of the vast airship, the better part of a hundred and fifty or so men and women of all ages, races and walks of life, assembled below decks in the vast hull. The only absences, Reuben and the ten crew that Crow had entrusted to aid in the planning for this most trying of missions. As he descended the wooden stairs, Selah greeted him halfway down, ready to stand at his side as he spoke to his crew.

"You will all be aware by now that the job we are preparing for is far more significant than those we are used to conducting. This is no mere bank heist or raid of a high society soirée."

Crow paused to look around the assembled masses, packed to the gunwales in the cramped hull space. He had to be sure he impressed the gravity of the situation upon his crew. They had to be fully invested in this mission, otherwise their misgivings may lead to disaster.

"I make no bones about this – what we are planning is likely to be dangerous. How dangerous? I cannot say. Can I promise it won't become lethal? I cannot. From the day I took over the captaincy of Arcos I vowed not to let unnecessary harm come to the ship or a single member of its crew. I broke that vow when Arlo lost his life. This is what we are going up against. We have always conducted our jobs free from unpleasantness or violence. But we are about to go head-to-head with the High Commission, right in the heart of their beloved United Republic."

His composure slipped as he spat the last out like a sour taste in his mouth. He took a deep breath, steeling himself for this next part.

"You have all seen them. The shadow wraiths. We are not the only crew they have targeted. Their appearances seem to be closely related to increased activity from High Commission Inquisitors and Standard Bearers. Particularly concerning activity that they have never previously been known to involve themselves in. I believe they are in some way connected. Certain events I don't fully understand and am not yet ready to discuss have led me to one conclusion – we need to investigate and get to the bottom of what they are and stop them."

Shock, tinged with fear, rippled through the assembled men and women, men and women Crow had led for many years. Men and women he entrusted with his life. He knew this was not an easy ask, but he needed them to trust him or disembark before events transpired to a point of no return.

"I understand your trepidation, believe me. I have misgivings of my own about this situation and wish more than anything it was not myself that has to ask this of you. We will not be alone. Selah and I have secured assistance from Maxwell Gladstone back in Rookhaven. Some will join us at Black River, the rest will be positioned in and around Copper Lakes. If we all arrive en masse it would be suspicious. We will be leaving Arcos outside of the city – she is too obvious and now quite likely on the radar of the High Commission. We will source a small armada of assorted airships – big freighters, leisure vessels, hunting craft, working vessels, cargo ships – as best we can in Black River. Arcos will be left with enough crew to defend and run her should this be needed well away from the action. I know what I am asking of you, the risks involved in this job. There is no financial gain to be had here, but I fear this is something that must be done if we are to have a chance of survival. I have no right to expect or ask this of any of you, but I must. We will need all the crew we can to stand a hope. I trust every one of you and am asking you to trust in me. I would not be asking you to stay through this with me, with us, if it wasn't such a pressing situation. If you cannot entrust me as fully as I do you, you may leave this crew and Arcos without reprisal. I will not think ill of you, or view you in any other way than with the gratitude that you have earned for serving with me. There is no expectation on you to do anything other than that which is best for you, though I do implore you to stand side by side with me through this. You have until we dock at Black River to have arrived at a decision."

He cast one last look across his crew, the best he had ever served with in all his years aboard this airship. He turned and headed back up the stairs to the main deck, seeking refuge in his cabin.

As he returned to his cabin, he passed Hester heading below deck. They caught one another's eye, a slight nod of the heads acknowledging one another and conveying only a small amount of gratitude Crow felt for her assistance, knowing she was heading to talk with the crew. Entering his cabin, he made straight for the drinks cabinet, pouring two large whiskeys as Selah shut the door behind them.

"Edison, I am sure they will stand by us, you have looked out for them at every turn."

He dropped himself into his chair, swinging his boots up onto the desk with a heavy sigh.

"I hope you are correct, Selah, I really do."

The captain knocked back his drink, draining the tumbler in one long swig. He placed the glass down on the desk and tipped his head back, eyes shutting the world out.

SEVENTEEN

I t had been the better part of two hours since Crow had addressed his crew. He was three whiskeys in before Selah put a stop to that. No matter the outcome of the crew discussions going on below decks, no matter how stressed he might be feeling, she could not let him drink himself into oblivion for the day. There was too much at stake, and too much to be done on arrival at Black River. He made for the drinks cabinet a fourth time but she was much quicker, getting across the front of it before he had rounded his desk.

"Selah, could you move out of the way, please? I need a drink."

Selah stood her ground. She respected Edison but did not fear him. She was the balance he needed, helped him remember he didn't have the luxury of having everything his way as captain of such a vast airship.

"Selah, I am not messing about, you may think I am, but I assure you I am not. Move, *please*. I will not ask again."

"Sit down."

"I'm sorry, I must have misheard you there, could you repeat that?"

"Sit. Down." Selah glowered at him, a steely intensity

that cut him to the core. "If you please, *Captain*."

Shocked at being ordered by his oldest friend in such a firm and commanding manner, he dropped into his chair. He looked to the ground and away from Selah, though he could feel her eyes burning through him.

"I am sorry, Crow, but you cannot get half-cut and bury your head under the pillow, especially not now. There's too much riding on this. You need to be focused and ready. The crew needs you. I need you. Don't let any of us down, please?"

The weary captain remained silent for a long moment. Selah feared she was about to lose him on this one. Right now, she had to bring him back onside. He looked up, holding Selah's gaze. Though he always loathed conceding she was right, he knew she was. More often than not, she was correct. There were a lot of people relying on him right now to get them through this.

"I know. I know. I dread to think how many people we are going to lose once they're done talking down there. It's really stressing me out. What if they all go? Hell, what if half of them go?"

"Then so be it. You cannot force them to stay. You wanted them to have the freedom to choose. We just cannot expect or demand that anyone stay on as we fly into what could be a very dangerous situation. None of us knows what to expect going into this. What I do know for sure is that I am going nowhere. Reuben, Hester or the other nine either. And we have Gladstone's men and any other support he manages to secure in Black River. Whatever we have beyond that is a bonus."

The pair lapsed into silence, lost in their own thoughts. Both were nervous about what they may be about to wade into, but both also knew they had to see this through, no matter the outcome. A firm, loud staccato echoed around the cabin from outside the door, pulling both from their thoughts and making them jump from the fright.

"Come in!"

The door opened a crack, the face of Hester peering around it. She looked sheepish and seemed to be focusing more on Selah.

"Hester, come on in."

Selah beckoned her over the threshold and into the dimly lit cabin. Even in the brightest part of the day, Crow's cabin seldom pushed the shadows away, existing in a near-permanent state of gloom. Hester entered, looking more like a nervous child than a hardened, confident and bubbly member of the crew that Edison and Selah had known for many years. She skulked over and sat across the desk from Crow, while Selah tried to feign a casual air, leaning upon the ledge of one of the tiny windows.

"I'm sorry, Captain. I tried my best to get them all onside. They all understand why you gotta do this, but some just didn't want any part of this mess we all seem to be walking into."

Crow looked crestfallen, his face the picture of a defeated man. He held his head in his hands, elbows on the desk.

"Hester, how bad is it? Are we done for if we even get out of this one?"

"We lost three. The Brothers. Not sure anyone knows

their names fully yet, only been on the crew three months. I tried, but they didn't want the risk this job poses. I explained they could leave per your words, no ill will, but they cannot rejoin after this. I think they're sure you'll take them back in a heartbeat after all is said and done."

Crow's head snapped up, the spark and passion back in his eyes. If anything, he seemed aggrieved that the departing trio thought him so malleable.

"It'll be a frosty day in Hell before those good for nothing, idle arseholes set foot back on Arcos! Over my dead body! Selah – I want it noted, even in the event of my timely or otherwise demise, those wasters are not to set foot again on my ship!"

Selah could not hide her shock at Edison's enraged outburst, especially with a mouthful of water that she had to fight to not spray over the desk.

"And you," he spun back to Hester, jabbing a finger in the air in her direction. "You have absolutely nothing to apologise for to me or anyone on this ship, for that matter. I cannot believe what you must have said to keep all of the crew on board with us through this. Losing the three idiots has done us a favour. I've not heard one redeeming thing about any or all of them. With something so large ahead of us this airship is better off without them!"

Hester's shoulders sagged, the weight of the burden lifted from her. She slumped back in her chair.

"I was so sure you expected me to keep everyone with you in this, I've spent a good half hour preparing myself to come and tell you this news. I thought you were going to go ballistic."

"Come now, Hester. You've worked under me for plenty long enough that you can drop the formalities. You know how I feel about that. I had worked myself up so much that I was certain you were going to tell me half or more of the men and women on board were set to disembark for the last time at Black River. To lose three men is beyond manageable, especially those three. You've done an incredible job down there if that's all we've lost!"

"I don't think it was a question for anyone else, Edison. You've always looked out for everyone here. Everybody knows you would do everything conceivably possible to try and protect them and give them the best possible life compared to where they came from. It didn't even take discussion, they all wanted to be here. We spent much of the time talking through the plan in some more detail. Everyone wants to get involved, people have pitched for what they feel they're best suited to help with – prep work in Black River or shadowing Arcos to its hiding place and ferrying crew back to town. All of them want to be involved when the action goes down. You've got a determined, fiery crew down there, all standing right with you on this one, Crow."

"In that case, Hester, we better make this work. Come, my dear Selah, we have much preparation to do!"

Pulling on his waistcoat and top hat, Selah could see the old Edison Crow still inside somewhere. Falling in behind him, she glanced over at Hester and rolled her eyes. The two women followed the captain out onto the deck.

He strode across the deck with purpose and a renewed vigour. Hearing that so many of his crew would stand with him, even in the face of such overwhelming odds, lifted his spirits. He busied himself ensuring Arcos was running smoothly, and ensuring crew were prepared to hit the ground running on arrival at Black River. Selah and Hester had joined Reuben up at the helm and observed the almost jubilant Edison as he darted around the main deck, not unlike a bee flitting from flower to flower in a meadow. Sometime later, he ascended the steps to the wheelhouse, seemingly bouncing from one step to the next.

"Reuben, my good man!" The exuberant Crow clapped the larger pilot on the shoulder firmly enough to rock him. He beamed from ear to ear with a newfound joy.

"Captain. Good to see you feeling more chipper."

"The sun is shining, the sky is blue, what's not to be chipper about?"

Selah tutted disapproval and muttered, "I'm sure we'll find something, probably somewhere behind that blanket of black cloud we seem to be flying straight towards."

"My dear Selah! There is no need for such glumness, every cloud has a silver lining! Even if that lining appears to be an almighty squall of rain…"

His certainty deserted him for a moment as he riffled through his coat pocket seeking his trusty old spyglass. Extending it, he put it to his eye and peered ahead of the bow, seeing a torrential storm that they were flying directly into.

"How long until we make port, Reuben?"

"Assumin' that there storm don't cause us too much of

a nuisance? I'd reckon a couple of hours at worst. Though I got a feelin' you can add at least another hour, maybe more on to that."

"I trust we are in a most capable pair of hands to see us through this storm. Selah, I want you, Hester and the rest of the Terrific Ten in my cabin post haste! We need to be ready to go as soon as we have Arcos tied off."

"The Terrific Ten? Where in the name of all things great and good did you conjure that bit of bullshit from, Crow?"

Hester snorted with laughter at Selah's uncharacteristic retort. She doubled over, gasping for air, while Reuben's broad shoulders rose and fell with his deep, booming chuckle.

"I feel that is quite self-evident, my dear. They are a fantastic group of people, terrific no less, and there just so happens to be ten of them! Now, meet me in my cabin as soon as you are physically able!"

And with a snap of his fingers and a flourish of his coat as he span, he bounded off for his quarters, leaving three utterly bemused, chuckling figures in his wake.

❁❁❁

Crow was in his cabin, the large table cleared from the chaos it had been of late. He had the maps showing all of the identified locations for hiding the airship, placed as accurately as possible around a map of Copper Lakes. He had a list of contacts in Black River that Maxwell Gladstone had given him to seek support from. With their arrival only a couple of hours off, he didn't want any delay in their preparations. The storm seemed to be strengthening, and though Reuben was the most capable pilot he had come across, he feared the worsening weather would test even him. A sharp series of knocks pulled his attention to the door. Before Edison had a chance to beckon his guest in, Selah had opened the door, a strong wind throwing stinging droplets of rain inside as she entered, followed by Crow's self-titled Terrific Ten.

"Ah, welcome! Please, do come in and make yourselves at home," Crow said with a tinge of sarcasm directed at Selah as they all trooped in, taking seats around the table. He turned away, walking purposefully towards the drinks cabinet once Selah had taken her seat on the wrong side of the long oak table to stop him.

"Crow, we discussed this earlier…"

"I know, my dear, I know. Clear planning requires a clear mind!"

And with that, he produced two large decanters filled with crystal clear water. Fresh and cool, it was a welcome refreshment knowing they were all likely to be sitting in the stuffy cabin for some time.

"Okay, where did we get to before we departed Rookhaven?"

"We've got the weapons, or at least a huge head start on that one – the hold is packed with small firearms, explosives and an impressive assortment of bladed implements. There's more than enough for the crew to be well armed."

"Great job, Hester, that's a good start."

"We found a shipyard about ten miles outside of Black

River. We should dock in town to offload the crew and rendezvous with some of the hired vessels. We can have one or two follow Arcos to the shipyard. They said it's going to be tight timewise, but they should be able to get the armour and cannon refit complete by the end of tomorrow."

"Thank you, Booker."

"We should be able to sort out the final details for the additional manpower and vessels when we get to Black River. We might even be able to get hold of Mister Gladstone."

"Good idea, Selah, I think we need to see if we can speak with Maxwell before we go any further. Hopefully, he can offer some more good news before we head off to Copper Lakes. I, for one, will be happier if we can speak with him before we go anywhere."

"Captain, we should consider splitting off so we can make the best use of our time in Black River."

"Agreed. Abel, Fi, Eliza – I want you to organise a skeleton crew to run Arcos to the hide. We will need enough to also man a few vessels to shuttle the crew back. While we are discussing that, I think we need to settle on the ideal location for hiding her."

Fi stepped forward. Having sourced the charts and maps, she had spent a little time familiarising herself with the details on them, the pros and cons of each of the four locations.

Pointing to one of the maps, Fi spoke confidently "There is a large clearing here in Hearthstone Forest. It's the farthest location from Copper Lakes, and there aren't any major paths or routes through there. The real issue here, though, is it's open from the air – any passing airships will have a hard time not spotting Arcos down there. We'd need a lot of time and resources, not to mention manpower, just to try and hide her there."

Selah stood up and interjected here. "No good, time is something we won't have an abundance of on arrival. We need to be able to hide her and get out of there as soon as we can."

"Fair call. There's a bluff up in the Dragon Tooth mountains up north, but I'm discounting that one right from the off – it's no good. We've no way of knowing how the weather is looking – if we get up there and there's a blizzard, neither Reuben nor you will be able to see us down safely."

"I think that's the right call, Fi. This mission is risky enough without needing to add any more excitement to proceedings."

"Smugglers Isles is always an option. No rational person goes to the islands, and those mad enough to go there tend to avoid other individuals at all costs. Discretion is assured as smuggling gangs are too paranoid to fraternise with others. There are docks there too."

"Hmmm, it might work. Can we be sure Arcos will be safe?"

"That'd depend on how many crew you can leave to keep watch over it. Though the other inhabitants tend to avoid one another, there's no way you can leave the ship unattended. You'll not have a great deal left when you come back to it."

"Shit. No good, we can't spare many men for ship-sitting duties. We've got to be able to leave Arcos somewhere secure. Ideally somewhere no one's going to find her."

"Fourth and final option then, or we're back to the drawing board."

"What've you got Fi? Tell me you've saved the best for last!"

Fi tapped the fourth map on the table. About fifteen miles southwest of Copper Lakes, six miles west of Black River.

"Is that the Overlook Mountains? Fi, that's a pretty crazy flight. Crazy enough it might just work! What's your plan?"

Fi tapped another spot, up in the heart of the range.

"Silver Falls? Pretty inaccessible, which is a bonus, but where the hell do we hide an airship this big up there?"

"I did a bit of digging, spoke to some people. There's something not on any of the maps. Behind the falls is a cavern. It's enormous, right behind the main fall. With so much water crashing over the falls, the cavern can't be seen. It's big enough to dwarf Arcos and we should be able to leave her there, secure and hidden. It'll be a tough journey, though – the amount of water flowing over the falls is huge so you're going to need everyone focused and working together to get past the fall and into the cavern."

Edison and Reuben shared a glance and a slight nod of the head.

"Great work, Fi. I don't see that there is another feasible option beyond Silver Falls. It's risky, but once through, Arcos should be safe. I think those of us here along with

Reuben will be the skeleton crew. Hester – I need you to organise two crews for smaller airships to follow us out to the Overlook Mountains and ferry us all back to Black River."

"On it, Captain."

"Everyone else, above deck. We need to prepare for arrival. Let's go.

EIGHTEEN

As Arcos came upon Black River, the sky grew hazy, a black smog staining the cobalt blue a murky black. The sun was reduced to a smudged, hazy yellow orb straining to shine through the smog. Through the breaks in the belching sooty clouds, in the distance two vast lakes shone a coppery light in the early autumn sun, a beacon drawing the eye into the capital city. The vast clock tower bridging the two lakes stood tall above the city, its clock face only obscured by distance. The air around it appeared iridescent with rainbow spray thrown up from the gallons of water tumbling through the hissing, steaming mechanisms. All this in stark contrast to the outlying city of Black River. All of the buildings, once the clean white of the limestone used to build them, were now all tinged with black soot. What few hardy trees and plants grew there were dulled thanks to a black dusting all over. The people of the town all worked in the mining, processing or burning of its principal resource – coal – and all seemed to wear a permanent coat of coal dust, ingrained deeply in their skin.

Though much of the town was covered in grime from the ever-present plumes of soot from the refineries, mines and factories, the town's namesake was one of the few points of clarity in an otherwise sooty place. The Black River flowed down from the vast peaks of the Overlook Mountains, ever on the horizon reaching their gnarled claws skywards. The water was crystal clear and ice-cold, no matter the season. The colour and its name came from the sheer volume of coal-seamed rock making up the bed. The onlooking crew from passing airships would be forgiven for thinking that the river was a wide gouge in the earth showing the inkiest of black beneath the surface, such was the depth of it.

With so much going on, too many thoughts swirled through his mind. Edison had always loved the opportunity to take the wheel and steer airships through the skies. It brought him a sense of calm and peace that few other things in this world could. He had dismissed Reuben for the last hour of flight. Having negotiated what turned out to be a much smaller storm than first thought, Reuben took his leave to get some rest ahead of a tricky flight into the Overlook Mountains. The captain raised his old spyglass to his eye at intervals, rechecked their bearing on the ornate deck compass and adjusted the enormous wheel with the slightest of well-practised movements. The ghost of a smile played across his face. A look of true contentment, thought Selah, as she watched him from her perch against the railings. A look she did not often see on him. How long will it last, she wondered to herself. *If we somehow make it through this, what comes next for us?* Trying to dispel the dark clouds swirling and expanding in her mind, she turned her face into the mild sunlight and closed her eyes, imagining easier skies ahead.

✿✿✿

Crow piloted the airship on the calm, warm currents towards the docking pads on the outskirts of Black River. The dock area was nothing remarkable, much like a million other such facilities in thousands of working towns the world over. The hard standing area that served as a hub that the pads radiated out from was littered with wooden cargo crates and myriad hoses for fuel and hydrogen, water and pumping waste like a nest of snakes. Half a dozen dock workers leapt to their feet from their resting positions, the arrival of Arcos providing a bit of excitement for a workforce used to small cargo and pleasure craft – barely enough work for one man, let alone six.

Crow deftly eased Arcos into the docking pad as his crew threw the docking ropes over the railing. Gangplanks dropped from several hatches along the side of the ship and the crew set about preparing it for its challenging flight into the Overlook Mountains. Arrangements were finalised as the crew headed into town to meet with the various contacts set up by Gladstone.

"Fi, I need Reuben and yourself to work out the route through the mountain passes. Use my cabin, I need you to be as certain as you can that we have the best route. We cannot risk damaging the ship on the way in."

"Aye Captain."

The pair headed up to Crow's quarters, leaving him and Selah on deck.

"Crow, let's get to the post office, that has to be the most likely place to have a phone line. We need to make contact with Maxwell Gladstone."

"Go on ahead, Selah. There's something I need to look into first. Make contact with Gladstone and finalise details with him, I will meet with you at the public house."

"Crow, this isn't the time to be running off on secretive errands now. Whenever we land at someplace new you disappear on me and won't tell me what is going on. Now really isn't the time for secrets."

"Selah, trust me, there is nothing to hide. I will see you at the public house shortly."

With that, Crow walked down the plank and across the dock platform to the lift.

Selah wandered the smog-filled streets, her boots leaving prints in the soot that lay thickly on the old acid-rain etched paving slabs. All around her the sounds of the city rang out. Steam flowed through mile upon mile of worn copper pipes, hissing out of pressure release valves on its way to the metropolis of Copper Lakes. Mechanised beasts groaned and rumbled and bellowed deep inside the mining pits. The processing plants that generated energy from the coal vibrated and hissed night and day, supplying the capital with power and superheated steam. The High Commission had installed a sprawling green space in the heart of Black River, a sweetener to encourage the town to produce steam and power for Copper Lakes and to remain loyal to the Republic. The large open space featured landscaped planters at its heart that, from the air, formed the hydra sigil that was known the world over.

Selah strode purposefully through the park, once lush and green but now tinged with black soot. Tall trees stretched up to the bleak sky, their leafless gnarled branches reaching high, their brittle ash-coated leaves littering the lawn. Reaching the eastern gate, she crossed a street bustling with coal-smeared workers in the late afternoon sun. The bell over the post office door rang a delicate chime as Selah opened the door, heading for the clerk standing at the counter.

"Good afternoon, Miss. How might I assist you?" The elderly postal worker adjusted his black waistcoat and tarnished shirt, excited to see an out-of-town customer in the office.

"Good afternoon. Does this branch have a telephone line? I'd like to place an urgent call."

"That we do, young lady. Down the hall, on your right. Should be plenty quiet for you. If you need anything, just ask. There's a connection fee, whether you speak to your contact or not, mind."

Selah reached into the pocket of her long black leather trench coat and produced a large silver coin.

"I do hope fifteen shruckles will cover it."

"Standard fee is six, Miss. Then there's a call time rate depending on how long you're on. We'll settle when you're done." Selah gave the kindly elder man a nod of acceptance and made her way down the narrow hallway. A musty smell infiltrated her nostrils. Looking around her she could see peeling wallpaper, water damaged wood panelling and mildewy damp patches on the old, threadbare carpet. The town of Black River may fall under the hydra flag of the

United Republic of the High Commission as one of its most important resource generating settlements, but it did not see nearly the amount of investment it dearly needed.

The phone was mounted to the wall, the mouthpiece about halfway up. The earpiece hung towards the mouldy carpet, from a frayed cord showing bare copper wire through the woven outer casing. She bent down and picked up the earpiece and retrieved the number for Maxwell Gladstone from her inside pocket. She spun the rotary dial entering the first digit, waiting for it to return before entering the next, repeating the action. Selah always thought that for a new technology supposed to make life easier and communication faster, the process of dialling a number seemed inexorably slow. Given how long it felt like it took to dial, who in their right mind decided on fourteen-digit phone numbers? With the final spin of the rotary dial, Selah lifted the earpiece to her left ear, momentarily considering leaning upon the mould-streaked wall. The long, drawn-out rings continued for some time without an answer. Selah gave up, replacing the earpiece and disconnecting the call.

She stalked down the hall back around to the main shop, annoyed she had not got hold of the man they were putting their faith in, entrusting their lives to.

"No luck, young lady?" The old man took pride in his job and would not have looked out of place dealing cards on the underground riverboat casinos. He sported a once-white button-down shirt, deep red crushed velvet waistcoat going thin in places and a visor cap with his wispy white hair flowing over the top. His watery eyes, a certain sparkle still gleaming deep within, peered at her over a pair of well-worn half-moon spectacles. She sighed deeply, looking down at the counter.

"None, I am afraid. I did not need that right now."

"Better luck next time, Miss. Anything more I can do for you this afternoon?"

"No, thank you. I should be going."

The old man reached for a lockbox under the counter, pulling it out and placing it on the old wooden surface. He took an old brass key on a chain from his breast pocket and unlocked the box. He counted out nine old bronze-coloured coins, sliding Selah her change. She thanked the man, pocketed the coins and left the post office. As she opened the door to leave, the door chime tinkled overhead once more.

As Selah walked back over the street towards the park she walked through on her way in, a figure watched her progress from a side alley that ran between the post office and a small general store. He watched her disappear. Pulling the hood of his black robe over his face, he turned and walked back towards town.

The public house was a dark, dingy space. Though it was still the middle of the afternoon, the weak autumn sun struggled to filter through the smog-filled air. The soot encrusted windows hadn't admitted sunlight in years. Dusty storm lanterns suspended from the low ceiling flickered, sending shadows dancing over the walls. The barman pushed puddles of stale beer around the chipped bar. The public house slowly started to fill with the crew from Arcos as they finished their tasks. Crow entered the bar area and took a seat at a table with his back to the wall, affording him a view of the door, bathrooms and stairs to the rooms. He always ensured nobody could sneak up on him.

He sat alone, observing his crew as they unwound, slowly sipping at his pint. Edison pulled his pocket watch from within his cloak and thumbed the clasp, opening the ornately carved gold cover. Just as he snapped it shut, Selah walked through the door. *On-time, as ever,* Crow thought. She sat at the table, across from her oldest friend, and signalled for a pint from the barman. The pair sat in silence until the barman brought over her drink and headed back to the bar.

"How did you get on, Selah? Has Maxwell got everything in place?"

"Unfortunately not, Edison. I couldn't get hold of him. Something doesn't feel right about it at all. Especially as he told us to contact him when we got here."

"What the hell? That lying, low-life, bottom-feeding, two-faced bastard!"

"Sounds like you're looking for me then, Captain Crow." Maxwell Gladstone spun a chair around backwards and took a seat leaning over the back.

"Gladstone, what the fuck?"

"Thought I'd surprise you and come on down here. If I'm committing money, ships and people to this cause of yours, I want to be out there. Can't ask people to act for me if I'm not prepared to step in myself."

Crow's anger slowly dissipated, though he continued to glower at Gladstone.

"Is everything in place over at Copper Lakes?"

"I've got people ready all over the city and plenty of eyes on the Commission Hall."

"How many, Mister Gladstone?" Selah seemed highly suspicious, anticipating the worst from a man like Gladstone.

"Somewhere north of three hundred around the city."

"Three hundred? I'd hoped for more," Crow lamented. "But with my crew that brings us just shy of five hundred. We can make that work."

Maxwell Gladstone looked from Crow to Selah and back, unable to contain a wide smile spreading across his face.

"I've got another hundred purely focused on the Commission Hall. Then there's a hundred and sixty I managed to arrange to surround the city at all the core entrances."

Crow's troubled expression turned to one of shock, then rapidly to one of hope. With so many people on hand, there was a chance this might just work.

As the afternoon darkened into a purple-hued evening, the crew gathered in the pub, and a sense of ease fell over everyone. Reuben walked into the pub with ten crewmates and beelined for the table where Crow, Maxwell and Selah sat.

"She's ready, Captain."

"How'd she handle, Reuben?"

"Slower and takes longer to manoeuvre, but between us, we'll get her through the Overlooks."

"Brilliant. Get some rest, Reuben, we need to leave at first light."

Crow stood, shaking hands with Gladstone.

"All being well, we won't see you until after everything is done, and the dust settles. Go safely and see you on the other side, Maxwell."

"Go safely, Captain Crow."

"I hope I am worthy of the support the crew have shown me, Selah."

Back aboard the revamped Arcos, replete with additional weapons and thicker armour plating on its hull, Crow sat in deep contemplation with Selah for company.

"Don't be so dramatic. You earned their trust and support long ago. You earned mine even further back. You've never given a single one of us reason to doubt or question you, even now."

"I feel hopeful that things will work out for us, but I am asking a lot of everyone. This is huge. I am asking them to put aside their superstitions for this."

"Crow, there is no way the crew would have said or done anything differently."

NINETEEN

TWENTY YEARS EARLIER

Merely surviving had not been good enough for Edison Crow for quite some time now. He had progressed to petty theft – pickpocketing unsuspecting passers-by in the street. It was a quick fix for some small cash. But it only served to make Crow desire a different life, something more. Selah had remained with him, the pair seemed to balance each other. It may have been seven years since they had met, but her irritation with him had not yet waned.

"I've got a job for us, my dear Selah!"

She rolled her eyes and continued down the alley she was skulking along. Crow had to trot to keep up with her.

"Just hear me out, Selah. This is something more than just picking pockets for loose change. It could be our chance."

His enthusiasm was infectious. She paused, then turned to face the gangly teen standing before her. The wound he suffered the day she first met him had left a twisted pale scar beneath his left eye. His dark hair had become thick and messy.

"Keep talking, Edison. Let's hear what you've got for me."

148

"Tomorrow night a wagon is set to leave town at eleven. It'll be collecting cash from the post office. Once it gets beyond the old walls, it'll meet with a High Commission escort. Before that though, it's gotta pass through Five Bridges. I say we hit the wagon as it passes through there – drop down as it passes under the first bridge, grab as much as we can and be off by the third bridge."

Selah looked away, pensive, thoughtful, silent for some moments. Finally, she let out a long, slow sigh.

"Fine, Crow. You might have something. But, and I cannot stress this enough, I will be setting this one up. I plan it and run it," she said, her voice rising just the slightest, and she jabbed him in the chest to punctuate each word: "And. You. Follow. My. lead."

"Ow, fuck! Okay, Selah, calm it. This is your take, your plan, your lead. Quit jabbing me!"

"I'll be at the North Gate at ten. Five minutes and I'm gone. Your choice if you're there."

Selah was organised. Meticulous some might say. She had checked out the Five Bridges road, looked at the bridges themselves, and watched the people flowing in and out of town. The first bridge was the obvious place to get on the coach. It had a low footfall, even during the busiest times of the day. She was sure that the fourth or fifth bridge would be better than the third that Crow suggested. The fifth offered better escape options in case things went wrong. Most wagons seemed to take about ten minutes to cover the distance between the first bridge to the fifth. This was one part of the plan that bothered her – it could be more, it could be less, a lot of factors could come into play. Selah, loathe to admit it though she was, would need Edison. His infectious positivity grated on her no end, but a second pair of eyes would see them grab more shruckles and ensure they didn't miss their exit. That fifth bridge had large ornate iron rings all along both sides. It was the oldest bridge. For as long as she could remember, she had thought what looked like large ornamental mooring rings seemed silly on a bridge so high up and nowhere close to water. Only now did she see a potential use for them.

After a busy afternoon, Selah had her plan. She needed to lay her hands on some bags to stash the loot in, before getting in some rest ahead of that night's escapades. She walked back over the third bridge and made her way back to town.

Edison Crow leant against the wall, his left leg bent, foot resting casually against the crumbling bricks, of a run-down pub across from the North Gate. Dark blue trousers, patched at the knees, scuffed, worn brown jacket with the collar flipped up in the hope of hiding his identity, not that he ever got noticed as one of Murkvale's hundreds of street dwellers. A tatty, frayed-around-the-edges cord flat cap finished what he considered a disguise, even if it marked him out a bit in this part of town. He peered through the cracked window of the old pub at the clock. A quarter past nine. Timing was never his strong point, but he was adamant he was going to be on time to meet with Selah. He needed to prove he was more than just a common pickpocket. He had ambition but lacked the means to achieve it alone. *I need to work on my time keeping if I'm to get anywhere. If we're to get anywhere,* he thought to himself.

It was a bitterly cold evening; a light sprinkling of snow had begun to fall. Crow stamped his feet and blew into his hands before stuffing them as deep into his jacket pockets as he could without adding to the holes already there. His breath, a plume of steam, billowed upwards into the wintry shower. Selah appeared at quarter to ten, two large messenger bags for each of them. She strode quickly and quietly through the square, the snow settling just enough that she left the faintest of footprints. She shoved two bags at Crow, apparently annoyed by something.

"It wasn't meant to snow."

"I am sure it is only a minor setback, Selah!"

"What if the wagon leaves early?"

"If it does, it does – that is always a risk. But we cannot give up based on what-ifs."

"Is this what it feels like when you pick your marks normally? How do you manage the unknowns?"

"It's quite simple – I cannot worry over that which I do not know. I can prepare, I can plan, I can tail a mark until I know them almost as well as they do. But the tiniest change in their routine could scupper everything. And if it does, so be it. Onwards to the next mark."

"That is just so casual, though. A job could end up being the making of us, it could get us out of this dive town and on to a better life."

"It could, Selah, it very well could. Until that happens, though, I take each day as it comes, roll with the successes, learn from failures, because we will suffer both; more failures I would wager."

Selah looked at Crow, really looked at him and properly saw him for once, not just as the irritating teenager she so often thought of him as. She looked away almost as quickly, turning away from him. Though she would never tell him so, she was coming to realise she needed his confidence as much as he needed her practicality and intuition."

"Come on, it's time."

She jogged towards Five Bridges, Crow close behind, as the snow fell heavier, the only sound the crunch of their boots in the fresh snowfall.

The arterial road that scythed its way through the heart of Murkvalle was swathed in darkness at this hour. The two scruffy figures were the only ones out in the worsening snowstorm, shivering in their inadequate, scavenged clothes. They huddled in the lee of the buttresses of the first bridge. They did not speak, both lost in their thoughts about the impending job. Their breath plumed into the frigid night air. A sound drifted to them from the south, in the direction of the post office. The muted clip-clopping of the hooves of two horses, the wagon rounding a bend at the bottom end of Five Bridges. Though it was on time, the snow had slowed its progress. *This will be easier than I first imagined*, Selah thought complacently. She stood up and poked her companion in the ribs with her scuffed leather boots.

"Get up, it's coming."

The pile of rags moved and materialised into a gangly youth. With all the confidence and exuberance of his age, he jumped up onto the parapet of the wall, squatting down on his haunches ready for the approaching wagon. The heads of two large shire horses passed beneath him, as he tensed his muscles. Just as he was about to jump, Selah placed a hand on the wall and swung her body around and over, falling gracefully and landing as deftly as a cat on the roof of the passing wagon. As impressed as he was by her skill, Crow almost forgot to leap himself, landing far less smoothly, nearly toppling backwards. Pausing only for a moment, the pair dropped themselves over the back, hauling the unlocked doors open. The interior was stacked with wooden chests filled with gold, silver and bronze-coloured coins. More shruckles than either person had ever seen. Selah began to wonder if she had wildly underestimated the number of messenger bags they would need.

"Get filling, Crow," she spat in a hushed tone.

They grabbed chests, stuffing them roughly in their bags. Emptying the coins would have meant they could carry more but they could not risk the noise. In his eagerness, Crow dislodged a chest as he lifted another down from the top of a shelf. It clattered to the floor, breaking open and spilling coins all over. Selah and Crow froze as the driver slowed the horses. After a brief pause that felt like an eternity, the wagon jolted to a start again. The pair let out their held breath. Crow leaned out around the side, realising the fifth bridge was fast approaching.

"On top, now!" he hissed, jabbing his finger towards the roof.

He scrambled up to the roof, leaning down once more to hoist Selah up with him. As the bridge neared, something drew the attention of the driver. He looked over his shoulder, spying the two street dwellers and their bags. He didn't shout, but placed a tarnished whistle between his lips, its piercing shrill rending the silent night air. Shouts and the rhythmic thud of hooves grew louder as guards of the High Commission converged on them. The pair jumped, snatching at the large, rusted iron mooring rings on the side of the bridge. Crow hauled himself over the wall when he heard a shout.

"Crow!"

He scrambled onto the wall again peering over. The ring Selah swung from was pulling free from the wall. The bitter cold had caused the aged masonry and metal to deteriorate, something she had not checked or planned for. Reaching down, Crow stretched for his companion, as the ring gave up its precarious hold on the wall. She managed to snatch at his wrist and was hauled roughly over the parapet just as the guards sped up, now long clear of the fourth bridge. They tumbled in a heap in the drifting snow at the base of the wall, scrambling to regain their footing. Gunshots sounded, deafening in such an enclosed street. Bullets pinged off walls, the whine of ricochets all around them.

"We've gotta get out of town! Lay low somewhere for

the night, separate. We'll be harder to find! Try to mask your footprints. I'll be waiting in the forest beyond the West Gate in six hours. Look for the sign!" With that, Crow took off across the bridge. After a split second to catch her thoughts, Selah sprinted as fast as the snow allowed in the other direction, aiming for the warren of streets and passages of the slumbering city.

The sky was tinged purple with the first light of dawn. A frosty mist hung low to the ground as the city began to wake. Crow had spent hours giving the guards the run-around – traipsing back and forth throughout the city. He double- and triple-backed on himself, disappeared into buildings, snuck out of windows and slunk along dingy alleyways. It was the work of someone determined to escape. Eventually, he snuck into the storm drains, a torrent of melted snow filling the waterways. The curved walls offered nowhere for him to escape the frigid water. Getting wet was something he could do without, what with a harsh winter storm howling at every gutter opening. Crow dropped down off the ladder into shin-deep water with a deceptive current. The bricks beneath his feet were slimy with decades of build-up from sources he'd rather not think about. It was going to be a slow, foot-numbing trek out of the city. The grey, foamy water meant it was impossible to see what was below. A broken or missing brick, debris hidden below, so many things could lead to a fall that down here could be more than just a turned ankle.

He sloshed his way out of the storm pipe as the sun started to show the faintest glimmer of light on the horizon. Now, as the sky painted from purple to the deepest fiery orange, he huddled amongst a stand of trees, seeking shelter from the biting wind in a thicket of bushes. He watched the road that approached from his left turn towards the ancient walls of Murkvale before it passed near him. He scanned every face as life returned to the city with daybreak. He sought the face of Selah in the growing crowds flowing in and out of the imposing portcullis gates. The paranoid voice in his mind stretched its icy fingers deep into his brain, sending shivers down his spine – he could not help but keep an eye out for the men of the High Commission.

Masses of people thronged to and fro about their daily business, bundled up in what passed for warm clothing to protect from the harsh winter weather. Hunched figures bundled under cloaks and jackets and whatever they could scavenge ebbed and flowed in and out of the city gates. An hour before their agreed meeting, Crow, from his hide beneath a stand of holly bushes, caught sight of a figure who stood out from the crowd. They were swaddled in a heavy black cloak that billowed behind them, striding with purpose. A scarf was wound close about the face, hiding any details that could be recognised, only the slightest gap left for the eyes. They carried themselves in a very particular way – tall, head constantly moving from side to side, looking for any sign of threat. Their stride was purposeful, confident almost, but ready to explode with power should they need to flee. Crow knew who he was looking at – Selah. He had scoped the edge of the forest when he had arrived and had seen a crow's nest in a tree a few rows back from the tree line. He tossed a rock at it, scaring two large birds noisily into the morning sky, drawing the attention of the figure. She made a quick check of her surroundings; she was certain she had not been followed but always erred on the side of caution. Pulling the hood of her cloak low over her face she casually strolled along the quieter path heading away from the makeshift market that was set up along the main road into town, before slipping into the trees.

Crow called out in a hushed whisper, "Over here!"

Selah strode with pace deeper into the shadows to where the voice had come from. As she neared, he crawled out from under the bushes and started walking deeper into the woods, Selah speeding up to keep pace.

"Edison, last night. I fucked up."

"We got out, didn't we? We've got four large messenger bags filled with shruckles. Even if we've got chests of singles, I reckon each bag is worth four, maybe five thousand. That's gotta be at least twenty, Selah! I've never seen that kind of coin in my life, I don't know about you."

"But I nearly blew it. You said we should've got out at the third bridge – it's got ladders on either side, that would've been much easier to make our escape. I was too bloody stubborn! I was so sure the fifth bridge would let us bag more cash and still manage to disappear. I'd noticed the mooring rings and knew they would be the perfect handholds to get up on the bridge."

"And you would be right, Selah, though a closer look, a little tug on the ring, a look at where it bolted into the wall, would have shown the integrity of the ring. Or lack thereof. A simple miss and, all things considered, we've come out on top."

"But it could have ended in ways not worth considering! If you hadn't caught me when you did, the mounted guards would've had me. A stay behind bars would have been the least of my concerns. Injuries would have been low on my list of concerns too, I'd wager. I hadn't even thought about our next steps. You got me out of a mess, Crow. If I'd gone in alone, I would never have got out of there. I was so sure the day I hauled your arse over the wall that you were going to be a complete burden, that you'd cause me way more trouble than you were worth. And I'll be truthful, you irritated me no end with your constant positivity and grand plans. I should've trusted you more. For that, I am sorry, Edison."

"No need, my dear Selah. All that I ask now is you put a little more faith in me. I may even prove to be a deal sharper than you credit me for!"

For the first time in the seven years Crow had known Selah, she showed signs of humour, the faint glimmer of a smirk ghosted across her face. He nudged her with his elbow amiably, pointing deeper into the forest.

"Come on, we need to get away from Murkvale. I would not be surprised if the city is teeming with those High Commission hired grunts. I think we need to keep going west."

"What do you propose, Crow? We cannot get caught with the contents of those chests!"

"Keep going west. I am pretty sure there are some less than clean towns that way, not under the High Commission flag. Bed down for the evening, get a room and a hot meal. I need some clean, dry clothes – a night in the storm drains has me soaked through and chilled to the bone. Tomorrow we buy passage on one of the smugglers' vessels. With luck, we'll get ourselves work onboard and be off the streets!" He strode on ahead with confidence and joviality. She found it infectious.

"Thank you, Crow. I owe you."

It was late afternoon when the pair arrived at the smuggling town of Iron Lake. The falling sun painted the sky a pallet of yellows and oranges, reds and pinks. Crow was shivering, never having fully dried out from his agonisingly long walk through the flowing storm drains. Making their way through the bustling town they had to elbow their way through throngs of people wheeling and dealing in illicit wares and services, as they made their way to the docks. Selah entered a small shop selling reclaimed clothing to see what she could find for Crow. She emerged ten minutes later with two packs stuffed with clothes. For Edison, there were black trousers, an off-white button-down shirt, a crumpled waistcoat in the richest of blues and an ankle-length brown waxed leather coat. A pair of slightly scuffed leather boots gave him a complete change of clothing. She had acquired herself new clothing while she was there – better to try and change their appearances than end up recognised by the wrong pair of eyes.

Unused to having money, Crow snatched a loaf of bread and some apples from a food vendor with a table out the front of his shop. The pair took off sprinting through the slushy, dirty snow covering the streets. They only slowed once they neared the dock. Catching their breath, they looked about their surroundings, spotting a boarding house. A quick sprint across the cobbled square and they were at the front door and inside in a flash. Payments in cash ensured a no-questions-asked room booking for the night. A hot meal and an early night and they could buy their passage on an airship at first light.

Something was wrong. He was being shaken roughly about the shoulders. Frustrated aggression was felt in the slap across his cheek. He could feel a warm breath on his ear as a hushed voice hissed angrily at him.

"Wake up! Crow! Come on, time to go!"

He groaned, scrunched his eyes shut ever tighter, tried to pull the bedsheets over his head. Before he could do much, another firm slap rattled the teeth in his head.

"Hells dammit woman, I am awake!" he bellowed, his usually jovial demeanour departing him.

"Be quiet!" Selah hissed at him. "Don't wake the whole bloody town, will you!"

"What's the hurry? It's the middle of the bastard night, Selah!" his hushed voice belied his irritation.

"Get up and see for yourself! Look here, across the square."

His eyes now adjusted to the murky light in the room, even in the shadows he could see the excited glint in her eye. He jumped out of bed, almost knocking over the chair that held his new clothes. Out of the window, the whole square could be seen. On the far side was a wide street that led to the dock. In the distance, the lanterns of the dock picked out a hulking shadow. An enormous hull, part of a huge pontoon and part of a long cannon barrel were visible. A wordless glance between the pair spoke volumes – this airship could very well be their ticket to distant lands. They dressed quickly in their new clothes, making themselves as presentable as possible. Their belongings stuffed in their packs and slung over their shoulders, messenger bags hidden beneath their coats, the pair was halfway down the staircase taking them two at a time before the door to their room had a chance to snick closed.

Edison trailed Selah as quickly and quietly as he could, though managed to trip over a collection of rubbish bins outside a fishmonger. The noise and mess were deafening in the silent streets. Selah spun, turning an enraged stare on him as he hauled himself out of the debris. Shaking her head, she took off towards the dock, Crow eventually following, trying to keep his footing. As the pair burst out of the end of the street, they skidded to a stop on the uneven cobbles. The airship they had seen from the window in the gloom was all the more impressive up close.

Sleek and long, the wooden planks of its hull were

waxed, dark and gleaming. The brass framing was polished and shimmering huge propellers and slender pontoons glinted in the deep orange of the rising sun. Enormous cannons with vast gaping maw were black as night. The airship looked brand new, and was the largest by some margin, docked at the wharf-side. A large flag flew from the bow bearing a single word, the name of this impressive piece of engineering – Arcos.

"So, let me get this right, two random kids stroll up to my nice, shiny new airship and decide they want a slice of the wealth?"

The captain, a large man – towering above the two figures standing before him – folded his thick, tattooed arms across his front. His long dark brown hair, greying at the temples, blew about in the strong winds. The man was an imposing figure. His long beard – brown flecked with copper whiskers and the occasional grey – framed a face littered with crow's feet. His eyes, a steel-grey colour, had a vibrancy to them. He had a barrel chest and an ample gut that still gave hints to a man more than capable of holding his own. His steely eyes bored into them uncomfortably. Crow, recovering quickly, turned the charm up.

"Captain, my good fellow! We appear to have got off on the wrong foot here. Allow me to clarify. We do indeed seek passage aboard your fine vessel, in return for becoming members of your fine crew. We seek not a slice of the wealth, sir, and as a show of good faith, we ask no cut of proceeds for any jobs over the next three months. We will also pay you two thousand shruckles for our places aboard Arcos. We will work diligently in any capacity you ask of us."

The captain's bushy eyebrows knitted together in a deep frown as he considered the proposition put forward.

"Three thousand," the grizzled man growled.

"My good captain, is two thousand not a fair offer? After all, we are paying to work for your good self!"

A broad smile played across his face, though did not reach his cold eyes.

"I think you have the entire situation all wrong, boy. I have a reliable crew and a brand-new airship. I have everything you need. In any bargain, the party with in-demand goods or services has the upper hand. You want a place aboard this fine airship, I think it is only fair that you recompense me suitably. All I ask is a mere three thousand shruckles, and never a coin more."

Selah jabbed Edison in the kidney with her pointy elbow and gave him a harsh stare. She shook her head almost imperceptibly. His charming grin slipped for the briefest of moments, realising there was no way to break the wily captain.

"I think we have ourselves an agreement, my good sir." He proffered his hand.

"Captain Rohgar, welcome aboard Mister...?"

"Crow, Edison Crow. And my dear friend here is Selah. A pleasure."

He shook Crow's hand and turned, walking up the gangplank. Crow and Selah followed close behind as dark storm clouds gathered on the horizon.

TWENTY

PRESENT DAY

The day was dawning, the sky out in the direction of Copper Lakes painted a fiery orange. Clouds started to crowd the horizon over the mountains, thick and black, hostile. Sheets of rain poured down upon the land as the storm continued its relentless march across the dawn sky. Crow stood at the helm of Arcos, looking out in the direction of the Overlooks. A skeleton crew of twenty manned the vast airship, far less than the ideal minimum for optimal operation. Crow had ensured he had Reuben, Fi and Booker aboard – he knew he would need some of his best crew around him if they were going to manage to get Arcos safely through the torrent of water cascading over the falls. This wasn't his first rodeo, however. Edison Crow was all too aware of how crucial a strong support team would be. Two shuttlecrafts would follow alongside – one led by Selah, one by Hester. Mycroft and Abel were along for the journey with four further crew members. That made for eight crew members that had plenty of experience and wits sharpened to a deadly point running the support vessels.

Reuben appeared at Crow's shoulder, his face set and serious.

"Captain. I've spoken with the others. Selah and Hester are all set, they'll follow your lead."

"Thank you, Reuben. Are we ready to cast off?"

"Aye, sir. Engines are idling, pontoons filled. Give the word, Cap'n, and the crew'll cast off the lines."

"Do it. Let's get this hurdle out of the way. Things are only going to get more difficult from here."

Edison manned the helm in stoic silence, lost in thought. He knew he would not be able to rest in his quarters. Better to be useful than pacing like a caged animal. He had barely spoken a word since they had cast off two hours earlier. The crew on deck scurried about, a hive of activity keeping the vast airship in the air on such short staffing. They had managed to outpace the torrential storm out over the lowland steppe, but the weather was looking to be less than welcoming as the flat grassland gave way to the craggy foothills of the Overlook Mountains. The wind had picked up dramatically, tossing Arcos about like a rowboat in an ocean storm.

She pitched and rolled and bounced in the strong wind; Crow fought with all his strength to maintain their course. He fought to keep them airborne. The long grass of the steppe beneath them seemed to flow as if it were water in the strong wind. The sight was mesmerising, spectacular. If he wasn't breaking a sweat and straining to continuously correct the wheel, Edison would be at the rail, marvelling at the spectacle below him. The small shuttle crafts on either side of Arcos were fighting just as much as he was to stay true, if not more so, as light and small as they were.

"Captain." Reuben slammed the door shut behind him as he entered the wheelhouse, a look of deep solemnity etched across his features.

"I have a whole new appreciation for you, Reuben. I know piloting Arcos can be tough, but you take the helm more often than I. This storm is a bastard." His arms were tense, and the thick tendons in his neck bulged under the strain.

"Tha's what I come to talk to you about, Crow."

"Shit, Reuben, when you drop the Captain this and Sir that, I know we've got problems. What's come up?"

"I been over in the observation tower. What we seein' ain't good. Snow's falling in the pass we gotta fly through. Fallin' sideways by the look. Edison, we flyin' right into a blizzard. A bad one. Sure you wanna keep workin' with this plan?"

"I have to, Reuben. I need a resolution."

"I mean this. Wouldn't you be happier leavin' Arcos somewhere easier to get to?"

"I appreciate the sentiment, Reuben. I don't think there is an option open to us outside of the one we are staring at right now. That cavern behind the falls is by far the best option we have open to us right now."

"I thought that might be the case. Never let anyone say I didn't try my luck." A ghost of a smile twitched at the corners of the older man's mouth.

A hearty laugh burst from Crow, something that hadn't happened in some time. It sounded so easy and natural despite what was ahead of them.

"There's not a man, woman or child that would dare accuse you of not trying your luck, certainly not aboard this fine vessel."

"If we're gonna do this, you'll be needin' me up here with you. As if you ain't already strugglin' enough, it's only gonna get worse once you get in that pass. We are going to need lookouts up front and on both sides. And you gotta slow it down. Too fast through here and not one of us has a hope of makin' it to the other side."

"I can always count on you to remind me of the gravity of a situation, old friend."

"Less of the old."

"Take the helm, Reuben. I think I ought to radio Selah and Hester, warn them of what is to come."

"Aye Captain."

Reuben reached across Edison, taking the wheel as Edison let go and stepped away from the helm. He gave a nod before making his way to the radio room.

The room smelled musty, cobwebs hung from the lantern fixtures and the long-unused equipment was coated in a thick layer of dust. Crow discovered the one working lantern in the radio room and lit it. Its pallid glow did little to dispel the shadows. He muttered and grumbled to no one about the state of the radio room. One of the drawbacks to only ever having a fleet of one was this room was rarely needed. *Maybe we need to change that*, he thought irritatedly to himself. He took a handkerchief from the inside pocket of his coat. Crow wiped it over the control panel on the radio so he could read the dials and knobs on its front. Looking around the gloomy room, he spied an old chair, the padding had gone flat, in a corner. He walked over to it, beat the seat cushion and broke into a coughing fit as a cloud of dust plumed around him.

As he cleared his lungs and the coughing abated, he swiped at his red, watering eyes with the back of his sleeve. Dragging the decrepit old chair across the dirty floorboards leaving trails in the dust, he set it up before the old radio unit. Sitting down cautiously, half expecting the old chair to collapse under him, Edison flipped the main switch on the unit. The tubes hummed as they warmed up for the first time in years. Bulbs along the top used to indicate the frequency cast his face in an otherworldly orange glow. The speakers hissed with static, startling him, the volume set too high. With that little shock out of the way, he set about manipulating the frequency dial by the most minute of increments seeking out the range Selah and Hester would be communicating over.

"Why in the name of all that is good did we not set this bloody radio while we were still together at the dock?" He yelled in frustration, pounding his fist into the table, casting up another plume of dust and triggering another coughing fit that racked his body.

The old radio hummed and hissed and whirred at him as he slowly twisted the dial, up and down through the frequency range until, finally, he heard voices. Distant and crackly, two females were talking over the radio.

"Hells knows why he didn't check and tune his damned

radio before we cast off!" An angry voice came over the speakers.

"Calm, Selah. None of us expected the weather to turn sour as much as it has. Though I must say, seeing the blizzard down in the pass, I'd be much happier if we were all able to communicate."

"Well, how fortunate I managed to get this old wireless working and tuned to your frequency, wouldn't you agree, my dear Hester?"

"Captain! Good to hear from you."

"Hmmm, yes, if only you'd sorted that radio earlier, we wouldn't have been following you blindly all day, you stubborn fool."

"Come now, Selah, you know me well enough to know I arrive at the correct conclusion on my own, more scenic route. Anyway, enough of the pleasantries – to business."

"Looks like a whiteout down in the pass, Crow. We are just about managing to keep the ships aloft, and we at least have manoeuvrability in the narrow canyons and passes through the mountains. It is going to be difficult, make no mistake."

"Captain Crow, will Arcos be nimble enough through there?"

"Honest answer, Hester? I couldn't say. She has lost some of her agility and pace with the upgrades. The thicker skin will allow for a few small bumps, but I don't particularly want to test that notion too far. I suggest we stay in contact for the entire journey. You both should sit back as far as you can while still keeping us reasonably in view. I will get the crew to light Arcos like a beacon – we will be able to see hazards a touch sooner that way and will hopefully be more visible for you."

"Sounds fair, Crow, better than us all bunching up and running into trouble."

"Very well. It's taking everything we have to keep Arcos true, but between Reuben and myself, I think we will manage. I will have her speed trimmed as low as possible, mind, slow and steady to give us all the time we can to think ahead. I'll go dark for a moment, I think it best I get this radio moved to the helm – better we hear things as soon as possible, rather than running the crew ragged passing messages back and forth. I will be in touch shortly."

"Aye Captain."

"Go well, Crow."

Crow stumbled back up to the helm, shoving the door open with his back. A flurry of snow followed him in. He mumbled and complained to nobody in particular as he struggled through the door with the cumbersome, heavy old radio unit. Reuben raised an eyebrow as he watched Edison lurch across to the map table behind him, dumping the radio down heavily.

"Woulda maybe been easier to have moved it before we cast off, don't you think?"

"Yes, thank you, Reuben. It never ceases to amaze me how close you think to Selah, even when she isn't here."

Crow set up the radio, powering it up. Nothing happened. He flicked the switch off, then back on. The tubes buzzed intermittently before shutting off again. One final, frustrated toggle of the switch and the tubes finally warmed up and stayed on. The orange bulbs on top glowed, dimly at first but brightening as they settled.

"Hah! Yes! It's working!"

He sat, fiddling the dial to try and locate the frequency that Selah and Hester were using. He wished he had written it down before he tried to lug the heavy old unit from below decks. Reuben stayed silent as Crow mumbled and complained to himself under his breath. His patience wearing thin, Crow didn't use the same level of finesse as before to tune in to the correct radio frequency. He twisted the dial back and forth, his frustration growing, until he finally found the correct setting, hearing Hester and Selah talking over the radio. They were discussing the risky flight they were about to take up into the mountains.

Reuben looked over his shoulder to address Crow.

"We'll be enterin' the pass in a few moments, Captain."

"Very good, Reuben. Stay focused and prepare to drop our speed."

"How low?"

"Honestly, as slow as Arcos can go and still maintain forward progress. Visibility does not look good. I want as much warning of obstacles or problems as we can get."

"Aye Captain."

Edison thumbed the button on the transmitter and spoke to the two vessels tailing him.

"Selah, Hester – we will be approaching the pass shortly. I want all crew on the lookout, take nothing for granted. Reuben will be cutting our speed shortly. When he does, hold back. We cannot afford any collisions. Whatever happens, keep us in view. Use us to guide you through the pass."

Both Selah and Hester replied in the affirmative.

A sharp, piercing whistle sounded from Reuben and was crystal clear even over the radio. The crews aboard the two smaller vessels could see lanterns begin to glow in the snowy air, turning Arcos into a beacon.

"How slow are we talking, Crow? We should get Arcos sheltered and the rest of us out as soon as possible."

"Reuben is trimming speed now, I've asked him to go as slow as he possibly can, and still maintain forward progress. I know we ought to get in and out urgently, but we cannot risk it. If this storm worsens any, we could be in real trouble."

"Aye Captain."

Crow set down the transmitter as he felt the vast airship slow greatly. He looked at Reuben and gave a slight nod.

"Proceed, Reuben. Let's see what awaits us."

The constant buffeting side winds of the steppe abated as they flew into the mountain pass, only to be replaced by a fierce headwind. The crew out on deck were bundled up in thick, fur-trimmed coats, gloves, hats and scarves, which did little to protect from the icy chill. The wind was blowing fiercely, the snowflakes and ice crystals flying almost horizontally, lowering visibility. Crow had been out on the deck for a walkabout to check in with his crew.

Returning to the wheelhouse, the wind shoved the door shut with a crash so loud it made Crow cringe. He stomped about in a futile effort to warm his feet. He was frozen to the core, stubbornly electing to wear his customary leather coat over his cuirass and his thin leather gloves offering little protection from the wind.

"Visibility is dropping, Reuben, go easy. The lookouts will flash the red lanterns towards us if they spot a problem."

"Good shout. We'll be climbing soon, out of the pass, so we oughta be wary – crosswinds, rocky outcroppings, obscured peaks. It's all a risk."

Crow turned to the radio and picked up the transmitter.

"All okay behind?" he queried tentatively.

"I've had better flights, Captain, but we're keeping up with you and maintaining visual." Hester somehow always managed to remain upbeat even in the face of adversity. It's why she was one of Crow's favourites.

"I am not sure we could have picked a worse day for this, Edison. Still, at least the snow and ice will preserve our remains and keep scavengers away when all three airships go down." Selah had a penchant for dark humour.

"Ahh, my dear Selah, I cannot get enough of your ever buoyant and bubbly outlook on life. We will need to climb shortly towards the falls. It's going to lift us out of the pass, so keep your eyes open, things get really tricky from here on in."

"Oh good, and there was me thinking it was going to be a boring flight." Selah's voice dripped with sarcasm.

"Take care and stay in communication. Fly slow and steady, maintain visibility."

Crow put down the transmitter and turned back to Reuben at the helm.

"Take us up, Reuben, let's get Arcos in the cavern."

Reuben gave a curt nod. He toggled a switch on the console panel by the wheel. In the eerie, snow-filled quiet, a hiss filled the air as hydrogen flowed from the tanks below deck into the pontoons. The airship ascended smoothly despite the strong headwinds. They had a long, slow flight ahead of them.

The storm began to subside the further they climbed. The sky was a brilliant cobalt blue above the swirling storm clouds obscuring the pass below. The air was frigid, biting at any exposed flesh. Coming around the largest mountain in the Overlook range, they heard the roaring sound of an inconceivable torrent of water rushing over the falls. With nothing coming close in size, it had to be the location they sought, though nobody could see the cavern behind. They had to trust the maps were correct. Swinging Arcos around the rocky outcrops and the jagged spires thrusting up towards the frigid sky, Reuben pointed the bow straight at the falls.

"Not a particularly wide cavern, best I can tell."

"Not wide at all, Captain. Won't be a lot of clearance either side, though looks like it goes back a ways."

"I can't see anything beyond the water, so that's a small blessing. We have to hope it will be enough."

"Enough, Captain?"

"I don't foresee an issue, Reuben, but if something goes very wrong and we are tailed back here it will be like shooting big fish in a small barrel. Arcos will be easy pickings."

A deep frown furrowed his weathered brow. "Aye, true enough, Captain. Rear cannons won't be much good if they block us in, and side shooters will be useless." Reuben grew silent, a shadow fell over his features as he lost himself in thought.

The situation troubled Crow as well. The lack of escape bothered him greatly – if an attack befell Arcos, she would be in trouble. After a long, silent ten minutes, he heaved a weary sigh as his mind settled on the only conclusion he could see.

"We need to reverse in."

"Reverse? Captain, you'll have no line of sight! Too risky! We got no idea what exactly is on the other side o' these falls! Surely you ain't serious?" Reuben's eyes grew big, he glared at Crow as though he had developed a serious bout of debilitating insanity. He wasn't far wrong, the plan was madness.

"I am afraid so, old friend. The bow points out, you'll have full use of the widow-maker at the bow. Punch a hole in any attack and high tail it straight out before anyone has a chance to regroup."

"I don't like this, Captain. You'll never see what is behind."

"Duly noted, Reuben, but we have no choice. It has to be this way."

He sighed again, looking weary and resigned. He

racked his brain for other ideas, nothing leaping forth.

"Shit! Yeah, you're right, Crow. We gotta do this right, mind. Arcos will have to go slow, too much momentum will keep her movin'. Too fast and there won't be a chance for the props to stop spinnin' before we can shift gears to forward and slow her down. This ain't gonna be a simple sailing, Crow."

Crow couldn't help but let out a genuine belly laugh. It took root so firmly it doubled him over, squeezing fat tears from his eyes.

"Are you okay, Captain?"

This set him off with another gale of laughter. He slowly regained his composure, catching his breath and swiping at the tears tracking down his cheeks. He stood up and looked at his old friend and pilot.

"Twenty years. Twenty years we've known each other, lived, worked, smuggled, stolen and survived together. You've pulled me out of many a scrape, stopped me from doing some really stupid shit in my earliest days here – stopped old Rohgar kicking me off the ship. In all of that time, despite my continued efforts, you have never called me anything more than Captain, perhaps Captain Crow if I have got you annoyed. Twice in one conversation, you called me Crow. I must have you really annoyed."

He fell about laughing again. Reuben stared at him for a moment, before succumbing to laughter himself. Quickly the pair regained their composure, the weight of the coming days bearing down on them all.

"So, how do we go about this one, Edison?"

"Do you trust me?"

"Do I have a choice?"

"Well, you could take shore leave – permanent or temporary."

Reuben looked back at Edison, eyes wide, eyebrows arched almost to comical proportions. He made to speak, but the words wouldn't come and left Reuben looking like a fish out of water, floundering for air.

"Relax, you aren't going anywhere – I am not losing you off my crew. And besides, shore leave wouldn't help."

"It-it-it-it wouldn't? Why not?"

"Because I wouldn't leave you here in the Overlooks, but this sailing has been anything but plain. I am not sailing us out just to drop you off, you'd have to wait until we have Arcos hidden away."

"You can be a real bastard sometimes, you know that, Crow?"

"Of course I can, you have to be to do what we do." A big smile spread across his face, a mischievous glint in his eye.

"Now then, as for how we get from here to there, well, you're not gonna like this."

"I'd established that bit, lad. Now come on, what are you thinkin'?"

"We need to get Arcos lined up and put some space back to the cavern. Set the props in reverse and give the engines everything. Once we're halfway there shut them down – that should be enough inertia to carry Arcos through. Switch the props forward. As soon as the stern passes the falls give the engines full power again, which should slow her down. We lower the power as we clear through the falls."

"Your madness may be rubbing off on me boy, but it might just work. I want a crew on deck, though. I want 'em around on all sides, fore and aft with whistles. We need all the eyes on this we can get. They can sound their whistle if we drift too close to the walls if we stray off course."

"Agreed. You round up the crew, I'd better radio the others to let them know."

Arcos drifted and swayed in the strong winds tearing through the mountain valleys. Reuben fought to keep her steady and lined up. Crow was hunched over the radio having relayed the details of the plan to Hester and Selah and now needed them to be ready to follow and lift him and the crew off Arcos.

"Crow, you know you are mad, right? If you mistime any part of this – get off the gas too late, don't apply enough forward thrust, don't have her lined up just right – it's game over. The cavern opening may be plenty big enough to get Arcos through, but who knows what is waiting behind the waterfall. It might narrow massively, sharp outcrops, stalactites, stalagmites, the works. Even the slightest perforation to the pontoons would be devastating. The least of your worries would be grounding out." Selah's voice rose, not something anyone heard very often. She was the voice of reason and calm within the crew, not prone to outbursts of emotion of any kind. She seemed to have forgotten she was still holding down the transmit button as she let out a long sigh.

"Selah, I know there's a risk. There's a risk in everything we are doing right now. This one is far from calculated, but I don't see how we have any other choice in this. Arcos is too noticeable, too big, too obvious. She won't get into Copper Lakes without drawing too much attention. The Commission will be over us like a rash if we try to pass over the city walls. We have to get her hidden away until this is over."

He listened to the static and silence coming back over the radio to him. Waiting for Selah to react, respond, say anything. Just as he was about to say something, anything to break the silence, he heard the tell-tale crackle as she held the button on her transmitter.

"Okay, Crow. Just be careful. And let's get out of here as soon as we can."

"Of course. Selah, Hester – be ready. As soon as we radio that we're in and stopped, be ready to follow us in. With that much water cascading down you are going to have to fly in fast. We'll get Arcos secured and shut down. Then we'll all jump ship to your vessels."

"Aye Captain."

"Let's do this, Edison."

The small crew rushed about on deck, spacing themselves along the perimeter railing, wearing whatever they had at hand in a vain effort to try and stay dry as they passed through the waterfall. Reuben held Arcos steady as whistles rang out around the vast airship – eighteen piercing tones tearing through the crisp air. Everyone was in position. Crow stood at the far end of the wheelhouse – the enormous map table and large, brass compass between him and the wheel where Reuben stood. Arcos – one of the larger airships in operation – was not designed to fly backwards. The windows in the rear wall, nothing more than small, round portholes more intended for admitting natural light into the room, offered Reuben next to no visibility. Crow opened the most central one, sticking his head out. He relayed information to Reuben, pulling his head back in, before sticking his head out of the window again.

"Okay, it looks like we're pretty well lined up. Full reverse now, Reuben!" Crow stuck his head out of the window.

Reuben selected reverse and pushed back rapidly on the throttle lever, engaging full power. A loud rumble came from deep within the airship as the motors wound themselves up. A strong vibration shook through Arcos, not used to having so much raw power applied so suddenly. The airship lurched backwards as the propellers bit into the air, driving her on to a disconcerting pace for something so large. As Arcos approached top speed, Reuben shut the engines down and selected forward, allowing her to drift towards the waterfall. Crow called back to Reuben as the stern reached the cascade.

"Hold steady, Reuben, the stern's getting wet!"

They felt a strong tug on the rear of the airship, the sheer force of water pushing the back end downwards. Reuben applied some lift to try to counter the force and slowly increased the throttle to slow the ship's momentum. A sharp whistle issued from the rear left of the deck.

"Slight right, Reuben. Listen for any more whistles."

Crow put his head back out of the porthole as the wall of water seemed to get ever closer, a bitter spray stinging his rugged cheeks. He returned to the cabin, slamming the window shut just as they broke through the wall of water.

"More throttle, Reuben, I don't think we are arresting our momentum enough!"

"Aye Captain."

The noise grew, the sound of the enormous motors now echoing around the spacious cavern as they powered up further. As the airship slowed, whistles rang out. Reuben fought to correct their course as much as possible, but before long the whistles became too many and the echoes made it impossible to detect where they were coming from. He drove the motors up to full power. A shrieking sound, louder than thousands of nails screeching down countless chalkboards filled the space, deafening everyone in earshot. Arcos scraped her starboard flank along the rough rock walls. She shuddered to a halt. The whistles fell silent. Reuben shut the motors off, the propellers spinning down. Voices rang out as the crew set to work, firing rock hooks on cables into the rugged cavern walls to help tether Arcos in place. Taking a moment to steady himself, Crow caught his breath.

"Fuck! That was a bit close, Reuben! There was a brief moment there I thought we were all in deep trouble, that we weren't going to stop before we met with the back wall! But you did it. I should have had more faith in you."

"Ahh, pay it no mind. If it helps yer, I thought we was

pretty fucked too, 'til she stopped and we didn't explode, anyway."

The pair laughed as the stress ebbed away. The two smaller vessels punched through the curtain of water, drifting sideways to avoid hitting the stationary airship.

"Looks like all went to plan then, Crow," Selah's voice crackled over the radio.

"We made it, and that's what counts. Come and dock up with us so we can get going."

"Aye Captain."

The two ships took up positions alongside Arcos, dropping narrow boarding planks into place. Selah and Hester disembarked to meet with Crow on deck. Reuben stood amongst a huddled group of the twenty crew that manned Arcos on its sailing up through the mountains.

"I anticipate the journey back being much quicker without Arcos to manoeuvre around the rocky terrain."

Reuben walked over, leaving the small huddle of ten or so crewmates.

"All set to depart?"

"Some o' the crew and me was wonderin' if we should leave half of us back here. To guard Arcos like. Would also mean we could grab you lot outta Copper Lakes when things go sideways. Much safer than leadin' half the High Commission forces up here."

Crow paused, mulling the idea over in silence. He had to admit it made sense, though he was annoyed with himself for not coming up with it.

"Would I be right in assuming that ten would include yourself, Reuben?"

"Aye, Edison, it would. I think it would be for the best that way."

"Much as I want you down in Copper Lakes for this, I think you are right. You and a minimal crew here on Arcos should be able to keep watch over her. Keep the radio on, keep in contact with us. If something happens, you'll be out of the way, out of danger. The rest of you, get on the airships – it's time."

Crow watched everyone board the smaller vessels ready for the journey back to Black River. He turned to Reuben, his right hand extended.

"See you on the other side, old friend."

"Go well, Captain."

Edison Crow shook hands with Reuben before turning away. He strode across the deck and climbed the boarding plank. Within five minutes the two smaller airships had throttled to full power and punched through the torrent of water hiding the cavern entrance.

TWENTY-ONE

Two small airships approached over the horizon, tearing across the grassy flats of the lower mountain steppe. They appeared to swell in size as they were watched into the docking platform. Seemingly out of nowhere, a swarm of figures appeared to greet them. The moment the gangplanks were dropped, Crow stepped down from one of the vessels and headed over to meet Selah as she disembarked her airship.

"We should get moving as soon as we can, Crow. The sooner we get into Copper Lakes the better. I suspect the Commission is going to be increasing their forces and stepping up patrols."

"Very good. We need to get everyone over there immediately. But we cannot just swarm the city, too many vessels coming in at once and something will look off, even to the least interested observer."

"I suppose it was just as well then that I sent the rest of the vessels a radio transmission before you finally got your radio working. They should have left at intervals and from different directions. Hopefully, that should make them less noticeable. Some will be docking outside of the city, the rest inside. If we get going now, we should arrive by late afternoon."

Crow nodded his agreement to Selah, and she returned up the gangplank to her vessel. He turned to see Hester ordering the crew about on her small airship, readying it to cast off. A handful of the crew remained on the docking pad, scurrying to and fro, making final preparations and gathering final supplies. He turned to address the busy crew on the dock.

"I want us airborne in five minutes," Crow bellowed. "Let's move!"

Murmurs of assent rippled around him. He turned on his heel and strode up the plank to join Selah aboard her airship. He strode to the bow rail, Selah close behind. She knew he was in a serious, thoughtful frame of mind, the way his eyebrows seemed to knit together spoke volumes.

"We need to get inside the city, Selah. I have a suspicion that every gate in those ancient walls will be manned. Inquisitors checking papers in and out. The Cabal won't be far behind. Foot soldiers will likely be in the streets, in the alleyways, keeping an eye on the waterways."

Selah frowned as she thought about this. "So why would the docks be any less protected? All the talk points to Anvil being in town for the Freedom Weekend. There's no way any airship wanting to dock inside the city limits isn't getting checked."

"Which is why we won't be onboard any airship mooring at a dock inside the city walls. It is also why we won't be walking – or swimming – into the grand capital of the great and wondrous Republic."

"So, what exactly do you propose, Edison? Everyone else will get in no problem. You and I? Well, we've allowed our faces to be too visible over the years. We haven't exactly been the most inconspicuous of roguish aviators, have we?"

"The skyway." A playful smile spread across his face.

"The skyway? How in the hell is that supposed to help us? Those steam-spewing carriages that hang under rails that criss-cross above the city streets are gonna be a tough solution. There's no way we can access the stations from the roof."

"Ahhh, my dear Selah, I have that one planned out already. You will need to have someone take the helm. And you aren't going to like it." Crow chuckled to himself, a sound filled with a mischievous joy that made Selah grow wary.

"Crow, what in the fuck are you planning? I don't like a great many of your plans. I *really* don't like the ones you *tell* me I won't like."

"We need to get into Copper Lakes unnoticed. As I see it, this is our only option. Have Booker or Abel take the wheel, they need to fly us as low and as slow over the skyways as possible without raising suspicion."

"Oh no! Edison, I don't like where this is going. There have to be other options open to us, surely!"

"If you can come up with a better plan during the two or so hours we have before we get there, I am most happy to hear it. But if not, you will need to jump overboard and stick the landing on one of those fancy, polished carriages."

"You're right, Crow, I really don't like this idea. Not at all."

"Come now, Selah, I am always open to better ideas, but as I see it, we don't have many options available to us. We need to get into the city undetected. The roads and waterways are completely out of the question. Too many opportunities to be found out. The docks will be just as heavily monitored. By all means, approach me with something better if you have it before we are close to the capital, otherwise, we have to go with it."

Selah scowled intensely as Crow disappeared below deck. She turned back, leant on the rail and stared out to the horizon, contemplating their next few moves. Everything they were walking headlong into was utterly crazy. The risks were huge. If things went to plan, they might just get some answers. Crow might also resolve whatever it was that was weighing heavy on his mind. The crew had all noticed he was distracted, though he wouldn't talk to anyone about it. At worst, well it didn't bear thinking about. Would they all come out of it? Unlikely. Once things kicked off, they would be stuck inside the city walls surrounded by hostile forces. They were going to have to fight their way out against the biggest concentration of Commission soldiers seen anywhere. Chances are they weren't all going to get out. It was a sobering thought. But what choice did they have? Things had come too far. They were being framed for two multiple murders. Murders they didn't commit. And there wasn't a single member of the crew that was going to leave Crow at this point. Even Maxwell Gladstone's men were fully invested in an opportunity for a big takedown. Maybe not emotionally invested like Crow and his crew, but the chance to take down an entity the sheer size of the High Commission would bring a level of notoriety money couldn't buy.

Selah took a deep breath of fresh air to settle her thoughts and her nerves. Even someone as stoic and dependable as she could easily suffer nerves when the stakes were so high. She focused on her breathing, calming herself so she could think clearly. Straightening, she walked across the short deck and down the steps. Sitting at a small table, she found Crow hunched over. A small overhead lamp cast a dirty cone of yellow light around him, faintly cutting through the gloom. He was mumbling to himself as he scrawled notes on a chart showing the aerial tracks that crisscrossed Copper Lakes. Crow laid a parchment paper map of the city over the skyline charts, giving him a good idea which rails traversed which parts of the city. He needed to be sure he made the correct choice. Everything depended on it.

"Ah, Selah. Good. Just looking at the best approach for our attack. We need to hit them early and hit them hard. The crowds are going to be at their peak today. Tomorrow the people are expecting to hear from their decrepit Commissioner. I, for one, will be astounded if Anvil isn't bedridden by now – they'd be lucky to get a radio transmission from him. He must be well into his eighties. That aside, tomorrow everyone will be crammed in the main square outside the Commission Hall."

"Isn't that the perfect cover for us?"

"No. I think the Cabal Inquisitors and foot soldiers will be watching the crowd, for sure. But there will still be a substantial contingent in the streets around the city. They will be expecting any enterprising sorts to attempt something when everyone assumes the forces will be fully focused on the city square. If you, I, or anyone for that matter is caught on the streets, questions, uncomfortable questions, are going to be asked. Who in their right mind wouldn't be in the square waiting for the Commissioner's address if they weren't up to no good?"

"Fair point, Edison. But Anvil's henchmen will be swarming the streets today too. How is today any better?"

"The crowds will be milling about today. Street performers, musicians and the like will be present on nearly every corner. A carnival atmosphere is sure to envelop the city. Too many distractions, even for the most well-trained of Cabal. We can use it to our advantage."

Selah became more animated as she started to catch on to where Crow was going with this. "So, we strike while the city has its guard down? Catch them sleeping and see if we can make in-roads before they have a chance to regroup."

"Exactly. If we can have distractions throughout the city as well, divert attention as best we can, we stand our best chance. We need to time this. The second we show our hand, the Cabal will rally. Some may rush the source of distraction, but a large number will aim for the Commission Hall. They'll set up a defensive perimeter. Nobody can strike before time or it will be the end of us."

"So, we need coordinated disruption. Between our crew and Maxwell's thugs. Scuffles to draw attention, the bigger the better. It may be extreme but perhaps we need to blow stuff up to ensure we draw attention. What do you have in mind? Go after Anvil?"

"No, I suspect Anvil is a mere figurehead at best these days. A puppet that appeases the masses but wields little if any power anymore. Though I believe answers lie at the heart of their organisation – the Commission Hall."

"You must be mad. I know something is on your mind, something you won't tell us. And I know it is something beyond those damnable shadow wraiths. What are you going to do? Stroll up the path and knock on the front door and ask if the master of the house is in? Not a bloody chance!" Selah snorted with derision, shaking her head.

"Of course I'm not, but thank you for your flippant observation." He pulled another chart out from under the city ordinance maps. This one appeared to be architectural plans for the Commission Hall. Old plans. By the date scrawled in the corner, they seemed to be the final approved plans that the construction would have followed.

"What are these?" Selah indicated what seemed to be corridors radiating out beyond the edges of the plan.

"My ticket inside. These appear to be the only set of plans that were never made publicly available. And those, I believe, are tunnels beneath the Hall." He circled a finger around a hollow octagonal space in the subterranean levels. "And that, my dear Selah, is a mysteriously unmarked chamber. It's deep and large. Why that would not be noted is beyond me, but I suspect I'll find some answers down there."

He drew a final chart from underneath the stack, placing it on top and smoothing it out so Selah could see it. It looked no different on first glance to the previous city ordinance map. She leant in and noticed sets of dotted parallel lines running all over the city, even beyond the walls. She lifted the chart to look at the architectural drawing, comparing the path of the lines and seeing they matched the tunnels radiating from the Commission Hall.

"These are the same tunnels? If so, they spring up all over the city, and in some cases beyond, it seems."

"Precisely. And this map is also not publicly known. Look here, Commission insignia. It is a private document. I'd wager that very few people beyond Mordecai Anvil have ever seen this. If it is to be trusted, and I am inclined to think it is, then this is how I get in. I'll need to be dropped here." He pointed to an alleyway by an old warehouse. "From what I can tell, it's no longer used. Fallen into disrepair inside and out. I'd imagine it unlikely to run into Cabal there, except for the odd patrolling soldier."

"So, drop down, where? In the alley? Could be risky. If we can get sight of the courtyard out back that might be safer – less chance of being seen."

Crow pursed his lips, deep in thought for a brief moment. The alley would be easier – even if the buildings around it had been allowed to decay and crumble in on themselves, the passage between the buildings would be kept clear at the very least of rubble and debris. The courtyard was an unknown – if it was littered with rubble, it would be an injury waiting to happen. A controlled entry, roping down to the ground, was out of the question too – if they were to avoid being noticed he would have to jump from higher than he was happy with and while the airship continued its course.

"I'd have much preferred the chance to scout the area ahead of time – see what kind of landscape I am jumping into. If I break a bone, we're done. Nothing more we can do. But I take your point. If the buildings around it are disused, then why would a lone out-of-towner be skulking around that area? I don't think I have a choice. Neither will you, Selah."

"What do you mean by that, Crow?" A note of suspicion tinged her voice.

"You need to get off the airship before it docks. You are going to have to jump to the ground or get on one of the skyway carriages. There's no choice about that."

She let out an enormous sigh. "You're right. I don't like it, but you're right."

Selah grew quiet, looking at the charts. None of the available options looked overly inviting to her. A drop to the streets raised too many issues. The risk of injury aside, she would have to hope she wasn't seen coming out of a side alley she shouldn't be down, or risk dropping in on a busy area of the city. No good. Water was no good either – there would be stalls and activities along the river and bordering the lakes. She knew she had to use the skyway. She groaned with the realisation.

"It looks like I'm going to have to make use of the skyway system. We need to get this right, though. What route are we going to be heading to the docks by? I need to use a track on that path, heading for the terminus."

Crow looked at the chart and traced a vague route with his index finger. It took the airship over a couple of different rails. Selah tapped one in particular.

"It looks like this one heads to the train station. It will be packed with visitors. I should be able to mingle with the crowds and melt away into the city. Then we can coordinate the distractions above ground to support your efforts. From there we may even get a run on the Commission Hall."

Crow looked at the chart again, considering all of the options.

"And you are meeting your crew at the station?" Selah nodded. "Brilliant. The number of train arrivals will likely be far higher than usual today. The crowds will be huge. There will be plenty of noise and steam all over the concourse, which will give you the perfect cover." He took one last look at the charts, mentally plotting the route on to the docking pads near to the Commission Hall. Crow plotted its path to ensure it looked natural and still covered the warehouse and the skyway line.

"You are going to have to jump to a skyline carriage somewhere around here, over the lake. It's the only place the airship can cross the rail, fly over the warehouse and not raise suspicions due to an odd flight path. Your safest bet will be to have Booker line the airship up with the skyline track. Jump just as the carriage passes under you and you should be able to use the steam to cover you."

Selah looked more uneasy than Crow had ever seen her, but she nodded.

"That makes sense. As it arrives at the terminus, I will take the first chance I can to slip down amidst the crowds."

"Very good. I think we are ready."

"As ready as I am going to be, anyhow."

"Come, Selah. We should get on the wireless. I'll feel happier when we confirm the plan with everyone. I want four of our guys to meet me in the warehouse, better I don't go down into those tunnels alone."

He extinguished the lantern above their head. They

moved for the steps, heading above deck to radio in with the rest of the crew.

"Captain!" Booker called out to Crow who, along with Selah, was finishing up in the radio room. The sliding door groaned open and the two figures stepped through to the cramped wheelhouse. It was a much smaller space than he was accustomed to aboard Arcos.

"Booker, what do you have?"

"Ahead and to the starboard side, Sir. Looks like Copper Lakes to me. Too far out to distinguish if there are two bodies of water, but it fits with our heading."

Crow headed out on the deck, to the bow of the ship. He reached inside his dark brown, waxed leather coat and pulled something out. He extended the telescopic tubes of the patina-stained, dented old brass spyglass. He breathed on the glass lens and retrieved a crisp white handkerchief to polish the glass to his satisfaction. Edison raised the spyglass to his right eye and ran it over the horizon, seeking the glinting body of water. The sun sparkled with coppery flashes off the ripples of the water. As he scanned along, he could see the old city built all around the lake. As he panned across, a spray of mist began to obscure his view, though a vast blocky structure showed as a shadow through the spray and rainbows. The iconic clock tower. He strode back to the wheelhouse to talk again with Booker.

"Good spot, Booker, that is most definitely Copper Lakes. You know where we are heading?"

Booker nodded his understanding.

"Excellent. Selah, we need to go and prepare ourselves."

Crow headed out of the wheelhouse and back below deck, Selah close behind.

Everything was in place. Crow had planned this job as meticulously as he always did. In his earlier days aboard airships, it caused a good deal of irritation and consternation amongst his fellow crew. With time, his crew came to realise there was no use in trying to persuade Crow into carrying out a quick job. No job would even get off the ground without him having looked over and analysed every detail to ensure it would go off without a hitch. Today was no different. He had planned this as much as he possibly could – analysed all the information, read maps and charts until they were imprinted on his retina. He knew all the ways in and out of the city and had a good handle on the secret tunnels running beneath Copper Lakes. He knew where the rest of his crew would be. As much as he could do, Crow had sought assurances from Maxwell Gladstone about where his men would be. There was nothing more to do but to get the festivities kicked off.

The small burgundy red pleasure airship lazily cruised through the air over the outskirts of the capital city of the United Republic of the High Commission. Down below, scenes of joy, frivolity and revelry played out in the streets. Stalls selling commemorative tat, food and libations of all varieties were manned by singing, yelling staff vying for the attention of the throngs of people heading to the main square for the Unification Weekend celebrations. At the same time every year, the High Commission hosted a four-day weekend of fun and festivities to celebrate the anniversary of the rise of the Commission, and the formation of the United Republic. Street performers and musicians entertained the masses as they gathered ahead of a public address from the Commissioner himself.

The noise from the crowds drifted up to the airship, though Crow would not break, would not look down at the goings-on. He was ready, focused only on the old warehouse as they lazily cruised towards it. He had donned his signature waxed leather coat but rather than his formal attire often worn on a job, he was dressed more practically. His heavy black boots, thick pants, a lightweight shirt under a new, thickened leather cuirass for protection. A nod to the stakes of this job, Crow wore metal armour – greaves, partial sabatons, pauldrons, a light breastplate and a pair of vambraces lined with viciously sharpened blade-like protrusions running from wrist to elbow. Two bandoliers crossed his chest filled with bullets ready for a pair of ornately engraved, long-barrelled six-shooter pistols. Strapped across his back was a long rifle. A small pouch on his belt contained flash bombs and small explosives in case they needed a quick entry or exit. Finally, he carried a wicked looking greatsword – long and sharp, polished to a high shine and devastatingly heavy sitting in its scabbard, while a needle-sharp knife was tucked in his belt. He carried as much as he could while allowing him the freedom to move.

Much as Crow felt uncomfortably restrained with the metal armour on his frame, weighing him down, he was no medieval knight incapable of movement at any pace. His armour was state of the art. The ideal blend of strong and resilient while also being lightweight. Its design allowed for a reasonable range of movement. He seldom ever wore the armour, didn't like the feel of it, or what it represented. For him, the need for armour meant the job was going to be so much riskier than any other job he would ordinarily accept. This was a job warranting absolute focus, a calm mind and a steady hand. His usual flamboyance and theatrics would be nowhere to be seen. There was nothing flashy with his armour. All of it painted a matte black. The only slight nod to his personality, the stylised crow painted in gloss red across the breastplate. The sharp protrusions on the greaves also bore the arterial red colouring, almost as if they were dipped in blood.

"Crow, the warehouse building is coming up now, off to the left!"

He climbed back above decks fully geared up with all of the ammunition, weapons and armour he could comfortably manage. Even at the slowest pace, they could get away with flying, the small airship would only be hidden from the main thoroughfares for ten or fifteen seconds. That left no margin for error. He climbed up and over the railing and readied himself to jump. The airship passed behind the warehouse and into its dark shadow. He jumped into the mild air. The fall seemed to take an eternity. His thick-soled boots struck the cobbles in what would have made for the perfect landing had there not have been dust and grit everywhere. Inertia toppled Crow into a most undignified tumble and roll. He sprung up but felt a twinge in his right knee and shoulder.

"Shit!"

He looked up, shielding his eyes in time to see Selah waving and indicating she was proceeding with the plan. He stretched out, releasing the muscles now talking to him after his less than graceful landing. He scrambled up over a heap of rubble and hauled himself up and through a hole in the crumbling wall to the rickety boards of the second floor. The tunnels were in the basement. *I hope the stairs are in one piece*, he thought to himself. He didn't fancy having to jump down from floor to floor. Standing as he crossed the threshold, he made a point to step with caution and care. He didn't want to make any noise if he could help it, or worse, bring the place down around him.

The first two or three paces were uneventful, and his confidence grew. He foolishly dropped his guard just enough to miss the minute shift of timber underfoot over the next few feet of floor. An ominous creak, long and low, secreted itself from the timbers somewhere beneath his boots. The rotten, termite-chewed floor shifted uneasily, giving in to the pull of gravity.

"Fuck. Fuck!"

He dashed towards the staircase in time to see it collapse in a plume of wood dust. Taking a chance, Crow took two large steps back before throwing himself over the void. He fell, grasping the edge of the opposite landing. Just as he began to wonder if his luck was turning, his grip betrayed him. He cursed his hubris as he lost his grip, tumbling down to the pile of rubble and splintered timbers below. He landed heavily, the wind knocked from his lungs as he lay upon a mess of jagged ruination. He coughed heavily as the air began to return to his burning chest. *So much for my quiet, subtle entry,* Crow thought to himself. He was thankful for his armour now, though. Battered and bruised though he felt, he was sure he had avoided broken bones or open wounds. Hauling himself to his feet, the dust-coated figure looked about his surroundings, hoping for an easier descent to the ground floor.

Picking his way through what looked like decades of detritus and scrap, he found the stairs to the ground in the opposite corner from his ignominious landing. He stepped gingerly towards the top step, easing his weight onto it, testing it. A minor creak echoed through the dusty space, brief and deep, but nothing more. Slowly, one step at a time, Edison made his way uneventfully down, ever closer to the firm footing of the ground floor. As his boot landed on the third from last step and he transferred all of his weight, the step creaked loudly and disconcertingly. In a panic to get down, Crow stumbled and staggered, tripping over his own feet to gain safety and find firm ground. His arms pinwheeled as he tried to arrest his fall. The wooden floorboards, though covered in an inch of sawdust and decades of dust, made for a bloodied nose on impact.

"Shit!" He dragged the sleeve of his coat under his nose, smearing blood over his top lip. Edison picked himself up, dusting himself off and half stumbled, half jogged to the double doors in the floor. He yanked them open, the crash as they bounced off the wooden boards echoing. He descended the rough concrete steps into the basement, enjoying their solidity beneath his feet. The air had a distinctly musty, stale taste to it. The basement had not been opened in years. Dust motes danced in a shaft of sunlight cast from a broken window high above him. Crow stepped off the bottom step and down a tight coarse-brick passageway, leaving the light behind him. A short way ahead of him, an orange glow highlighted a larger space than the passageway. Muffled whispers carried to him as he approached the subterranean room. They stopped abruptly as his scuffing footsteps echoed along the passage. The glow from the lantern was extinguished, and Crow paused before entering the larger space.

He drew his great sword and struck the pommel, shaped like the head of a crow, against the crumbling old masonry of the tunnel wall. The air rang with metallic clangs, with seemingly no discernible pattern or rhythm. To his crew, it heralded his arrival. Half a dozen paces onward brought him through the opening and into the larger space. All enveloping darkness swallowed him, silence with one exception – a muffled, distant dripping, as if from behind a wall. His arms were wrenched painfully behind him, as far as his armour would allow and then a little further. His legs were kicked out from beneath him. A sharp scratching sound gave way to the hiss and crackle of a phosphorous match flaring to life. An old lantern flickered and danced as the flame fought to take hold, to establish itself as a pitiful guard against the darkness. The meagre glow did enough to cast a shadowy glow upon the faces of Crow and the four men surrounding him.

"Well done, men!" Crow let out a dark laugh. "Exactly as we've practised – wait for the agreed signal. Even then, don't trust anything until you are sure. Now, if you all trust well enough that I am in fact who I claim to be, will one of you please help me up?"

The men holding Crow released his arms and helped him to his feet. The man before him lowered and holstered his gun, while the man behind nodded in recognition when Crow looked over his shoulder. He dusted himself down and approached the far wall. In it was a pair of large, thick steel doors covered in flaking dark green paint.

"Looks like these were meant to keep something in as much as keeping others out, if you ask me, Captain." The man holding the lantern aloft walked closer. "What in the hell gets hidden behind a door like that?"

"A very good question, Bernard. A question I fully intend to answer in due course. Come along now men, let's see what's behind door number one!"

TWENTY-TWO

The four-man team wasted no time in opening up the tunnel. The large double doors were locked from the inside. Despite looking old, many decades most likely, there were little signs of wear beyond the peeling, flaky dark green paint. The hinges showed no signs of rust, and there were no gaps anywhere around or between the doors. One man placed a large leather pack roll on the dusty, potholed floor, unbuckled the straps and unrolled it. Inside was a professional lock-picking kit, along with a range of hammers, pliers and other tools of use when trying to break a lock. Taking the assortment of pins, he set about working the tumblers of the lock with a fierce concentration. Everybody gathered around him as a series of clicks and clunks indicated his progress through the locks until he cursed loudly, giving up.

"That's one serious fuckin' lock, Crow. Whoever put it there really doesn't want anyone getting in – or out – of this tunnel. We'll have to take a less subtle approach."

"Okay boys, let's light some fireworks and make some noise."

Two men set about hammering on the hinge pins, working them loose before packing a clay-like substance around them. The remaining men set about pushing the fuse cord into it, unspooling a length out of the room and into the narrow passageway.

"Everyone out!" Crow barked. The men retreated down the passage as he struck a match on the rough wall. With a glance over his shoulder to ensure everyone was back far enough, he bent down and touched the burning match to the fuse cord. It took immediately, hissing and spitting with white-hot sparks. The bright flash tore down the passage and into the room. The five men crouched and covered their ears, tightly shutting their eyes. The hiss stopped almost as suddenly as it started, replaced by a boom so deep it knocked the wind from their lungs. Rubble and dust filled the enclosed space, the small crew descending into a fit of coughing as the air became thick. Returning to the room, they were disappointed to find the doors still standing as they had before, though now significantly scarred and blackened by the blast.

As the dust and debris settled, the men approached the doors. A noise stopped them in their tracks. An ominous creaking sound filled the small space. It grew louder, the sound of metal tearing and shearing against itself. In unison, the small crew took two large paces back just as the hinges gave way under the weight of the thick doors. The doors tilted inwards towards each other, held tenuously by their bottom hinges. The two six-inch thick steel doors crashed to the ground unceremoniously.

"I hope there's nobody down here, Cap'n." One of the men glanced around nervously.

"No use fretting now, anyone in there knows we are

coming. There's nothing like announcing our arrival to our unsuspecting hosts. Come now and be ready – I'd rather we aren't taken by surprise. I have no idea what to expect when we get down there." Crow looked around his men, a steely resolve descending over the crew.

"I know we don't go in for killing, not lightly anyway. But today is something different. We aren't knocking over a bank, dealing in illicit goods, smuggling or relieving the wealthy of their riches to redistribute to ourselves. The soldiers of the High Commission will not hesitate to act with hostility. That much is clear. I am quite certain that Commissioner Anvil would love nothing more than to whisk us off to an early grave. If you come across any member of their order, you have my word as captain, no retribution will be sought if you dispatch them. While peaceful discourse would be my preference, I highly doubt anyone in earshot of our entrance will be so welcoming. Do. Not. Hesitate."

Crow paused, looking from one man to the next, each nodding their agreement while unholstering pistols, handguns and rifles, ready to act at a moment's notice.

"You all know what I ask of you today?" Once again, four heads nodded their understanding. "Very well. You should have plenty enough explosive to finish the job, with a fair bit to spare. Apply it liberally, the city must see the Commission Hall tumble. It must fall, do not leave that to chance. Once we get to the end of this tunnel, if the charts are to be believed, there will be a perimeter tunnel. This runs the full outline of the hall. Ensure the support pillars are targeted, then bring the place down. Anvil is expected to address the crowds at two o'clock. I anticipate that the crowds outside will peak around noon. Do not give Anvil his moment in the sun. One o'clock – whether I am at the meeting point or otherwise, I want you to light this place up."

"Crow, sir. Selah will have us if we light anything before you are back."

"Well lucky for us I am in charge then. I may have left this little detail out when discussing it with my dearest friend. She would never allow it to go ahead. But it must. I must. Do not let me down."

Frowns and concerned looks etched the faces of the four-man crew, each ill at ease with such a final attitude to the mission. But each knew what was expected of them and mumbled in agreement that they would do what their captain asked of them. Crow looked around them once more then turned sharply on his heel and descended a long flight of stairs hewn out of the rough rock.

The air immediately grew cooler, a damp musty smell suffused the tunnel. The rock walls were slimy with algae brought on by decades of dripping water. Calcified formations stretched downwards from the cavern ceiling above their heads. No matter how light their steps, the pooled water on the ground made splashes that echoed in the rough tunnels. The party of five trooped as quietly as they could, not a word spoken between them. The sheer scale of their undertaking wore heavy on the men assembled. To a one, every member of this small crew was focused on the task at hand. They all knew how meticulously planned this job was. Everything needed to run according to plan.

In less than two hours the fun would really begin. The crew on the ground all over the city would set up distractions. They would incite panic in the crowds, small riots, anything to disrupt and distract the foot soldiers and the Inquisitors. Maxwell Gladstone and his men were taking things one step further. On the outer extremities of the city, they would be setting off explosions in disused factories and warehouses, alleyways, and smaller park areas. They would also be looking to engage the High Commission, diverting attention from the centre of the city in time for Crow to bring the house down.

Three-quarters of an hour passed before Crow finally exited the narrow tunnel. It opened out into a wider sweeping curved tunnel disappearing off to the right and left. The four men split into two pairs, lighting their lanterns from the flame of Crow's. Wordlessly two men peeled off left, the other two skirting the wall to the right. Crow took a moment to collect his thoughts before heading straight ahead. The tunnel was wider than the last, a small blessing. But he knew from the charts that anything could be lurking now. The vast Commission Hall was an impressive piece of architecture. Gleaming polished brass walls, steel trusses and buttresses formed a cold, grey skeleton. Huge glass windows broke up the vast gleaming walls. The east and west wings were made up of long four-storey spans ending in huge towers rising twenty storeys into the sky. In the centre of the building, the Grand Gallery sat wide and extended front and back. It was topped with a gravity-defying glass dome that rose three storeys higher. Crowning it, a black metal sculpture in terrifying detail of the Commission symbol – the five-headed serpentine hydra.

If you ran a line straight down from the dome, way down and five storeys beneath the ground, you would find a vast open space. A square chamber of some description, clearly shown on the architectural drawings, was suspiciously unlabelled. There was no way to know what it housed. But it had to be something important, why else would the Commission seek to keep it blank on the plans? And the only way to get to that mystery chamber was a twisting, turning maze of a tunnel that cut back and forth, hiding who knew what within its switchbacks. Crow drew his large six-shooter. He seldom had cause to use it. Since he purchased it, he could probably count the number of times it had been fired in anger on the digits of one hand. He had it custom made for him. Ornately decorated with fine filigree work, it glinted in the flickering lantern light.

His distaste for using it – or having to carry it because he may have to use it – made it feel ponderously heavy in his left hand. He didn't know what he was expecting, which troubled him greatly. Crow had grown to be meticulous, wanting to know every possible outcome ahead of embarking on a mission. He was feeling so unsettled he attached the lantern to a thick leather loop on the bottom of his cuirass. His right hand now free, Crow drew his greatsword from the scabbard at his hip. Though what good it would do him, he pondered, struggling to heft it one-armed. Crow stepped forward slowly, one foot in front of the next, and entered the labyrinthine maze of tunnels. Nothing would surprise him more than to find a beast of supernatural origins ahead of him, much as he hoped he wouldn't. He began the laborious journey through the tunnel to the mystery he had to uncover at its centre.

Ten minutes of trekking through the cold and the wet without event brought Edison no solace. It only served to unsettle him further. The greatsword became too ungainly, now bumping his thigh with every step where it rested in its simple scabbard. He held a needle-thin dagger now in his right – less lethal than the greatsword but eminently more manageable than the unwieldy weapon. Crow rounded the next corner and found the stone walls now bore sporadically placed stuttering torches. They cast a dim glow, barely enough to dispel the dank murkiness that seemed to press in around him. He was sure he heard something around the next corner. Indistinguishable. Unintelligible. Unsettling. He approached the corner with a rising sense of trepidation, his left hand raised, the gaping maw of the six-shooter pointed to the ceiling.

Then the noise appeared behind him. Brief. Fleeting. As if something had flown just behind him. He whipped his head around, looking to locate the source of the sound. Nothing but the flickering of the torch halfway down the tunnel and the mess of shadows seeking to play with his mind. Crow returned his attention to the corner. He rounded it quickly, hunched low with the gun straight ahead ready for whatever may be there. Nothing. Just another empty tunnel. Another stuttering torch in an iron holder halfway along the wall. That noise again, just on the edge of his hearing. It grew louder as he ventured down the tunnel, though nothing could be seen. He stopped suddenly. That noise. It wasn't a humming sound as he had first thought. Nor was it mechanical. It was a noise that haunted his dreams. It was a buzzing sound. He turned to flee back the way he had come. His slow and stealthy progress from earlier was gone as his heavy, splashing footfalls echoed through the tunnels and his breath tore from his throat. As he rounded the corner, Crow skidded to a halt. There before him stood a tunnel filled with shadow wraiths, their leader barely an arm's length away. He turned and ran back towards the centre of the labyrinth.

TWENTY-THREE

Selah felt a deep sense of unease as the airship neared the skylines. Of all the things today would bring their way, jumping onto a moving carriage gave her more concern than any other. She looked across the left side of the airship, following the route of the skylines. A grey smudge of steam indicated the approach of a steam carriage moving fast, high above the lower lake. The small airship manoeuvred itself on to a course to intercept the carriage. As the distance closed, they slowed their speed to match the carriage as it approached the rail terminus. Selah travelled light. She had relented to Crow's insistent requests that she wear metal armour, but she put her foot down at carrying firearms. Instead, she carried a pair of long daggers, one on each hip. She had foregone her cloak. This allowed her greater movement. On her back, she wore two handcrafted katanas. Honed to the sharpest of edges, they were equal parts beautiful and lethal with their leather-wrapped grips and highly polished blades. Though she seldom had cause to carry them, she practised with them regularly. Selah wielded them as though they were extensions of her body, Crow knew this, so did not push the issue of firearms. She did, however, carry a satchel of explosives, ready to sow panic among the massed crowds.

"Twenty seconds!" Fi bellowed from the helm of the small pleasure vessel. Selah looked up and saw the carriage, packed with excited tourists, as it came hurtling along the track. She climbed over the railing on the right of the small airship. Taking a deep, calming breath, she readied herself. The hissing, puffing noise grew, accompanied by a high squealing of brakes as it began its deceleration. The steam and coal-infused smoke choked her vision as the front of the carriage appeared beneath her. Selah released the handrail and blindly leapt out to where she hoped to find the roof of the carriage. She landed well, though her momentum carried her forward into a shoulder roll. She hunkered down in a low crouch to keep herself out of the acrid smoke belching from the small funnel at the front. The carriage jerked and jolted under braking, drawing closer to the shoreline and station.

The steam and smog enshrouding her lifted as the carriage slowed to a crawl, joining a queue, carriages painted in a vast palette of colours, all waiting to dock and disgorge their passengers. As the steam carriage inched its way forward, it crawled under a glass roof supported above the platform on ornate metal trusses. The carriage lurched to a halt. With a hiss of steam, the doors opened. Two well-dressed station attendants stepped forward to help the masses of excited day-trippers disembark. As they turned away, already focusing on the next carriage, Selah vaulted over the roof edge with a feline-like grace. She landed softly, sprung to her feet and melted off into the crowds streaming towards the station exit.

Even with her unusual choice to wear a long leather trench coat on such an unseasonably warm day, Selah hardly drew a sideways glance from anyone. The Commissioner's Day celebrations drew people of all walks from all across Auridia. People from the humid coastal tropics to the south or the dry and barren deserts of Auridia's interior found a balmy Autumnal Copper Lakes day to be bracing, enough so to keep their outer layers buttoned and buckled. She merely appeared to be one of the out-of-towners. As she exited the terminus, the flow of the crowds pulled her along. As the ebb of the crowd carried her towards the square, she spotted members of her crew mingling amongst the crowds, though all headed in the same direction. A vast plaza stretched from the largest park in the city down to the Commission Hall. It was surrounded by a high fence, black iron railings topped with viciously sharp, ornate spikes. The enormous gates featured a vast hydra, bent and shaped in wrought iron and painted in a blue so dark it was almost black. It made for an intimidating spectacle.

Selah meandered through the crowds, appearing to any onlookers as just another visitor enjoying the sights and sounds of the celebrations around her. Suddenly, she pulled her scarf around her face and a hood up over her head, just as she heard shouts of confusion and anger and fear erupt close to the huge fences. The crowds began to surge away as the shouting grew. Then the deep, chest punching boom of explosions. The masses, as one symbiotic organism froze, deer trapped in the headlights. A further burst of explosions off to the east broke the spell. Screams of fear rang out and the crowd began to scatter. Terrified people broke away in all directions, desperate to put distance between themselves and the Commission Hall. Concussive blasts echoed out around the city. Something was going on, but nobody knew what. Even the massed forces of Cabal foot soldiers and Inquisitors were rattled.

They may command full obedience from the people, but this was often due to fear and intimidation. After the initial, futile uprisings from ousted leaders, no person or organisation had ever dared to oppose the High Commission. This granted the Cabal forces a power beyond their physical attributes. Unfortunately, this also meant that for all their power and intimidation, the Cabal was uninitiated in organised attacks and serious threats. Many had never seen a gun fired against them in anger. Now explosions rang out around them from all quarters. Stern, bellowing shouts carried above the noise and panic. Senior Cabal Officiants broke the trauma, freezing their men in place. The massed forces ran into the fray, seeking the source of the explosions. The chaos within the city left the Cabal fractured as the forces scattered all over the city with no real leadership, direction or cohesion. The diversion was working.

Echoing booms came from the city above, small chunks of rock and showers of dust falling with each new blast. Selah. Her crew had started diversion tactics to clear the area. His eye was briefly drawn upwards to the ceiling somewhere above him. When he returned his gaze, it was right there in front of him. Hazy yellow discs for eyes and a fuzzy, indistinct appearance accompanied by the buzzing. Though the noise didn't seem to echo, it was as if it arrived immediately inside his head, bypassing his ears altogether. The wraith, it had just been behind him. Crow looked back, then in front, unable to believe what he was seeing. How was it possible that it could get ahead of him? He was a rational man, always had been. Edison Crow didn't believe in superstition or the supernatural, but there was something about the shadow wraiths that could not be explained logically.

Panic rose inside him, gripping his chest like a vice. His eyes darted about the barren space, his head turning front and back in unnerved, jerky motions. He was trapped. He would never admit it to his crew, hell, he'd never admit it to Selah, but he was scared. Not uneasy, but outright terrified. There was no way out. Nobody around to aid him. The six-shooter in his left hand felt ponderously heavy. He briefly snatched a glance downwards at it. The fear took control of his body, his arm snapping up in front of him. The flash from the barrel was blinding, only to be eclipsed by the deafening boom. The ringing in his ears would take hours to truly subside. But the buzzing – it was gone. The wraiths had gone. He was alone in the tunnels. A guttural, low groaning sound drew Crow's attention back to the tunnel stretching out ahead of him. On the ground, in the shin-deep murky water was a crumpled heap of a boy. He had some sort of metal helmet covering his head and large parts of his face.

Crow dragged him down the tunnel until they were under the light of a torch. The contraption on his head had some kind of goggles or lenses over his eyes. Big, round opaque lenses. Wires ran all over the top of the cap, some seemed to be connected to the boy, entering the skin at the base of the skull and in the back of his neck. On the back of the device, thin tubes filled with a blue fluid were plugged into small metal inlet ports on either side of his neck that seemed to have stopped pumping whatever they carried into the boy.

He looked around him, noticing bright lantern light from up ahead. The end of the tunnel opened out, another room just ahead of him. He scooped the boy up in his arms and carried him through the tunnel. The room before him was vast, matching the footprint of the spectacular metal and glass dome hanging high above him, above the ground. Octagonal in shape with other tunnels leading off from each side, the room was vast.

So, the plans for this part of the building weren't entirely accurate, Crow thought. Dotted along some of the sides were plinths. If this were a place of worship, you might even say they were more akin to altars. Crow laid the boy on the nearest altar, having completely failed to notice the vast machinery in the centre of the room. His frantic fingers worked to remove the wires and cables running between the metal helmet and the frail-looking boy.

Pulling the tubes out of the inlet ports, the boy gasped for breath, and as the helmet tumbled off his head, he looked wide-eyed straight at Crow, before passing out. Crow looked down at his hand, seeing some of the viscous blue liquid from the tubes had dribbled onto the back of his hand, likely when he pulled the tubes free. He sniffed it, though could not identify its odour. It was pungent and unpleasant. He wiped his hand on the ragged cloth covering the altar. He took a moment to look at the boy. No older than ten years, he was dirty and bruised. He wore a black top and trousers, tattered and frayed at the cuffs, patched at the knees and elbows.

He had a trickle of blood above his right eyebrow. It seemed to be where the bullet had struck the metal cap. It had pushed the metal inwards, slicing the boy. It may need a couple of stitches but nothing too severe. The boy seemed, albeit in need of a good meal, in good health. Crow would have to try and get him back to Arcos somehow. Fi could then work her magic and tidy him up. It seemed that the worst of his condition was born of that blasted metal helmet he was wearing. And who knew what that blue fluid was that was being pumped into him. He spotted a nasty red welt on his neck. No, a burn, a brand mark scorched into flesh. Angry and red around the outside, with knotted and puckered white flesh forming a hydra.

"Bastards!" Crow spat with disgust. The High Commission was using people to strengthen their vice-like grip upon the people whom they ruled over. Children. They were taking in street children and using them. His blood boiled. It was not as though Crow needed a reason to hate the Commission, but using children was the lowest of the low. Innocent, vulnerable children willing to do anything for a meal. Then the realisation struck him. The shadow wraiths. They were nothing supernatural, nothing to fear. If only he could communicate with his crew, they needed to know what he now knew. Lost in his thoughts, the room became a cacophony around him.

Steam hissed noisily as the sound of machinery rang out. A metallic grinding of cogs and gears meshing, and the squeal and thump of pistons filled the space. Crow spun, seeing an enormous mass of machinery – gears and pistons and pipes and valves and boilers and gauges. It filled the centre of the room. Crow had no idea how he had missed it earlier. As the machinery ran up to full power, he heard another sound just at the edge of his hearing. It rose to a crescendo, filling the space around him. An intense, high buzzing sound. A whooshing sound surrounded him briefly as the perimeter of the room was instantly surrounded by shadow wraiths. The sight raised his hackles and made his blood run cold. Though he knew the truth, they still instilled fear, such was the superstition built around them. He turned around, full circle, taking in the spectacle.

With his back to the machinery, he didn't see the robed figure step out around it. They stopped to watch the new arrival, before speaking.

"Ahh! The infamous Captain Edison Crow. Such a pleasure to finally make your acquaintance."

TWENTY-FOUR

Panic was spreading throughout the city. The explosions had ceased. Palls of black smoke rose into the blue autumn sky above the city. People were running everywhere – anywhere that wasn't the epicentre of the chaos at the Commission Hall. Edison's crew and Gladstone's cohort of men wore hooded cloaks and bandanas over their faces to aid in an escape, though it marked them out to the Cabal forces still struggling to regroup. Three Cabal Combatants entered the plaza ahead of Selah. Skilled in melee combat, she would have to take them down quickly. She drew her pair of katanas, testing their weight. Selah rotated her wrists, swishing the finely honed blades in front of her.

The Combatants picked her out in the crowds and chased her down as she attempted to draw them out from the masses of people. The soldiers struggled through the tide of bodies flowing against them, but one eventually broke free and rushed the cloaked assailant before him. Anger ran through him and he lost all sense of rational thought. As he approached, the cloaked figure before him sidestepped, leaving a leg out to trip him. He sprawled to the cobbles, rolling over in time to see the long shining weapon slice down and across his throat. He clutched at the neat wound ineffectually as the blood flowed in a sticky mess over the stones. He gurgled to catch a breath, losing that battle as his eyes glazed over, staring straight up with a wide-eyed shock.

His colleagues took a more measured approach, seeing how efficiently their quarry had dealt with the corpse on the ground. They attempted to flank, moving to keep one of them out of sight as much as possible. They hadn't expected Selah to flee into an alley. They gave chase, spurred on by the realisation it had no exit. The two soldiers rounded the corner to find Selah standing before a wall she could never climb. Continuing their chase, they underestimated her in their excitement. As they made to reach for her, she seemed to run up the wall. She sprang back off it, arcing over their heads in a spectacular backflip. Katanas in hand, as she landed, she stepped forward, thrusting the blades into the meaty flesh in the back of the Combatants. So quick and brutal was her attack they had no time to register a cry of shock before the life drained from them.

Selah paused, though appeared not to have broken a sweat. She looked as she always did, unfazed and undaunted, like she was strolling through the park. She tossed a disinterested glance at the two corpses over by the wall, using her black cloak to wipe off the blades of her katanas. She ran back down the alley, finding the square mostly empty. Shouts and screams rang out over the city. She assumed that Maxwell Gladstone and his men were busy sparking fights in the wake of the explosions. The city descended into utter chaos around her. Skirmishes kept the

High Commission forces busy, divided, spread too thinly to be effective.

Running through the streets, Selah found a group of Gladstone thugs circling a small cohort of five Combatants, throwing bricks at them before a gunshot rang out. It echoed off the walls of the deserted warehouses and factory buildings in this part of town. She despised the use of guns, they always dialled up the tension in any situation. Start waving one around and everyone else with a shooter developed a twitchy trigger finger. A scuffle broke out, blades slashing as the group of thugs stabbed and slashed at the soldiers before them. Their tactics worked sufficiently to terminally incapacitate their foes. Three other corpses joined them. Two women, no older than mid-twenties and a teenaged, grubby-faced lad, ended with ruthless efficiency, each with their throats slit, lay on the ground. Three of Gladstone's crew. There was no time to dwell on what had happened, though, with the survivors disappearing deeper into the city, and Selah melting away into the lengthening shadows.

Crow froze. The last thing he had expected was a voice amidst the throng of wraiths. The buzzing noise continued, though much quieter than he was accustomed to. But it was still there, discernible enough to be troubling. He surreptitiously drew a long knife in his right hand, his left unholstering the heavy six-shooter. His flowing cloak served to mask them from view. Turning, Crow eyed the stranger with suspicion and anger. Stepping forward into the murky light of the room, the robed figure slowly lowered his hood. Long, slicked-back black hair, thick mutton chops blending into a handlebar moustache. He carried an ebony cane, a silver hydra entwined around it. He put himself together in such a way to give the image of a man of perceived status, a man who thought highly of himself.

"Your reputation precedes you, my good captain. Your actions have been the cause of quite some interest within the Commission."

The man strode around the machinery, absently polishing the glass of several gauges, adjusting settings. The buzzing grew as more of the shadow wraiths seemed to appear. The helmet lying on the ground by his feet crackled and fizzed with electricity in response to his adjustments.

"We have all been very keen to meet you. You see, your actions have presented a problem for us. Especially all of your talk in that cesspit of a public house in Rookhaven."

"I'm sorry, who the hell are you? You clearly know me, but I am none the wiser as to who you are. You are too young to be the enigmatic Commissioner Anvil, and we all know his face. You're not one of his immediate subordinates either. I'd imagine a low-level Commission member, someone with lofty aspirations, dreams above their station."

The smug grin on the man's face faltered. He did not approve of being talked down to. It appeared he also harboured a complex; Crow had hit a raw nerve mentioning that he was unknown outside the Commission.

"Oh, believe me, Captain Crow, I will be known. You will know me. The High Commission would not have the power, the stranglehold over Auridia that it does if not for me. The entire organisation owes me. My name should – will – be remembered!" The stranger was losing his cool. His voice rose, spittle flew from his lips. His eyes grew wide and wild. Whoever he was, he had had enough of being the lackey, not being given the credit and status he felt were his due. His casual, fluid movements became erratic, jerky. A tic developed beneath his right eye.

Crow knew time was running out. With all that had happened, he had been seriously delayed getting here. He had lost track of time. He hoped he still had half an hour to finish his task here, though could have less than that. A cold sweat slicked his skin. But he had an opening. Whoever this man was, Crow was getting under his skin. He had to use that.

"This is all very nice, but I still have no clue as to who you are. And what will you be remembered for. If you aren't known now, you surely won't be known once the sun sets on this day. In time, even Commissioner Mordecai Anvil will only remain as a footnote in history. Nothing more!"

"Enough! I should not have to bear such insolence! Not from you, and certainly not from the decrepit old fools running this poor excuse for an organisation!"

"So, who are you to think you are so much better than the Commission?" Crow knew he was pushing his luck, goading the man before him. He was testing the waters, waiting for his chance.

"I am Atticus Rigby! It should be me preparing to address the people of Auridia today, not that shambling corpse, Anvil!" He became more erratic, pacing and gesticulating at nothing, mumbling incoherently to himself. Suddenly he span, turning his wild-eyed gaze on Crow. He pulled something from a pocket, a small box with three nondescript buttons, and what appeared to be some form of antenna.

"If not for me, the Commission would not be in possession of this marvel of modern engineering and technology! I became aware of it twenty years ago through college. Tracked its development. When I was apprenticed to the High Commission, I maintained an eye on it. I saw its potential. Not what it was originally intended for, but with simple tweaks, it offered us a way to control the people."

"The shadow wraiths."

"Precisely, my good captain. How astute of you to notice."

"Auridia is enormous, so is a nation of aviators. Aviators and sea captains alike, we're all a superstitious bunch. You played on our superstitions to keep people in line. I get that, but how does it help with everyone else?"

"Simple really. Airship crews travel all over Auridia, all over the world in some cases. How else do superstitions spread? Sow the seeds of fear and let it travel. Crewmen and women talk freely in public houses after imbibing a few libations. Grounded patrons spread the word to their families, barkeeps talk to other patrons. Word spreads. We ensure the wraiths appear more and more, perpetuating the superstitions. We cultivate the narrative. Shadow wraiths appear when undesirable behaviours occur, thus using them to keep the people in line."

"You use children to do your dirty work? That is twisted."

"Oh, but you are so wrong, Edison. It is genius. Scruffy street urchins, the lowest of the low, people that those more fortunate fail to see."

Rigby pressed a button on the control unit in his hand. In a flash the wraiths moved inwards, closing the circle around the two men.

"Isn't it amazing? An absolute marvel of modern technology and the very best in engineering. We have many more like them all over Auridia. Towers pick up and amplify the signal so we can operate the shadow wraiths in pretty much every single corner of this wonderful nation!"

"It is impressive, Rigby. This one device alone is a sight to behold. But more of the same?" Crow whistled impressively. He had spotted an opening – keep Rigby talking about himself, and he might just have a chance.

"Not quite the same, Crow. But close. The other units are more like substations. They all keep the signal going, allowing us to control the wraiths anywhere." He turned away from Crow, spreading his arms wide as he marvelled at the machinery. "But this, now this is where the real magic happens. Without this, there is no signal in the first place. All of the control is done from down here. This is where everything takes place!"

Rigby still had the control box in his hand as he massaged his ego, basking in his self-importance. Crow slowly raised his six-shooter. The wraiths did not flinch, obviously awaiting their instructions from the control unit. He steadied himself and fired. The sound was immense, echoing around the room. In an instant, the wraiths disappeared. Something about the destruction of their control box sent them who knew where. The box exploded in a shower of sparks. Rigby yelled in shock and pain, the bullet having passed through his hand. He fell to his knees on the wet ground.

Head bowed, his long hair covering his face, Atticus Rigby held his mangled right hand close to his chest. An animalistic sound rose from his chest, unsettling Crow deeply. It evolved into a maniacal howling laugh. He threw his head back to let it ring around the room. As the laughter died, he levelled his eyes on Crow, peering through matted, dishevelled hair.

"Oh, I underestimated you, *Captain Crow*. That was fast thinking – remove the control unit, remove the weapon? Very perceptive of you." Rigby dropped his head again as another fit of laughter racked him. He regained his composure, shaking his head with a crazy grin stretched across his face. "Unfortunately, you underestimate me, underestimate us. You think I would carry the only control unit down here into the undercroft, knowing you would be here? You poor, naive fool. There are many more around, all of them programmed to the hub here. And right now, the full power of the Cabal forces will be on their way here. Your little attempt to get inside has failed."

Explosions rumbled overhead. Close. Too close. Rigby looked up, an expression of surprise and concern clouding his face. It sounded as though they were coming from inside the Commission Hall. The noise was immense, shaking the cavern walls and showering dust and minute chunks of rock down upon the two men. The boy on the stone plinth groaned, still not regaining consciousness. Crow knew he had to finish this quickly if the boy was to survive. Crow looked down on the broken shell of a man before him, kneeling on the ground nursing his wounds. A satisfied smile broke across his face.

"It would appear it is you who has underestimated me, my dear Mister Rigby. You see, that is the sound of explosive charges being detonated throughout your grandiose Commission Hall by people working with me. It seems you and your beloved High Commission have downtrodden far too many working people. Hard, back-breaking jobs in unpleasant environments for a pittance of pay. What you weren't expecting, and maybe haven't even realised is that I arrived in this great city with my crew of more than a hundred loyal people. Add in easily that number again of disenfranchised Rookhaven residents, plus those who have had enough of the Commission in Copper Lakes."

Rigby looked up at Crow, a gaze of manic fervour in his wide eyes.

"The might of the United Republic of the High Commission will be brought to bear upon you, Crow! I'll wager the Cabal and their Inquisitors are mopping up what remains of your ill-conceived coup as we speak!"

"Your forces are isolated, Rigby. Separated from one another. Explosions and small riots have been staged all over the city. Pockets of soldiers splintering to deal with multiple unexpected uprisings. A simple tactic, though effective I am sure you will agree. Against a unified force, we would have no hope of success. But spread thinly all over the city, their strength and will can be broken."

A raspy, unsettling chuckle came from the hunched figure before him. Rigby shook his head, realising his error even in his unstable condition.

"Divide. And conquer. Very good, very good. It seems you have us bested. But you seek something more. That much is obvious. You will not rest until you have your answers. Oh yes, we know your secrets, Edison. We know you seek more than wealth."

This chilled him to his core. How did the Commission know he was haunted by something? Distracted, lost in his thoughts, he didn't notice Rigby rising to his feet. The man dashed at him, spearing him at the waist and sending both men tumbling to the floor. They scrapped and scuffled, Crow finding himself pinned down. Desperation made Atticus Rigby dangerous, unpredictable. He rained punches down on the prone captain, peppering his face, catching him about the eyes and nose. He bellowed with rage at the insolence he felt Crow and his crew had shown in attacking the High Commission right in the heart of their Republic. Decades to build and moments to tear it down. Rigby spotted a substantial chunk of rock off to one side. That would teach the rogue a lesson in humility. The punches ceased as he stretched out to grab for the rock.

Crow took his chance and rolled the overbalanced Rigby and drove the long needle-like knife into his abdomen. Rigby's eyes momentarily gained clarity only afforded by shock. He slumped back onto the cold, hard ground, gasping ragged breaths through clenched teeth. A hoarse chuckle petered out to a fit of coughing, splattering his teeth and lips with blood. He knew his time was short.

"I-i-i-i-it would seem I underestimated you once again, Crow." Rigby was struggling and seemed to be drifting towards unconsciousness. His breathing was growing ever shallower and more ragged, his forehead pale and covered in perspiration.

"It's over, Atticus. All of this. The wraiths, the machine, the Commission. It's all over."

Rigby coughed again, the pain it sent through his weakening body was indescribable.

"It may well be," he gasped, "for me. For the Commission. For the republic. But – for you – things are just – beginning."

Crow froze. His earlier fear that Rigby knew something about his inner turmoil grew.

"What does that mean, Atticus? What do you know? Tell me!"

Rigby wheezed a terrible chuckle before more coughing. It seemed to take him longer to recover this time.

"That – which you seek. The answers – lie in your future. You will find them – hidden within – the shadows in the deep. Hidden by – the tides." Rigby's focus wandered in his delirium.

"What tides, Rigby? Hidden by what tides?"

"The tides – of time, Crow. The tides – of – the past. Your – past." He reached within the inside chest pocket of his jacket and withdrew a many-times folded piece of old paper, staining it with the blood now coating his hands. He managed to get it into Crow's palm, but the effort was too much. Atticus Rigby slumped back to the ground. His last breaths rasped in and out of his throat as his eyes seemed to settle on a spot somewhere above them.

"No, Rigby! What am I looking for? What am I going to find?"

Rigby's chest fell for the last time, his eyes staring. Unfocused, unblinking.

"Fuck! FUCK!" He pounded his fist in rage against the chest of the corpse of Atticus Rigby, the folded paper screwed up in his other clenched fist. Explosions way above in the city drew Crow's attention back to his current predicament. Whoever was setting them off seemed to be drawing closer to the Commission Hall. His entire focus came rushing back to him. Crow unbuckled the bag worn under his cloak, retrieving the few explosives he carried, hoping the rest of his crew had managed to successfully rig the perimeter pillars. He strode over to the vast machine, not knowing what he was looking at. He circled the hulking mass, finding an access panel on the back surface. Edison pried at it with his bare fingertips, forcing an opening in the metal big enough to reach in and place the explosive. He set the charge, hearing the clock mechanism start counting, shoving the panel back as best he could to maximize the effectiveness of the blast. He would have rather used a charge with a fuse, but he didn't have the time to carefully run the wire and make good his escape with the boy before the perimeter charges detonated.

He ran over to the plinth where the unmoving form of the boy lay. Crow leaned over his mouth, listening for the faint sound of breathing, feeling for breath upon his cheek. Satisfied that the child was at the very least clinging to life, he snatched up the helmet contraption and used the damaged wires to tie it off to his belt. He scooped the boy up in his arms, stumbling through the dingy room to a tunnel at the back. If the plans he had seen were correct, it should lead him up and out into the Commission Hall above. The explosions drew closer, growing louder with every few steps Crow laboured up. Dust drifted down, coating him with each new blast. Just when he thought his back was ready to give out, he could make out beams of light breaking through an ill-fitted door in a warped frame, clearly old.

He prodded at the door tentatively with the toe of his sturdy leather boot, testing it. There was a little give. He shifted the boy, hoisting him over his shoulder. Crow took a large step back before striking the door firmly with the sole of his boot. It splintered like dry kindling. The charge set in the machinery down below exploded. The rush of superheated air burnt at the back of his neck, pushing him forward into the circular reception hall. Stumbling forward as a cloud of smoke and dust billowed out of the doorway, Edison looked up. He was standing beneath the floating glass dome. He needed to get out, he had no clue how long was left on the charges that would bring the entire Commission Hall down around him.

Shouts echoed from the rooms and offices that branched off the reception hall. As he made for the nearest exit to the plaza, he stepped over bodies – senior Commission members, Cabal forces and many belonging to Maxwell Gladstone's posse. More shouts, closer this time, added to his urgency as Crow picked a path through the destruction and corpses to the grand double doors. He span around as three High Commission Aspirants burst into the cavernous entry hall. Young men, keen and eager to learn, to progress, and not afraid to do what they must to climb the ladder in their ascent to power.

"Stop! This is the Grand Hall of the High Commission!" With all of the bravado and confidence of youth, the young men ran towards their assailant. He barely made a sound, raising his gun. Crow saw the look of fear cross their faces in the split second it took him to fire off a trio of deafening rounds. The three slumped to the ground. Two fell immediately silent. The other, only groans of agony could be heard. A thundering smack of boots on marble echoed along the corridor. Crow readied himself, steadying his aim and pulling back on the hammer. Just three bullets left in the revolver – he had to make them count. Finger on the trigger, Crow was relieved to see the cadre of four with whom he had entered the tunnels below round the corner.

"Gotta go, Captain! Less than a minute left on the fuses we lit!"

Two of the men got the doors open, flooding the grand hall with warm autumn sunlight. They provided some cover for Edison as he stumbled his way down the steps, trying to get clear with the boy over his shoulder. Gunshots echoed around the city, a violent soundtrack underlining the end of the High Commission. Then the air was filled with thudding booms as the charges detonated, sending everyone sprawling. The ground seemed to roll like ocean waves. Struggling to their feet, two of the group helped Crow up and onwards beyond the imposing wrought-iron gates and out into the now-empty plaza. A rumble filled the air as the Grand Hall collapsed in on itself, dust and rubble flying as the caverns beneath gave way.

The party made a beeline for the narrow alleys and backstreets, seeking a way through the city to the wide esplanades of the Upper Lake. From there, they could assess the situation and find a way out of the city. In truth, Crow had not fully anticipated the plan succeeding thus far. To have brought down the symbol of the Commission, its seat of power, was never assured. Escaping the caverns beneath, less so. The boardwalks and terraces were packed, scuffles breaking out everywhere. Day-trippers attempted to flee, treading upon anyone and everyone in their desperation.

Locals, and those living in the squalid settlements outside the walls, the workers who laboured day after day to keep the city running, had come out in a show of force. Now that the Commission had been attacked, they seized their opportunity, an opportunity that had once seemed like nothing more than a dream. An opportunity to tear down the Commission in totality and remove its power. Benches and tables served as makeshift beds for the injured. Crow laid the boy upon a picnic table, noticing other children laid about, sporting the metal helmet devices the boy he had saved once wore.

Shouts from the farther reaches of the crowds rang out. Shouts of fear. One of his crew clambered up on a table, trying to catch sight of that which caused the commotion. Then a noise from across the water. The sound of motors. Boats, a vast armada of them, cut their way across the lake, carrying the newly regrouped masses of the Cabal military. The crowds seemed to press in around him, striving to get away from the surrounding streets. A cold feeling descended over Crow as realisation struck. The remaining loyal Commission forces had corralled the dissenters. Their coup was set to fail.

TWENTY-FIVE

ELEVEN YEARS EARLIER

Edison Crow and Selah had been loyal to Rohgar in the nine years they had spent under his command. More than that, they had been useful. As he sat in his quarters, the ageing captain pondered his two youthful charges. Crow was exuberant, effervescent with energy, enthusiasm and bold ideas. He also possessed a meticulousness, a penchant for wanting every aspect of every job planned out. He obsessed over the minutiae – scouting the area, knowing the targets, poring over plans, ensuring he knew all possible entrances and exits. He was fond of the boy's enthusiasm and his somewhat flamboyant presence but loathed the obsessive element.

Selah was the antithesis of her friend. Quiet and reserved, she seemed to be forever thinking. She eschewed bluster and theatrics for a more direct approach in comparison to Crow. She could become a little impetuous at times. Hot-headed even. It wasn't uncommon to find her reacting first and considering second. On their own, the pair had their good points and bad. But take them as a pair, and they could be pretty formidable. Not that Rohgar would ever admit as much to either of his young crew members. On the few

234

missions he had allowed the pair to run point, he had found himself growing frustrated at the days of planning put into devising, scoping and executing them. The last one was hard to consider as anything less than a success – having targeted a political fundraising gala and walking out with a very comfortable four thousand shruckles.

But the week of planning damn near drove Rohgar over the edge. He always had a simple approach to every job he had ever done – pick his target, hit hard and get out. He wasn't bothered about making a noise or a mess as long as he got out with something to show for it. It wasn't subtle or tidy, but he liked the system. That's why Crow and Selah found themselves sidelined on this latest mission. Even Reuben, the ship's wheelman, was on the ground for this mission. While stewing in his anger, Crow at least got the chance to man the helm, a task he quite enjoyed. The focus needed to captain such an airship spoke to him. It brought him inner peace.

Less so today, unfortunately. He had an ill feeling about the job. Rohgar was determined to take his biggest score yet. He wanted to write his name in the history books. That seemed to be his constant flaw – he feared being forgotten. But this job would ensure he would always be remembered. He planned to break into and rob the United Republic Mint. Rohgar had only devised his plan the previous evening after six large rums. Though many of the crew that were drinking with the captain encouraged him the previous night, as morning broke bringing sore heads and weary bodies to the deck, few believed it to be anything more than drunken bluster.

Crow and Selah were none too happy climbing up on deck in the soot-filled grey light of the early morning. As Arcos flew over the wide slate-coloured river, the imposing walls and guard towers of The Island loomed into view. Crow looked over the railing, a sinking feeling in his stomach. On the far side of the fast-flowing river, Murkvale hunkered on the muddy bank. When a younger Selah and Edison had broken free of the bindings that had kept them on the city's grimy streets, they had never planned on returning. At least this time they weren't back alone. The clouds always seemed to hang low over Murkvale, weighed heavy by the ever-present coal soot in the air. Reuben eased Arcos below the cloud line and over the low-lying city. The largest building was an unimpressive black structure at its heart.

The United Republic Mint only had one entrance and exit. Rohgar had a simple plan – drop the crew in, blast the doors, kill or subdue anyone inside and clear the place out. With hindsight, the amount of alcohol consumed the night before made the plan look so simple. Looking through his spyglass, Crow held his breath.

"Fuck. This doesn't look good," he muttered, handing the spyglass to Selah. She slowly panned across the scene. The doors looked solid, so too did the walls. There was no quiet way in through those. The only windows lined the upper tenth floor – most likely the office and administration floor. There were guardhouses at all main gates into the compound, with men patrolling the perimeter. They didn't seem to be armed, but that didn't mean they wouldn't be dangerous. Crow didn't like that The Mint seemed to be hemmed in by buildings and narrow alleys on all sides. It would not be easy to get in or out, likely by design.

Edison entered the wheelhouse where Rohgar was making final preparations for his plan. He had no patience and that troubled Crow. The captain would not hesitate to harm or kill anyone in his way – an attitude Crow despised.

"Captain Rohgar, I think we need to reconsider this job. I think the plan needs work. There seems to be only one way in, no windows at ground level. And what about the guards? I would wager there are many more guards I cannot see. This won't be a simple, quiet job."

He growled in frustration. "Will you quit yer belly-achin', boy?" He span around, eyes wide with anger as he hoisted a pair of large rifles and slung them over his shoulders, settling them across his back. He tightened a belt around his waist and positioned the holsters – one on each hip. "Yer yeller, lad. Worry too much 'bout a whole lotta nothin'. How 'bout you worry 'bout flyin' this here ship? Let me worry 'bout everythin' else."

Rohgar turned to the map table and picked up a pair of long-barrelled six-shooters and holstered them. The man at the wheel turned to Rohgar. "Captain, we oughtta move. Drop off in less than a minute."

"Thanks, Reuben, time to go. Boy, take the wheel." He strode out of the wheelhouse, paused, and came back in. "And don't put a scratch or anythin' on 'er!"

Crow took the wheel, Selah acting as a lookout. Twenty crew assembled on the deck ready to attack The Mint as Edison piloted Arcos over the courtyard. Ropes were tossed over the edge as the crew, led by Rohgar, descended to the ground. After a moment, explosions tore through the air. Rohgar led his men through a large smouldering hole blasted through the doors. Selah kept watch over The Mint as Crow piloted Arcos in lazy circles around the complex. He held a position far enough out to see everything, while also being close enough to perform a fast extraction if needed.

"They had better hurry up," Selah muttered, surveying the scene around her. The guards from the guardhouses had flooded the building following Rohgar's surprise attack. It looked like the modern airship was drawing all sorts of unwanted attention as it looped around and around The Mint. Small clusters of people congregated down on the streets, looking up at Arcos, shielding their eyes from the sun.

Selah looked over her shoulder and called out to Crow, "Trouble heading our way!"

"What is it, Selah? Like we need any more shit today!"

"More security inbound. Looks like they are trying to surround The Mint!"

"Since when did any Mint keep extra security off-site?"

"They're not Mint security. Not police or military either! They are all in black, look like cloaks or robes, heads covered. A dark blue emblem on them, impossible to make out any detail from here, though."

"What the f–" an immense blast stopped Crow short, pushing Arcos sideways. He fought to regain control again, steadying the ship. Gunshots rang out as Rohgar's crew desperately sought an escape.

"Shit, they're in trouble, Crow! We've got to get them out!"

"I know, I know! Fuck! Why won't the stubborn old bastard ever listen to us??"

Hobbs often spent his entire time in the dark of the cargo hold, but appeared on deck, presumably his interest piqued by all the noise and goings-on down below. He burst into the wheelhouse, his wispy grey hair flying about in the breeze giving him a manic look. Many of the crew often debated if it was more than just a look. He lost grip on the door as he flung it open, sending it crashing against the wall noisily.

"We got problems, lad!"

"Don't you think I've noticed the problems on the ground, Hobbs?"

"So you seen the mortars settin' up?"

"Seen the what now? This is not the time for silly games, man!"

"Them robed fellers! They settin' up positions on the roofs nearby wi' mortar tubes!"

"Shit! Not good! Hobbs – get anyone that can hold a rifle to pepper them with shots, we need to slow them down!"

"Right you are, lad!" As quickly as he had erupted into the wheelhouse, the old man was gone again.

"Selah, we need to get the barrels of black powder from the hold."

"Crow we cannot fire the cannons, we may hit our own!"

"I want them all rigged with a fuse. Light the fuse and drop the barrels amidst the guards. Hopefully, the explosions will disrupt them long enough for them to get out. Go, now!"

Selah left the wheelhouse to round up the crew and start preparing the barrels. Crow kept Arcos moving as the crew fired rifles at the men on the roofs. Barrels of black powder primed with fuses were lined up by the railings. Crew scurried around under the watchful direction of Selah. As the airship rounded The Mint, she called for the first fuse to be lit and the barrel thrown overboard. Over the next two flyovers, a cacophony of booms rang out as robed figures scattered for cover. Rhogar was dragged out of The Mint by his crew firing guns at Mint staff and the external forces. Edison brought the airship to a hover over the courtyard. Ropes and ladders were thrown down over the railings for the retreating group. Rohgar was hoisted on deck, a bloodied mess where his right leg used to be. His skin had turned a pallid colour and his brow was slick with sweat. As the last of the crew snagged hold of the ropes, Crow manoeuvred Arcos up and away from the barrage of mortar and gunfire directed at them. He sought to put as much distance between them and Murkvale as he could.

Reuben was back at the helm as the crew worked to secure their meagre haul in the cargo hold. Selah and Crow joined some of the longest standing members of the crew in the captain's quarters. The on-board doctor, Maisie, an elfin woman of just twenty-eight, had the most medical experience amongst the crew. Not that it amounted to much. In her earlier life, she had worked at a state-run orphanage, having grown up in a similar home. She was more accustomed to nose bleeds, grazed knees, sprains and the odd broken bone, not a leg, mangled beyond recognition at the knee, rivulets of blood spreading over the hastily cleared map table. Skin, bone, muscles and blood vessels a tangled, shredded mess. She had set the rest of the assembled crew to work cleaning and patching what they could of the multitude of wounds all over his body. His left eye was a mess, highly likely he would never see out of it again.

Rohgar mumbled incoherently as he drifted in and out of consciousness. He was in bad shape. If he made it out of this, he would have to count himself exceptionally lucky. Crow headed out on the deck, knowing he would offer little in the way of help in the efforts to save the captain. He leant on the railing, staring off into the distance at nothing in particular.

"FUCK!" he yelled, long and loud into the darkening evening sky.

Selah, on his left, leant over the railing. She squeezed his shoulder firmly. A gesture of solidarity, and the closest thing to affection that she had shown in the time Crow had known her.

"I should have pushed him to call it off, Selah. Letting him beat me down was a mistake. I could have stopped this whole mess."

"Don't be such a fucking idiot, Crow!" she snapped, with a venom in her voice he did not often hear. Selah turned to face him, the anger in her eyes burning deep into him. "Now is not the time to play the victim here! If Rohgar lives – and listening to Maisie back in there, it's a bloody huge if – then he owes that to you!"

"Did you hear what the others were saying? Five died down there! Two more besides the Captain seriously hurt, not likely they will make it, certainly not without serious complications if they do. The rest, a man and woman, suffered injuries. Nobody, not one single person, came up unscathed. Even Reuben! Took a bullet to the knee. Maisie had him patched up, nothing vital hit, but that leg, he will forever walk with a limp! Fuck! Selah, I should have done more!"

Her pupils narrowed in her steel-grey eyes, the rage growing inside her. For a moment, Crow thought she was going to erupt at him. That would have been preferable to the silence that crackled between them. He looked so helpless, defeated, like a mournful puppy. She despised the moroseness that had swallowed her friend. She struck him, a flat open palm firmly across his cheek. The stinging pain and shock brought tears to his eyes. His cheek reddened, a handprint-shaped welt stuck out vividly against his pale skin.

A young boy, Jack, ran across the deck towards the silent pair. No older than seven, everything was still an adventure to him. His view of the world had yet to become jaded, thanks to the captain having plucked him off the streets when he was barely a toddler.

"Edison! Hey, Edison!" he hollered with youthful exuberance, skidding to a halt in front of Crow. He bent over, his hands on his thighs, as he tried desperately to catch his breath. He stood again, still panting. Jack pointed back towards the wheelhouse. "Reuben. He asked for you."

"Thank you, Jack, I'll be right along." The boy ran off,

likely in search of another errand. Crow turned to look at his oldest friend.

"You better not leave him waiting. And for the sake of all that is good, don't even think of playing the victim with Reuben. You might be nearly twenty-four now, but don't think he won't cuff you round the head, far harder than I did."

He threw a dirty scowl in her direction, pausing for a brief moment. He turned on his heel, the bottom of his new waxed leather greatcoat flying out behind him as he stalked away to the wheelhouse.

Still seething from his interaction with Selah, Crow bore down on the wheelhouse like a storm front racing down from the mountains to the plains. He slammed the door behind him and slumped into one of the chairs at the map table.

"Yes, Reuben?"

"Well, ain't you just a big ol' bundle of sunshine, boy!"

"I am not in the mood for japes and jollity right now, so if you would kindly tell me why I am here, then we can both be on with our day."

Reuben frowned. He had served under Rohgar for just over fifteen years, and damn it if he was going to be spoken to like that by a jumped-up little upstart who came begging for a job aboard the airship.

"Listen here and listen good, boy! Nothin' gives yer the right to talk to me or anyone on this here airship in such a fashion. D' yer hear me? You and yer lady friend out there come an' ask the Captain fer a space on board, a place he didn't have ter give yer but he did anyhow! So, you ought to act wi' more respect! The pair o' yer!"

A sullen silence fell over the wheelhouse. Crow had a look of shock etched on his face. In almost ten years aboard the Arcos, most spent working with him, Edison had never heard Reuben snap or shout at anyone before. He let out a long sigh of frustration and exhaustion.

"Look, lad. It all went to shit down there. Fuckin' disaster."

"It was too risky, Reuben. He should never have led any of you in there. It looked like there was no way out other than the one set of doors."

"Aye, that were right. Not a door or window to be found. The bastard guards blocked us in. There were almost no coin in there, either. Money gets sent out every bloody mornin'! If the old bastard would've stopped and taken yer approach of plannin' and thinkin' first, he'd have known! We were fucked before we ever started."

"I implored Rohgar before you went down. I wanted him to reconsider it. He was just too bloody stubborn! Maybe I could have pushed him more. Though I suspect he would have never listened."

"I've known Rohgar for many a year. The man's as stubborn as a sabre tusk wi' food on his mind, and just as mean when he's got a mind. We both know you'd find it easier to turn this airship by hand than turn that man's mind. No point beatin' on yourself, boy. You tried, more than once. Ain't nobody gonna disagree wi' that. When he sets his mind to a plan, it's gotta be done, consequences be damned."

Crow sighed wearily. "People died today, Reuben. Fuck, the captain is in a bad way! It was set to fail before it had even started!"

Reuben paused a while, a pensive silence falling over the wheelhouse. The only sound, the occasional creak of the ebony and brass wheel as the elder man made the slightest of course corrections.

"Rohgar's been reckless of late. Too much so. You ain't the only person tryin' to get him to see reason. Most gave up sooner than you, though, boy. We oughta have listened to you. He was so irritated by your obsession wi' plannin' and detail he had us all believin' you were worryin' for nothin'."

"He made no effort to hide his disdain for my penchant for planning. I always suspected he was less than fond of me in general, and that just gave him one more reason to put me down."

"You never understood him then, boy. He looks fondly on ya, sees potential in ya. Even if you are more cautious. Not that any of it matters now, though."

Crow looked up at Reuben, eyes wide. Had anyone other than Reuben told him this, he would have had a hard time believing it. But he trusted Reuben. Most of the crew were nice enough, but a large number seemed to follow Rohgar – what he said was gospel. Reuben was different, though. Not the most sociable of fellows aboard, but he was a good, fair man. He always gave Edison and Selah a fair shot to prove themselves. Always backed them on the odd occasions when Rohgar gave them the chance to lead a job.

"If that was the case, why did he always look down on us, put us down in front of the crew? Belittle us at every turn?"

"He has himself a reputation, lad, an image. He needs everyone to see he's in control. Yeah, he could do that by earnin' respect off everyone around. The captain, he don't have the patience for that. He always seen it as easier to just knock people down a peg to make everyone see he's boss. Thing is, lotta people here respect you pair. Most youngers don't last a few weeks under his bullshit. Figure anywhere's better 'n bein' treated how he does. They get off at the next port and never come back. You pair, though, stuck it for, what, almost a decade?"

"Nine long years. But I was never going to let him wear me down. Neither was Selah. We have been through too much together to let him knock us down."

"And that's why the crew got a lotta respect for you both, on the whole. A few bad apples totally in the palm o' Rohgar. But yeah, not as many as he reckons on. But things are changin' now, lad. He's hurt. Hurt bad as I hear it from dear Miss Maisie. If he can manage to walk after this, with help o' course, that'll be somethin' amazing."

"Maisie is still working on him? I knew he was hurt quite badly, but not this badly."

"Aye. That's the issue. He won't be back. It's the end of him aboard Arcos. Too many people lost faith in him. They all know you and the girly tried to make him think. Know he were too stubborn to take advice and went in blind.

246

How can a crew trust a man too foolish to listen, to lead his men like lambs to the slaughter? He's not got any backing now."

"So, what happens now? Sell off Arcos? Divide the profits, and all slope off to join other crews?"

"Don't be so bloody stupid, boy. There's no chance this crew would split off. And not a chance we're gonna sell off the ship. Yeah, it may well be profitable for us to all stay aboard her, but she's more 'n that to us – she's home. She's family. But wi'out someone to pull it all together, we ain't gonna last long. Everyone is lookin' for somethin', lad. You, Selah, me. We all are. Different things oftentimes. But there's somethin' every one o' us onboard seeks. Belongin'. Rohgar, for his many vices and failin's gave us all that."

"So, who was his number two? Surely any captain has a right-hand man or woman?"

"Not Rohgar – he were too arrogant. Too sure in his ability to survive anythin'. That disappeared pretty quick when he realised we was cornered in The Mint. He were afraid. Hadn't banked on things not goin' as he saw 'em in his head. He realised he'd been too bloody short-sighted, rolled the dice and lost. You don't say a word, boy, but when he was hit, he cried. Begged and pleaded wi' me, pleaded that I don't leave him to die."

"Shit, that's not good. Did anyone else hear him carrying on?"

"Of course they did, all of us did. When we saw shit going sideways, we looked to him. He always had answers. Soon as those robed bastards stormed in, the fear in his eyes – he had no idea what to do. Jeez, I couldn't tell yer how we even got out! If it weren't fer you droppin' blast barrels and spookin' the guards, we may never 'ave 'ad a chance to get away."

"I wish I could have done more, Reuben, might have saved everyone. So, who takes over now Rohgar is no longer capable?"

"Tha's why I called you up here, Edison."

"I know it's serious when you use my name…" Crow looked at Reuben with trepidation.

"Where you think I been while you flew us outta that mess? Were below decks talkin'. Us olders been talkin' fer some time, lad. Rohgar's not up to it. The older he gets, the more reckless he becomes. Like he's affeared of gettin' on in years. You musta seen more close calls this last year or so. More crew gettin' hurt each time we go out. Then this mess. It ain't worth it. Someone's gotta take over, he knows it. The crew knows it."

"You've been aboard this vessel as long as anyone. You know it better than anyone, it has to be you, Reuben. You know the crew."

His brow furrowed as he shook his head, and silence settled in once more.

"No, not me. It were mentioned, and I shut it down. I ain't no leader. I get on well 'cos I know my job an' I do it well. Nothin' more. I'm a pilot. I'm an engineer. I fly this old girl, fix her up. I know every part o' her inside and out. But a captain gotta be more than a pilot. He gotta be a leader. Gotta know when to go, know when to hold. You gotta know how to talk to the crew, keep 'em onside when times is tough. You, Edison, you know how to speak. You know how to talk to everyone. Nobody's beneath you. Your jobs 'ave never yet failed. You think 'em out, plan 'em right. An' with Miss Selah at your side keepin' you honest, you'll be golden."

"Me? No way! Not a chance, Reuben! I can plot a mission, no problem. But run this whole ship? A crew of, what, two hundred souls? No way! For one thing, I am no navigator or pilot!"

"Edison! Hold it together, fer fuck's sake! We're all in agreement, lad. Unanimous. You got the right character fer it, not a single voice against you on this here ship. Us olders ain't goin' anywhere. All of us wanna stay on Arcos. It's our home, her crew our family. And we wanna stand with ye'. I'll fly the ship if that's a job you'd be wantin' me to do. But we need yer as much as you need us, lad."

"I'm not old enough to lead a crew! The last thing you need is a child running a crew this size! I am not cut out for it!"

"Will yer bloody listen fer one moment?" Reuben was beginning to lose his temper, shouting so loudly at Edison that even Selah, out on the deck, turned to see what the commotion going on in the wheelhouse was. "Yer no more a child than I am a king! How old are yeh?"

"Twenty-four in three months."

"Well fuckin' act like it, Edison! Yer a man, probably have been longer 'n most having lived as you 'ad afore joinin' this crew. You've got the knowledge to plan jobs, scout 'em out, yer meticulous. Yer confident. Wi' Miss Selah at yer side to keep you outta the clouds, so to speak, you'll be golden. And yer not on your own, either, we all wanna see you succeed."

Crow slumped back into his seat in pensive silence. He appeared lost in thought. Reuben needed him to commit, one way or the other, but knew well enough to let him think. It was an enormous ask to take on a ship the size of Arcos and her crew. Even greater when it would be the first ship Edison would captain. Crow sighed heavily, hunched forward with his head in his hands.

"What choice do I have here, Reuben? What if I said no?"

"Nobody's gonna make you do anythin' yeh don't wanna be doin'. You gotta want to be captain. The crew need a captain happy to be in charge. Make no mistake, it's a tough job. A lotta responsibility is on yer as captain. If yer not wantin' to do it, don't play at it. One o' us will step up to it, or at worst, we'll recruit someone."

Crow considered the situation some more, before walking to the door. As he opened it, he spoke over his shoulder, "Let me think about it. I need to speak with Selah."

"Aye, lad. It'll be wise to run it past her."

Edison nodded distractedly as he closed the door behind him, and strode across the deck to where Selah was, looking out over the land slowly slipping beneath the hull of Arcos.

⚙⚙⚙

"So, let me get this right, Reuben and the other long-standing crewmates have already been discussing succession plans? And by the sound of it, for a little while before today's utter mess?"

"That is how it sounds to me. Selah, this is no small ask, though. I mean, captain, of a ship. Not just any ship. We're talking about Arcos. She's huge, and the crew, a few hundred men, women and children. It's a massive responsibility!"

"Yes, Edison, yes it is. But how many street rats like us could ever say we have not dreamed of an opportunity like this? It's a miracle Rohgar ever took us aboard, and for that, we are eternally lucky. Obviously, you have proved yourself in their eyes. It seems like this crew needs stability to me. A captain that shows restraint when required and will act when warranted. Sounds to me you already have a level of respect from the crew and not just the olders. You know a good opportunity when you see it. You've pitched a job to Rohgar and his closer crewmen. You've polished those ideas, done the research and seen them executed flawlessly! We need that in a captain."

"You may well be right there, but I cannot do it on my own! I am just twenty-four, for fuck's sake! I am no airman, crude at best when flying an airship. I'm no navigator, either. And the crew, it is a huge crew to lead alone, Selah."

"And perhaps it always has been! Think about it! Rohgar led as a team of one. His decision was final, it took immense will to change his mind. And even then, it seldom worked. Would the last few jobs have been so close, so risky, if he had allowed input from others, had deferred to other opinions? Would we be preparing for a burial at sea for five decent crewmates if he had taken your concerns on board? Maybe, maybe not. Captaining a ship and crew this large is too big a task for one person. But maybe leading with support is what Arcos needs."

Crow leant over the railing, polished chrome gleaming in the weakening light as the sun slid towards the horizon. Though it was still too far away, he knew they were slowly sailing the air currents towards the coast. A beautiful piece of Auridian coastline known for being the final resting place of many an unfortunate airman – The Bay of Souls. They would likely arrive as the sun cast the ocean gold with the first rays of morning. The perfect light to honour and say goodbye to good people gone too soon. He let his eyes take in the vista before him as his mind processed everything.

"Reuben has already agreed to continue as our pilot. He knows Arcos as well as anyone. He has a way with the engineers too. We need that." He paused, looking at nothing, looking at everything.

"We? Does that mean you will do it?" Selah looked at him cautiously. She knew it wouldn't take much to tip Edison and did not want him to feel pushed into a corner with no free choice in the matter.

"If I do this – big if – I need assurances. First and foremost, from you, my dear Selah."

The look on his face was of the utmost seriousness. Now would not be the time for dark humour.

"From me? Of what, Edison?"

"For this to work, I need your help. We have worked well together in all these years together. Looked out for one another, saved one another on more occasions than I care to count. We intuitively know and understand one another. We might as well be extensions of one another. Will you work with me on this?"

Selah lapsed into one of her characteristic silences. It

seemed that she had a silence for every occasion; this one was a silence of deep thought.

"Okay. I will stand by and work with you. This is your chance, Crow, to be who you always said you would, to do all you said you would when we were children."

"Not me, Selah. We. We will do this, together. You and I are equals, always have been and will be as long as we stay together."

Selah straightened her lithe frame, head held high, turning to face her old friend. Not another word was spoken. Crow extended his arm and proffered his hand in agreement. Selah embraced him briefly. In that short moment, she conveyed everything he needed to know. He reciprocated, with no less affection and sincerity than he had received.

"Come, Selah. I think we'd best go and speak with Reuben. There is much to be sorted."

TWENTY-SIX

PRESENT DAY

The flotilla of boats drew attention as their diesel motors rumbled and rattled across the lake. Amidst the noise and distraction, the regrouping Cabal forces launched an attack from the streets, pressing the crowds further back towards the lake shoreline. Panic tore through the crowds, screams filled the air, nobody knowing what to do or where to go. Herd instinct took over, people surged in all conceivable directions, not knowing if it was the route to safety. Gunfire rattled from all directions. Crow and his crew attempted to drive through the crowd towards the assaulting Cabalists. If they could hold them back from the innocent day-trippers, they may be able to delay the inevitable.

More people swarmed from the warehouse district, attacking the Cabal, distracting them. The real threat, though, came from the lake where the on-rushing boats drew closer, firing mortars. Chaos. Noise. Bodies. Crow clambered up on the ornate column base of a streetlamp, trying to make sense of the disorder reigning around him. He saw other members of his crew do the same. To the south, four small vessels swooped in over the gate. Men

254

rappelled down from hastily dropped ropes. Support from Gladstone's men had arrived just when it was needed most. But everyone was still corralled, even with the Cabal forces fighting on both sides.

Shouts went up from the lake as sporadic gunfire and the noise of the motors being pushed to their limits drifted over the water. Arcos ascended over the vast clock that sat between the twin lakes. Turning side on to the desperate High Commission water assault force, ports opened all along its flank. Through some of them, large-bore cannon barrels were pushed through, sighting the boats motoring through the water. Thudding booms echoed across the city as the cannons pummelled the small armada. What boats were not obliterated under the onslaught scattered to the furthest shorelines, knowing their fight was over.

Arcos swung over the promenade, immediately above the Cabal soldiers. Black powder barrels were dropped overboard, short fuses ensured they detonated above the ground. Further explosions sounded from the direction of the site of the Commission Hall. It sounded like some of the charges had not originally detonated. The ensuing thunder-like rumble heralded the final collapse of the heart of the Republic as it tumbled in on itself, falling into the cavernous subterranean warren of chambers and tunnels.

The Cabal enacted a tactical retreat. To where, nobody knew, but under the power of the assault from Arcos and the now-combined force of Crow's crew and Maxwell Gladstone's ragtag bunch of mercenaries, they melted away in a hail of retreating gunfire through the streets. Cheers rang out from the downtrodden Copper Lakes residents.

Cries of relief and fear rang out amongst the visitors. Crow watched as Arcos turned in an arc, slowly flying overhead and heading to the central docking pad, barely big enough to accommodate such a large airship. He turned his attention to the situation on the ground.

Selah stood on top of a kiosk in the centre of the promenade that would have been selling all manner of souvenirs and trinkets that tourists would lap up. Putting her index fingers between her lips, she gave a long, shrill whistle, cutting through the raucous clamour of myriad different emotions. The hubbub died away as all faces turned to her. Crow hauled himself up on to the kiosk beside Selah, spotting his opportunity to take charge of the mess he now saw before him. With the attention turned towards him, he had to think fast. Surveying the scene, he took in the destruction around him, windows smashed and pockets of fires all over the city. He caught sight of the terminus, and clouds of steam billowing all around it.

"I know many of you are scared and uncertain right now! This was not how you had envisioned your trip! The safest thing now would be for you to all return to where you came from! The Skylines are intact. The threat is now over, so please make your way as calmly as possible to the terminus!"

The dazed and confused day-trippers cautiously gathered their groups and made a hasty departure towards the terminus. Children with tear-streaked faces clung to the skirt tails and jackets of their parents as the newly emboldened residents of Copper Lakes rallied with vigour to safely transport the visitors out of the city.

A warehouseman waded through the crowd, catching Crow's eye as he gently shouldered his way against the flow of people. Edison dropped down from the roof of the kiosk to greet the man, his left hand resting casually on his holstered six-shooter, just in case.

"No need fer any o' that kinda business, if ya please, sir. I only wanna parley some with yer, if I may?"

Cautiously, he took his hand off the butt of the gun. He glanced the man up and down, deciding he was likely of limited threat with so many of his crew around. Crow proffered his right hand, which was accepted. He noted the other man had dry, callused hands, the hands of a working man.

"Anderson Richards, worked fer thirty years or more in that there coal warehouse," he said, pointing to a vast red-brick building, the windows coated in coal dust.

"A pleasure, sir. Please, call me Edison, Edison Crow."

"We been hopin' and dreamin' fer many a year to see the back o' those bastards in their high castle. What you done today, not a man nor woman here coulda hoped fer in their wildest of dreams. If we were allowed the freedom to practise religions, I'd bet ya my lot that every one of us workin' types here in Copper Lakes woulda been prayin' to any who'd listen to see somethin' like we have today."

"I had never realised there was such sentiment towards the downfall of the High Commission. The way they are always spoken of, it would be hard to imagine that anyone disliked them. They always seem so well-loved, just look at the number of people who travelled to be here."

"Aye, those who got means are more 'n happy to grease

the palms of those what make life easy for 'em. Those who have to work to make the lives o' the few comfy will be made up to see the back o' those bastards. The Guards, the Cabal, they kept us in check. You wanna live? You work. You cause a problem fer the Commission? You disappear. Simple as. We never had the means to change that. Not 'til today."

Crow thought for a moment, casting his eye about the city. "What will happen here now? You cannot allow somebody as bad, or worse to fill the void. This is your chance to make right all the wrongs Mordecai Anvil put you all through."

"We'll come good, pay that no mind. Too many o' us been wronged by the Commission. There's people wi' plans. The city will rebuild, without the likes o' the Commission anywhere near it. I imagine elections'll be the obvious move, a return to the better days of old before Anvil turned up. Firs' things firs', we gotta see these people outta here. If you'll excuse me, sir, I better see to gettin' people out to safety."

"Go well, Mister Richards."

The two men shook hands once more, parting ways to see to their respective matters.

Reuben had moored at the main docking pad, now empty save for Arcos and a dozen smaller vessels that had joined the coup. He had rounded up half a dozen to ferry the small crew manning Arcos down to the rapidly emptying promenade. His small landing party tied off to the railings surrounding the shoreline and makeshift gangplanks were dropped down into place. Reuben disembarked the first small ship, hopping down to the ground and striding straight over to Edison and Selah. He surveyed the scene before him. Acrid, black smoke billowed above the skyline in pockets around the city. Dust still hung cloying in the air over the former Commission Hall. The visitors streamed towards the terminus like refugees fleeing a war zone.

"Holy fuckin' Hell, Edison! You crazy bastard, you did it! If there was ever someone that were gonna make it happen it'd be you, but even then, I weren't certain!"

Crow shook his head, laughing. He was in as much disbelief as anybody else. Since he had taken on Arcos, he had continued to plan and execute jobs with ever-increasing takes. The risks grew, but his meticulous planning made sure the jobs were as safe as they possibly could be. He knew tackling the High Commission was always going to be a tall order and had made his peace with the likelihood of his impending demise. To have succeeded in that was beyond his expectations. To still be alive had never entered his mind.

"You and I both! And to be fair, if it weren't for your timely arrival, I think we would be staring down the barrel of a very different scenario. Why did you come down here? Not that I am going to complain."

"We were listenin' in on the wireless, Captain. The more we thought about things, the more we figured you might need some help. When we heard you was readyin' to leave for Copper Lakes, we decided to leave the Overlooks.

There was no way we was gonna sit by and wait, we were so bloody helpless up there. We came down, makin' sure we took a wide route around the built-up areas and over to the far side of the lakes. Y'know the forests that border the city? Found us a clearin' and laid low. We was followin' the radio 'til it were obvious things was going a little sideways for ya."

"And we are eternally thankful you elected to completely disregard my orders and saved us from an absolute beating. If you hadn't arrived when you had, things would be much worse. As it is, I fear we will not have made it out without losses."

"Now let's not go beatin' ourselves up. You gave everyone a chance to leave. You knew from the start there was risks wi' a job this big. Said so straight outta the gates. Any losses are a tragedy, but we gotta carry on. We did the right thing wi' this job. We all knew that were the case!"

Crow sighed; clearly the adrenalin was wearing off. The gravity of the day was wearing heavy upon his shoulders.

"I know, Reuben, but it doesn't make it sit any easier. Any death on my orders is too many. I suppose I should be thankful we aren't all awaiting our internment, given the sheer scale of the day. We will honour them. I want every single person, alive or otherwise, accounted for before the day is done."

"Aye Captain. You want an honour service put together?"

"Thank you, but no, Reuben. Leave that to me."

Selah had been curiously looking at the unusual figures lying around the promenade. The small figures of dishevelled children, street children, with strange hat-like contraptions covering their heads and the upper part of their faces. She puzzled over the wires and tubes that seemed to bore straight through their skin. She walked over to Edison and Reuben, a puzzled look upon her face.

"Edison, what is going on with these, errrrm, children?"

Reuben stopped mid-stride, noticing the enhanced street children. He turned back towards Crow and Selah, his face reflecting a look of confusion, much like the one on her face.

"These are – were – the wraiths. Logic told me they could not be something supernatural, but superstition is deeply ingrained in us all. It wasn't until I was in the chambers beneath the Commission Hall. The bastards seem to have gathered up all of these street kids and used them. They used them for their means! I think they are all alive. This one was in the tunnels earlier, I think he is the one we've been seeing, the leader. I managed to remove the metal cap and think he might be okay with care. Selah, I want you to organise some of the crew to get them aboard. Get Maisie to work on them, with help. As long as she is careful, I think all of them can be revived. I think they deserve that chance."

"Of course, Edison. We'll see to it."

Reuben set to work rounding up all of the crew and Selah dutifully organised the repatriation of the street kids to Arcos. Edison looked around him, the sight of the prone children wearing him down. He slumped down on a nearby picnic table, his head in his hands.

Crow had returned to Arcos to oversee things. He felt of little use to anyone as he paced the deck like a caged animal. He solemnly watched over proceedings as the children were carefully stretchered up the gangplank. Maisie was on deck dishing out instructions, coordinating a makeshift ward in the cargo space below decks. He hadn't seen Reuben in the hours since they spoke, and it left him unsettled. A sinking feeling had settled in the pit of his stomach. He fully expected losses, not that it eased his mind at all. His racing thoughts were interrupted by a shout from across the deck.

"Edison! Edison, over here please!" Maisie was beckoning him. Aside from Selah, she was one of the few members of the crew comfortable enough to dispense with formalities and refer to him by name. Not that Crow would openly say so, but he wouldn't dare tell Maisie to do otherwise. He straightened his back, taking charge once more, and strode over to Maisie at the head of the steps leading below deck.

"Maisie, how are we getting on?"

"Twenty-seven children in all, Edison. Children! I would say the boy you brought us uncapped is the oldest. Perhaps twelve at a stretch. The rest, anywhere from there down to six or seven I would wager. What the fuck were the Commission doing with them? To them?"

She was incredulous. For Maisie to swear so openly, things had her rattled.

"That's a conversation for later. How are they?"

"I've not exactly had an opportunity to examine them all fully, Edison. But cursory inspections, all are breathing, all with a reasonable pulse. No obvious sign of consciousness. I am concerned about removing these contraptions on their heads. I don't want to do more harm. How did you get the boy free of it all?"

"Guesswork. Thankfully it seems to have worked."

"I need you to show me what you did, Edison. If I can at least copy what you did, I might be able to save them. At the very least, I will be able to get these awful things off them."

"Very well, after you."

The noise in the cargo hold was immense, a constant hubbub of chatter with the well-meaning crew trying to work out what best to do for their charges. Some focused on the easier task of patching up the walking wounded amongst the crew.

"Monitor the children, but do not touch those things on their heads!" Maisie shouted commandingly to the assembled crew.

Crow stepped up to the nearest makeshift bed. On it lay a tiny girl, pale of skin with dirty blonde hair. Her face and arms were streaked with soot and grime. He refocused himself on the cap. First, he carefully pulled on the wires, threading them out from the papery skin around the shoulders and collar bones. He checked the vials of viscous blue fluid, none leaking, before pulling the tubes carefully free of the metal inlet ports on the neck, careful of the needles on their end. Just as the boy had hours earlier, her body convulsed as she gasped in a deep lungful of air, eyes wide and staring ahead of her, before collapsing back down into unconsciousness.

"What in the name of all Hell was that, Edison?"

"The boy did the same. I suspect it has something to do with whatever that blue stuff that was being pumped into them is. I know nothing about it, so whatever you do, take care. That goes for anyone else working on them."

"Aye, we will." She turned on her heel and began issuing orders immediately.

Crow returned above deck in time to see Reuben as he strode up the gangplank. He headed straight for Crow.

"All crew accounted for, Captain."

Stretchers came up the elevators to the docking pad. Crow turned to Reuben.

"How many, Reuben?"

"Seven souls, Cap'n. Found 'em in the streets, fallen wi' the Cabal soldiers. They died doin' the best they could. Fightin' to the end and seems like they took some o' those bastards down wi' 'em."

"Thank you. Seven lives wasted. At least they are back, and we can give them a proper and fitting send-off."

"No, Captain. You're wrong there. A life given to doing the right thing, fightin' to the finish line, is never a waste. We will do right by 'em. Once they're aboard, I'll get Arcos airborne and I'll make for The Bay of Souls."

"Very good, Reuben. I want them honoured as soon as we possibly can."

After the excitement of the day, the ship suddenly felt a place of calm. The bodies of seven of his crew were respectfully laid to rest below deck. Maisie had worked long into the evening uncapping the children they had rescued. After removing the metal cap from the last of the children she had come to find Crow at the bow of the vast airship. She told him that all of the children had reacted the same, but none had shown any indications of consciousness. She returned to maintain her vigil over the children, and ensure the wounded were tended to as needed.

Crow leant on the railing, looking out at the dark indigo sky as night shrouded the land. The dark canvas was pocked with vibrant, shining stars that glinted like diamonds. He spotted something he had heard of many times but never seen before. A vast body in the sky. A pale greenish-blue surface swirled with clouds of the purest white. Iridescent ice and gas rings spanned its equator, reflecting sunlight, giving them a rainbow effect. It was the nearby planet of Chrolanthia. He had forgotten that its orbit would be bringing it closer to Sylbarania than it had been in years. He was transfixed, thinking about what it might be like to visit another planet. He had heard tales of a group of mad scientists attempting to create a means of travelling across the void to explore Chrolanthia. Outwardly he agreed it sounded mad, foolhardy, but privately the idea sang to the adventurer within him. All around him was quiet save for the steady hum of the motors and the creaking of the deck.

Footsteps striding confidently – if a little quietly – across the deck broke his reverie. Selah took a place beside Edison, perching against the railing. She was looking back in the direction of Copper Lakes. Crow looked ahead. The pair remained in companionable silence for some time. For all the professionalism the pair exuded, they had come to care for one another over the years.

"Are you okay, Edison?"

The question hung in the air for a moment, while Crow pondered it. He sighed wearily.

"I don't know, Selah. I honestly don't know. Seven people. We lost seven good people today. Because of me." Anger made his voice tremble.

"Oh no, you don't get to be the victim!" Selah spat back at him with such a venom his eyes grew wide. "You made it clear that the stakes were high. That the chance of dying was real and likely. Don't you dare play victim! They knew. We all knew! You did this all those years ago after old man Rohgar botched the raid on The Mint. Not now, not again."

"You're right, Selah," he sighed wearily. "You're right. When we get to the Bay of Souls, we will send them on with our honour and respect. Then we will carry on. It's the only way."

"And what about the children? What are we doing about them?"

"I really don't know. First, let's take Maisie's lead, get them back to health, see what we can do for them."

"Then? We don't have space aboard Arcos for them. Not enough food or water."

"I know that. I haven't got that far. We cannot take them with us to La Ville de Cuivre. But I haven't worked it all out yet. All I can say is, there was no way I could leave them behind. They deserve better than that."

Selah stared out over the dark landscape unrolling

beneath, a carpet of pine trees broken up by lakes of all sizes reflecting the glow of the moon. Despite the solemnity of the occasions that always brought them out this way, she loved the natural beauty in this area. She would often imagine losing herself amongst the rough trunks of the trees, traipsing over a carpet of needles, the comforting scents enveloping her.

"Of course you couldn't." Selah broke the peaceful silence. "Bringing them aboard was the right thing. I just don't know what we will do once they recover."

"We have to find somewhere to dock Arcos soon. I know very little of La Ville de Cuivre, and will not risk bringing her into a potentially hostile location. Maybe we can find somewhere that wasn't under High Commission control, somewhere with a respectable home. Give these kids a better chance at life than we had."

"That sounds the best option, Edison. Leave it to me, I will set to work on it with Fi."

Crow nodded agreement. As Selah's footsteps receded, Crow returned his gaze to the horizon.

The slight breeze had dropped away, and the sounds of animals in the forest had grown silent, as if in solemn reverence for The Bay of Souls. It always seemed as though nature had a way of knowing what the place meant. Stars shone through the inky blue canvas of the early morning sky. The crew of Arcos assembled on deck. Reuben steered the airship about, its port side facing in towards the shingle shore of the bay and the seemingly endless pine forest stretching back inland. Arcos hung just metres above the surface of the deep bay. The scene was backlit by the earliest deep orange tinges of daybreak. Crow had overseen a few of these solemn memorials and realised anything he could say would be nothing more than hollow, meaningless words. Words that would not bring back those that the crew wished they could. It would provide no comfort to those no longer living. Seven figures in black shrouds were held at the railing.

Crow walked down the line in silence. He turned back to face the bodies and uttered in a strong, solemn voice, "Your jobs are done. Go well in your journeys."

On cue, the seven shrouded figures were gently rolled over the railing, splashing faintly into the dark water below. He was grateful for one tradition – shrouds were packed with weights to help draw those inside down to the seabed, where they would rest in eternal peace. He was always terrified of the idea of a shroud coming loose, the corpse inside floating free, or the weight not being enough to draw them beneath the gently lapping waves. The crew drifted away to their usual tasks, though the ribald jokes and questionable shanties were missing. Crow maintained his vigil, staring at nothing.

"It's so peaceful here, I find it so relaxing. Especially when there's a bit of a breeze through the pines, and the sound of the waves on the stones below. It's as if the souls are speaking, telling the world they are at peace."

Crow had not heard Fi approach, though it didn't spook him. She always carried herself silently. She was a relaxed individual, easy to be around. Aside from Selah and Reuben, Fi was one of the closest people to Crow.

"Of that, you are not wrong, my dear Fi. Though this is a place of death, it does not have to be a place of calm and peace. This is precisely why I always stay up here after we shepherd our people onwards. A chance to reflect on the world."

"You know that nobody blames you, Captain?"

He sighed. Crow thought to himself that it seemed he had done a year's worth of sighing today. "I know they don't, but it doesn't always mean I don't burden myself with the guilt. It was my decisions and actions today that led to their demise. I just have to try and comfort myself in the knowledge that they, too, knew the risks of our actions and elected to stand beside me."

"I get that. It can't be easy being in charge. But that's why you've got us. Selah's always got your back and, if you start bitching, she'll kick your arse as well! You got me, Hester, Abel and Booker, Reuben, Maisie – we've all been on your crew for longer than most crews live for on other airships. We've got your back because we all know you've got ours. Now suck it up, buttercup – there's shit to be sorted and a crew to be kept busy."

"You're right, Fi. Have you found a suitable location?"

"There aren't too many places that ticked all the boxes. But I found one place, and not too far away from here. Pike River. It has a large docking station, plenty large enough to accommodate Arcos. Looks like it has full docking utilities, too – fuel, resources, maintenance and repair facilities."

"That sounds perfect. Reuben said she took a little

damage in his haste to depart the Overlooks and a little more combat damage. Nothing a few days in dry dock won't resolve. And how about the High Commission?"

"They tried to get a foothold here many times. Tried to sweeten up those in power, the elite of the town. Never got anywhere, though. Like most of the settlements and border towns of Auridia, they take their attitudes to power from across the borders – they're more of an independent state."

"Fantastic, the last thing we need right now is to walk into a High Commission enclave baying for our blood. That's what we are aiming to avoid. How is access to La Ville de Cuivre?"

"Seems like it has plenty of places to dock in and around the city, loads with the capacity for Arcos."

"Reuben will be remaining in Pike River for a while yet. As will the majority of the crew. Being across the border in The Free States, I know too little to risk the entire crew and the ship over there. Selah and I, Abel, Booker, Eliza and yourself will be coming with us, assuming all seems well in Pike River. We need to find a way to get there without Arcos."

Fi's brow furrowed in thought. Crow thought she had something in mind.

"Leave it with me, I think I have a solution. Give me half an hour."

"Very well, come see me in my quarters."

TWENTY-SEVEN

A short sharp series of raps on the double oak doors announced the arrival of Fi. She swung the door inwards and practically ran in. The door slammed behind her as she dashed over to the map table, hurriedly clearing charts out of the way. She unrolled a battered chart. Not one he was used to looking at. There were the faint outlines of towns and cities over which snaked mile upon mile of black lines. Railway lines. On the outskirts of Pike River, a small-town station with lines radiating outwards, connecting the remote fishing town to all compass points. One line ran across the border and into the Free States. It snaked its way down towards the southern coastline. It ended at the large terminus station on the northern edge of La Ville de Cuivre. Fi traced the line with her right index finger, tapping it on their destination.

"If they have a sleeper service from Pike River that will take us all the way, that would be perfect," said Crow.

"But it would likely take two or three days to get there on a fast run, with minimal stopovers," replied Fi.

"So much the better. We need as little attention to still be on us and what happened back in Copper Lakes. A few

271

days should be enough to let the heat die down some. There will be time for Reuben and the crew to have the Arcos fixed up and back to her shining best."

"Are we to be off immediately following our arrival, Captain?"

"No, we should take the day to collect ourselves. There will be jobs to be done, granted. But I think we should all dine and drink together as a crew that evening. Allow the crew to let off a little steam. Not too much, mind, we still have the children to tend to."

"About the children, Sir. How are they doing?"

"I confess, I know nothing more on that score than when I spoke with Maisie earlier. Other than for the briefest moments when their caps were removed, they haven't shown any signs of waking as yet."

"If I may, I'd like to go and help Maisie with them?"

"You have my blessing, Fi. I need to rest, today has taken it out of me. Update me in the morning please."

"Aye Captain."

She left the map on the large table and left Crow alone in his quarters.

As day broke, Crow was already awake, and had been since an hour or so earlier. He had relieved Reuben of duty so that he may rest. It wasn't an entirely altruistic move, though, as he often delighted in manning the helm while the crew slept. He found solace in the gentle creaking of the ship and the whispers of the wind. He was far more likely to be found piloting Arcos during the night or early hours. It was his way of unwinding.

As the leaden sky brightened, it spat drops of rain down upon them, distorting his view a little. Pike River materialised on the horizon, its lights burning brightly in the gloom, refracting on the glass of the wheelhouse. The door opened, the strong, bitter odour of freshly brewed coffee sweeping over him. Fi placed a steaming mug filled to the brim on the map table behind him. She took a seat and looked out of the windows at the dull landscape below.

"That Pike River, Captain?"

"Unless I have made an incredible mess of navigation – entirely plausible, I should add – then that is indeed Pike River. If we maintain speed we should be there in an hour, two at the outside." He reached for his mug, taking a long, comforting sip of the hot, bitter liquid.

"Two hours would be amazing; I could grab a little shut-eye before we dock! I've been down with the children all night. Was all I could do to get Maisie to go get some sleep. It's been a busy night, something's happening."

"Something good, or…?"

"Good, I think. It would've been somewhere around two or three this morning. All of them, they're still unconscious. But, they all got, well, restless. Fidgeting their arms, murmurs from them. At first, it was all at once and ended simultaneously. Almost as though they were still functioning as one. But then the restlessness started and stopped throughout the early hours. Each child different from the last. It's as though whatever connection they've had forced upon them is breaking down. Maisie's hopeful that they will come to, soon enough."

"That sounds somewhat promising. I had another look over the charts when you left last night – there appears to be a vast hospital in Pike River. As best I could tell it has an enormous children's ward. I think we ought to try there and see what they can do."

"I'd better let Maisie know. She'll be pleased to see them get looked after in a proper setting, but somehow she seems to have become rather attached to those little buggers."

"Pay it no mind, my dear. Reuben will be back before long; he always likes to be in control for docking – if I didn't know any better, I'd think he didn't trust me not to graze the docking platforms! When he does, I'll speak to her about it. In the meantime, I suggest rounding up the rest of the crew and making ready to dock."

"Aye Captain." Fi left the wheelhouse as the rain outside worsened and forks of lightning brightened the grim sky.

Crow knocked on the door of a small room off the hold, little more than a cupboard in reality. Maisie had commandeered it as a makeshift office and quarters. It meant she was always on hand at what served as an infirmary.

"Come in." A tired voice beckoned him through the door. He opened it just enough to squeeze himself through and shut the door behind him.

"Captain. How are we doing?"

"Less than two hours out, I would say. We're going to be docking at Pike River. It's on the border with the Free States. As best as I can tell, it is well outside the reach of the Commission, so we should be untroubled there."

"No hassle for even just a few days would be bliss right about now, Edison. I think we all need that. You included."

"You won't hear any disagreements from me on that score. I won't have quite so much time, though. Selah and I, Fi, Eliza, Abel and Booker will only have the day in Pike River. Tomorrow we depart for La Ville de Cuivre."

"Wait, why not all of us? What are you up to, Crow?"

He raised his hands in a placating manner. "Calm down, Maisie, I am not out on a sneaky mission of my own. Nothing so sinister, in fact. I know little of the Free States. I am quite sure they have no ties to the Commission, no feelings towards them in any way. That said, I suspect Arcos is quite known after recent exploits back in Copper Lakes. I'd not be overly shocked if my own face has found its way into some news outlets. I cannot risk the ship or her crew walking into the unknown. Reuben will remain aboard, as will Hester to help man the ship and take charge in my stead. The six of us will be catching a sleeper train from Pike River to the coast. It will likely be at least two or three days' travel. Once there, I plan to spend at least a few days scoping out the city and ensuring it is safe for the rest of the crew to join us."

"And what of the children? I trust that Fi has updated you on their status?"

"That she did, Maisie. I hear there is a sign of improvement from the children. Is it a definite change, or just a tic?"

"I suspect it to be genuine signs of recovery. Now those metal contraptions are off, and that blue whatever it is they were being pumped full of seems to be working through their systems, it seems like their bodies are taking over. I had a closer look at those helmet things last night. It looked like there was something over their right temple. It looked like some sort of transmitter or something. It had two metal prong things, they seemed to puncture right into the bone and then some. That machinery, beneath the Commission Hall, the one you blew into countless worthless pieces. It must have been what Mordecai Anvil used to control them, put them where he wanted them, speak the words he wanted them to speak."

"I believe that to be the case too. I had never noticed the prongs, though it was the right side of the boy's helmet that I had shot. What you've done is nothing less than incredible. It's amazing you have got a response from them."

"I know, I know it is. But I am frustrated."

"About what?"

"That I cannot do more for them. I suppose there are limitations to nursing them here on an airship. They need more care than I can offer them. But what do we do?"

"Pike River has a hospital, larger than any I have seen. If the plans are accurate, it has a vast children's department. I think it is worth a look. Pay it a visit when we get there, make a decision. If it looks right, work with them to get the children transported over there in the days that follow."

Maisie fell quiet, pondering over this plan for a few moments. Her brow furrowed as she thought it through.

"I don't like it, Edison. If we just leave them at the hospital, I'll feel like I am abandoning them."

"I understand that, but we need to be rational. Firstly, they have been unconscious the entire time onboard Arcos. Secondly, what treatment can we offer them right now? The care you have given them is nothing short of amazing, but it has limitations. An airship infirmary is not the place to offer the care they need. The hospital might just be the one place that can turn them around."

Silence. The pair lost in their thoughts.

"I intend to do more digging as soon as we dock, Maisie. If it isn't the right place for them, I won't consider turning them over to the care of the hospital. I want to be assured of their care and ongoing welfare."

"I cannot care for them any further here, Crow, you are right. Please be sure they will be okay before we turn them over."

"You have my word."

Crow stood and eased his way out of the small, cramped office. He paused, casting his eye over the space before him, filled with beds. He could hear the soft sound of breathing, the occasional susurration of bedding as bodies stirred. A far more comforting sound than the unsettling silence when the children were mostly comatose. Quietly, he headed back above deck to oversee their arrival at Pike River.

Their arrival under leaden skies did little to dampen the frenetic activity upon the deck and on the docking pad. Viewed from a distance, the crew hurried about their tasks like a colony of ants scurrying around in the dirt. Crates were unloaded, the holds restocked as arrangements were made for repairs, gleaming coins exchanging hands hastily to ensure jobs were done correctly. No words were required from Crow. The crew knew what was needed from them and hit the ground running as soon as Reuben sounded the whistle, indicating that the airship was secured. Crow left Selah in charge so that he could explore the town, see what he could discover about the hospital. Selah, with Reuben, took the lift down from the docks and set off. Pike River did not have all the fancy trappings of Copper Lakes. Neither did it have the oppressive, almost claustrophobic feeling that Rookhaven had.

People ran from cover to cover avoiding the falling rain. Drainpipes gurgled and spilt water across the cobbled pavements. They passed through the manufacturing district, populated with warehouses and workshops, the air filled with the smell of sawdust and hot metal, the sounds of sawing, the hiss of metal workers quenching white-hot ironmongery. The pair approached an enormous workshop. The clang of anvils, the sounds of wood being worked and the hiss of hydrogen in a maze of pipes filled the air around the airship workshop.

"This is me, Miss Selah. I need to get repairs to the ol' girl organised and all that heavy metal platin' removed. It's weighin' and slowing her down. If you'll not be needin' me in town, I'd like to get things movin' so we can be ready to leave just as soon as you and the cap'n give us the word."

"No problem at all, Reuben. I will see you back on board Arcos."

"Aye, that you will, Miss."

Selah watched as Reuben made a beeline for the workshop manager. He engaged him in warm conversation. It seemed so natural and easy. He was clearly in his element, surrounded by manual labourers. It made her realise what a diverse crew she worked with. Reuben disappeared with the manager into an office to arrange the works needed on Arcos. She turned and walked on further into the rain-soaked town, a number of errands in her mind that Crow was relying on her to organise. She still enjoyed the walk, the cooling rain on her face grounded her after the utter madness that now seemed far longer ago than it was.

As she entered the main square of the town, Selah saw a large inn on the bank of Pike River. Opening the old, varnished door, the smoky interior offered a brief respite from the unrelenting rain. She approached the barman, moisture from her saturated cloak dripping on to the rough floorboards.

"What can I get for ye?"

"Accommodation, I hope. We've just docked our airship and need somewhere to stay."

"You after rooms fer the night?"

"It will be closer to the week. Payment upfront if I can book out your inn for our crew."

The barman looked wary. Often airship crews drank too much and instigated fights. It could be more trouble than it was worth. He was about to voice his concerns until the serious woman before him produced a bag from inside the folds of her cloak. He heard the clink of coins inside. She tossed it on the bar. A greedy look in his eye, he ran numbers quickly. It didn't matter what the value of the coins in the bag, the noise they made told him there was enough to cover at least two weeks' boarding costs.

"I think we have an accord, lady. The bar and rooms are yours once the customers clear. Wi' that many people in here, though, I don't want no trouble from any of you."

"You have my word and the word of my captain. I assure you that he will make sure you are covered upon his arrival later."

He nodded acceptance and turned away to serve his patrons, after passing her a glass of brandy on the house. It's the least he could offer given the price she was paying for the inn, she thought. She took a seat by the window with her drink, looking out at the swelling river as it flowed through the heart of the town. Occasionally, steamboats would chug up and down the waterway carrying materials and wares to and from the factories and warehouses. Small fishing boats anchored on the river, their crews casting nets and lines and hauling up their catches. She nursed her drink, savouring the moment of peace. It was the first time she had stopped to take stock since Copper Lakes. The brandy warmed her as it slid down with an oakiness to it. Finishing her drink, having made it last as long as physically possible, Selah stood and left the inn. She followed the billowing clouds of steam and smoke rising from the train station.

The station was filled with noise and the press of bodies. Porters were decked out in well-worn suits and caps, marshalling people towards their platforms. Passengers rushed to board their trains. And the engines, engineering marvels. Hulking beasts snorting steam into the air. Huge wheels bore them on their journeys far and wide. Vast pistons and seemingly unending lengths of pipework. These mechanical beasts came in all manner of shapes. Long, sleek and streamlined. Short, squat and powerful. One thing in common they all shared, however, was that they were huge.

The noise and smells filled the air and momentarily Selah was overcome by all of the stimuli around her. She had been around airships for years now, but these majestic trains were a sight to behold, even for one as stoic as Selah. She managed to collect herself, striding over to the nearest porter.

"Excuse me, Sir. Where would I find the booking office?"

"Not a problem, miss. Head over to platform twelve, just off over that way. Can't miss it, right at the end of the concourse." He pointed over in a direction obscured by trains and steam.

"Thank you." Selah strode purposefully away across the station concourse, soon disappearing in the mists of steam. She threaded her way through the throng. Every individual seemed perfectly synchronised, dodging and weaving around one another. Finding her way to the booking office, she saw the line was long. It offered her the chance to crowd watch, an opportunity to get a feel for the town by observing how its people act.

The queue moved inexorably slowly. Finally, she made

it to the head of the line and was greeted by a young girl behind a glass window.

"How may I help you?"

"Six tickets please, for tomorrow. Your earliest service to La Ville de Cuivre."

"That'll be a sleeper service, ma'am. Three days, three nights, arriving first thing on day four. It departs at four forty-five tomorrow."

"Perfect, I will take them."

"That's one hundred and seventy-five shruckles a ticket please."

Selah counted out twelve hundred gleaming coins into the deposit drawer.

"There's two hundred each there, can you book a whole carriage for us for that price?"

A greedy glint stole into the girl's eye. "Yes ma'am. The rear carriage will be fully reserved for you and your guests. The next carriage in is the dining car. You'll have no disruptions or anythin'." She wrote the details on the tickets and passed them back through the drawer."

"Thank you." Selah scooped them up and they disappeared somewhere deep inside her black cloak.

Lights flickered on around the town. Not the gas lanterns Crow was used to seeing, though – lanterns that needed to be lit by children shimmying up and down the poles – these lit themselves. They flickered and flashed in the twilight. You could hear them humming if you stood beneath them.

Electric lamps, thought Crow. The world was changing around him. He was a part of that change now.

He paused for a moment, taking the sights of the town in. It was a large place, surrounded by farms and woodland. The buildings were old but looked well kept. Edison looked up at the darkening sky. The moon, full and fat, rose high, a backdrop of stars twinkling behind it. Not even so much as a wisp of smog clouded the sky, no factories anywhere nearby. Pike River, though within Auridia, identified as a Free State. In the Free States, communities worked together, traded freely with whoever they liked. Life was easier. Walking through the streets, Crow felt it. The atmosphere felt so much lighter. Pockets of laughter rang out. People greeted one another warmly in the streets.

Edison entered the bar to the smells of beer, tobacco smoke and the sounds of upbeat music. Voices rose above the music, cheerful and relaxed. Crow hadn't heard that amongst his crew in far too long. The High Commission, the shadow wraiths, there had been far too much going on for them to unwind. A smile spread across his face, knowing that they were safe, at least for the moment. Some downtime was something they sorely needed. Close to a week in Pike River would be ideal.

He strode up to the bar with a spring in his step, his shoulders felt lighter. Everything that had come at him lately had worn him down more than he would care to admit. He ordered himself a large whiskey and a round of drinks for the entire crew. Cheers rang out and the singing grew louder. He settled himself into a corner of the bar where he could observe the evening's proceedings.

Later, Selah joined him. They shared platters of food in companionable silence. With the food cleared, the pair discussed their plans.

"How did you get on?" Crow took a long sip from a pint of local beer. He grimaced then sighed contentedly. It was a lot stronger than he was accustomed to, but he liked it. Selah cradled a glass of brandy between her hands, observing the revelry amongst the crew, a ghost of a smile on her face. Rarely for her, it seemed to reach her eyes. She looked relaxed, Crow thought. Possibly the most relaxed he had ever seen her in the many years they had known each other. It was a look that suited her, he thought. He made a mental note to try and avoid drama as much as he could from now on. For the sake of himself and his crew. Though he knew he still had one last piece of the puzzle to lay to rest first.

"Everything's sorted. I've booked this place out for the week. It's cost us a small ransom, mind you."

"I believe it will be worth it, Selah, if it keeps us free from prying eyes. So, if all went to plan, I trust the tickets are booked?"

"Of course. It's an early start. Four forty-five the service leaves. Apparently, we will be on the rails for three days. Assuming no delays, we should arrive at La Ville de Cuivre around sun-up the fourth morning."

"Perfect. It should allow us all some downtime before we hit the ground again."

"I paid a little extra, two hundred shruckles each. It got us the rear carriage of the train. The next one along is the dining car. More privacy. We'll know if anyone tries to follow the train, and anyone entering the car that's not one of us will be an unwanted guest. I thought it made sense."

"Good thinking, worth every extra shruckle, I think. I very much doubt we will be troubled now, but better to be safe. A nice early start tomorrow is by far my preference. I'll not lie to you, Selah, I will be a lot calmer once we arrive. I know we are likely in the clear now, but until I see the coast and check the city out for myself, I will not be settled." He sat in silence for a few moments, sipping at his beer absent-mindedly. "I think we ought to make our own ways to the station. Arrive at separate times, not communicate until aboard. I cannot take any chances."

"Agreed. We'd better consider turning in soon. And you might want to cut the other four off, or they'll be sure to miss the damned train. Is everything else in hand?"

"As much as can be. I saw Reuben back at the docks earlier with a burly fellow. He said he was from a ship fitter here in town."

"Quite likely, I left Reuben at one to go about my errands earlier."

"Very good. The pair was rather animated, especially by Reuben's standards. Seems to me they have everything in place to get Arcos sorted out."

"Brilliant. What about the children?"

"Maisie has met with the hospital. She's loath to admit it, but I think they impressed her with what they can offer. She will work to ensure the children are stable, then oversee their safe transfer into the care of the hospital. I doubt we will see her now before we leave."

"It's going to hit her hard, giving them up. But I am

sure she knows, deep down, it is the best thing for them."

Edison sighed. "It is, Selah, we all know it, her included. But she feels responsible for them. She will be fine in time, but it will affect her somewhat." He finished off his beer and rose from his seat. "I think we should call it a night, early start and all. Let's go and tell the others before we turn in."

As he turned to where Fi, Eliza, Abel and Booker propped up the bar, Selah followed him.

TWENTY-EIGHT

It was pitch black outside the window when Crow awoke. It was so early even the songbirds were still asleep. A hot shower and he had his finest suit on and his bags packed. He eased the door open quietly, walking almost completely silently down the hall. He stopped outside a door. Nondescript. The same as any other on this hallway. No numbers on any of the doors. He lightly tapped its surface. Selah stepped out dressed in a way Crow had never seen before. A long flowing deep blue dress, almost black. Silver stitching and trim. Dark brown bodice laced tightly. Black heeled boots polished to a shine and laced to the knee. A long, loose coat matching the dress. Somewhere hidden under all the cloth would be weapons aplenty. Small and dangerous, and in easy reach. Her hair fell down her back in tousled curls. On top, a short top hat with a curled brim, a peacock feather in the hatband adorned with a large silver brooch of a bird. A crow.

He took her bags from her and stepped aside to let her out of the room. Edison could not help but pause; he had never seen her like this before. She looked refined, elegant. An air of confidence poured from her. His appearance had not gone unnoticed either, Selah finding herself viewing her oldest friend with changed perspective after all that had gone on. Regaining his composure, a warm, wide smile spread across his face, his eyes sparkling with joy.

"After you, my dear." He indicated for her to head downstairs before him. The pair descended the stairs, making no sound. The bar area was dark, the only light the dim flickering orange glow from the town's basic electric lamps. Their room keys doubled as access keys, allowing them to unlock the main door. Out on the street, looking over Pike River – the namesake of the town – the pair briefly observed the hushed comings and goings of the early rising fishermen. Crow hoisted their bags on his right shoulder and offered Selah his left arm. "Shall we, m'lady?"

A wry smile on her face, Selah swatted his arm playfully with the parasol she carried, before linking her right arm through his.

"You idiot!" She chuckled at his expense.

The pair wandered around the building to the front that overlooked the town square. On the opposite side of the square was the taxi office. Crow walked arm in arm with Selah to the booking office, paying for a carriage to take them to the station on the edge of town. They were led to the nearest carriage, a glossy black affair with gold leaf finish. The gleaming brass steam horse glinted in the light from the candle lanterns on the carriage. Steam billowed from the nostrils and mouth. The thing was incredible. Both could not look away, having never seen such a piece of engineering. As large as a shire horse, crafted from highly polished brass with gold and chrome tack. The flanks were left open, exposing a network of pipework and gears.

The driver urged the mechanical beast forward as it stepped out of the garage. The mechanics whirred and clanked, and the steam hissed as it galloped through the streets, its metal hooves sparking brightly on the cobbles in the early morning darkness. Within minutes it drew to a halt, the horse rearing much like a skittish horse of flesh and bones. From the shadows, a porter stepped forward with a trolley. He began to unload the bags onto it. Crow stepped around the carriage to help Selah down.

"Ma'am. Sir. May I see your tickets please?"

Selah produced them from a pocket within her elegant coat, handing them to the young porter with a polite nod.

"Sleeper service terminating in La Ville de Cuivre, very good, ma'am. Platform eight, if you'd care to follow me." The porter headed up the ramp with the trolley. Selah looped her arm through Crow's as they headed for the station concourse. They followed their porter as he threaded a path through the crowds. Even at this early hour, the station was packed with bodies travelling to work, holidays, day trips and all manner of journeys in between. They hurried to keep up with the porter until the locomotive came into view.

If the sight of the brass horse had been a spectacle, the train engine before them was beyond their wildest imaginings. It was huge, almost two storeys high. And long. It's sleek angular lines and flowing curves spoke of power and speed. The huge wedge on the front, not dissimilar to a cattle catcher, brokered no mercy to any creature in its path, large or small. The livery carried through from the locomotive to every single carriage behind it. A deep, rich burgundy finished with silver and gold leaf pinstriping. Gloss black roofs on every carriage. Wheels, pistons and crankshafts and connecting rods were polished and gleaming silver. Brass pipework and six enormous chrome chimneys completed the most impressive locomotive either of them had ever seen. Two flags bearing the insignia of the free states fluttered lazily on the front corners ahead of the vast boiler.

"Quite the sight, isn't she?" Neither Selah nor Crow had noticed the porter pause with them. "Pride of the Golden Seas she's called. Biggest, fastest and most powerful train running in the Free States. You got mighty lucky getting booked on her for your journey – tickets usually get snapped up the minute word gets out she is running the service."

"She is certainly something special," Selah marvelled.

"You'll have plenty of time to admire her on your journey, but given the length of the train, we are still a fair walk to your carriage. If you'll follow me, I'd like to have you settled on board as soon as we can, ready for departure.

"Lead on, good man." It was the first Crow had spoken since setting eyes on the incredible locomotive.

Selah and Crow were shown to their cabin on the carriage. It seemed that the extra money she had paid for the tickets was worthwhile. The doors and windows were all lockable from the inside only. A nice touch. And better still, each cabin was huge – two large double beds, seating area with chairs and desk, record player with records and a private bathroom. This was going to be a comfortable journey. Having arrived two hours ahead of departure, the porter suggested they partake of an early breakfast in the dining wagon. All meals were included in their ticket price, so they were only too happy to oblige. Having set their belongings in the room and hung their hats and coats, Selah and Crow headed into the next carriage. Edison pulled out a chair for Selah, settling her before taking his seat.

"Now this I could get used to," Selah opined. She looked around at the opulent surroundings. Polished dark cherry wood everywhere, glowing lanterns casting a thin light around the carriage. The bar area had a polished brass rail running around it and plush stools along its length.

"No buffet tables or anything, though," Crow noted, relaxing into his seat.

A man dressed in a fine, pinstripe suit with bowtie and white gloves approached to take their breakfast orders to be cooked on request. Before long he was back with a cafetière of hot, strong coffee. The smell was intoxicating, far better than any coffee the pair were used to. As their food arrived, Selah noticed amongst the now-filling tables the familiar faces of her crewmates. Without so much as the slightest nod of the head, she made eye contact as a means of greeting. A trolley wheeled out from the galley area was stacked with plates, dishes and bowls with all manner of mouth-watering foods. Sabre-tusk sausages, steaks of ursanid meat cooked medium rare, the largest eggs with vibrant yellow yolks that were rich and silky. Exotic fruits and thick, creamy yoghurts. In all of their years on the streets, they could never have imagined such a spread. The pair indulged and enjoyed the enormous feast greatly, leaving not even so much as a morsel of food behind. Full to bursting and in need of a rest now, they gingerly rose and headed back to their cabin.

The journey had been a welcome, uneventful period of luxury, decadence, and indulgence. A much-needed respite for everyone involved. As Edison and Selah returned from dinner on the second day, Crow slipped an envelope beneath the two other doors in their carriage. He would need to see them before they arrived in La Ville de Cuivre. They would all meet in the lounge room the following night, after dinner. Crow was beginning to feel jittery now as he drew closer to the next chapter. A worm had worked its way into his thoughts ever since he had gone toe to toe with Atticus Rigby. How had he and the Commission known he was haunted? How had they known to come after him so much?

Selah took the chance to luxuriate in a hot bath, leaving Crow alone. He sat in a chair at the desk. He withdrew a crumpled, bloodstained scrap of paper from his inside pocket that he had carried with him since that moment. He turned up the lamp on the desk, dispelling the shadows a little further. He laid the paper on the blotter pad, spreading it out and smoothing it with his palms. Just a few lines of text scribbled in hurried cursive handwriting.

The Shadows that trailed the Crow, he sought to dispel.
In the city, with twin lakes, he came into the light.
The wretched wraiths banished to the darkness,
Waiting to strike again.

The Crow knows not that shadows cloud his past,
And loom large over his future.
To clear the mists of time and seek what lies
Amidst the Shadows in the Deep, the Crow must fly to the
    City of Copper.
Follow The Blood Trail to its end, and the Crow will be
    one step closer.

"Fuck! What the hell does this bullshit even mean?" Crow mumbled to himself, not hearing Selah come out of the bathroom wrapped in a robe.

"What has you so confused, Edi?"

"You are unbelievably lucky nobody else is around to hear you call me that! If you hadn't saved my arse all those years ago, I am not sure I would let that slide." Crow glowered, though his frustration softened a little in the face of Selah's mischievous teasing.

"Joking aside, Crow, what's up?"

"You know why we are coming to La Ville de Cuivre?"

"You said Rigby mumbled something to you as he was dying."

"That he did. But he also pushed this into my hand. It doesn't clarify things at all."

Selah reached out for the note, a curious look on her face. "May I…?"

"Hmmm? Oh, yes. Be my guest."

Crow rose from the chair, allowing Selah to take his place. He strode over to the drinks cabinet, pouring two exceptionally large drinks. He returned, drinks in hand. He placed them on the desk, condensation pooling around them on the varnished surface. Returning to the cabinet, he grabbed the crystal decanter and slumped into the chair opposite Selah with a weary sigh. He knocked back the glass, grimacing at the harsh, earthy taste, and poured himself another large glass. Selah frowned as she read the note, mumbling its words under her breath.

"What in the name of the Almighty is The Blood Trail? That's got to mean something to you. Think, Edison!"

"Do you know I hadn't considered thinking about this little conundrum and if it actually resonated with me on any level? Of course I've bloody well thought about it!" Crow lapsed into an irritable silence. Angry. With Selah. Himself. Most of all, he was angry with that weaselly bastard Atticus Rigby for dropping yet another mystery into his lap.

"You're right. I wasn't thinking. It doesn't mean anything, though. I've never heard of The Blood Trail. In all truth, I had only loosely heard of La Ville de Cuivre."

Crow sighed, feeling guilty for his outburst. "No, nor have I. It is beyond mysterious."

"What are we going to do?"

"We continue. Two more sleeps and we will be pulling in to La Ville de Cuivre. We must carry on. We get a feel for the place, ensure it truly is Commission free. We need somewhere to call home, at least for the time being. Maybe this could be it. In time, I hope that we can uncover some of what is going on. And in the meantime, we get the rest of the crew together. Start taking some jobs. Get back to something approaching normal. As normal as things get for our merry band, anyway."

"But what do you plan on doing about this little puzzle here?"

"What can we do? We have less than nothing to go on. We will need to do our research once we are settled. I expect we will be staying for some time. In the meantime, let's keep a low profile, not draw any unwanted attention our way." Crow fell quiet, his brow only slightly less furrowed than before.

"Are you okay, Crow?"

"I will be, with a good night's sleep. I thought once we had ousted the High Commission the biggest of our concerns would be behind us. It seems as though we've just waltzed right into another troublesome mystery to unravel."

Selah stood and moved behind Crow. "You need to go easier on yourself. These troubles and burdens are not yours alone to shoulder. You've always looked out for the crew, let them support you as well." She laid her hands upon his shoulders, feeling a tightness, the tension of everything they had been through as a crew in the recent days and weeks. She rubbed the muscles, to ease some of his tension. She leant down close to his ear and whispered: "Now, will you please come to bed?" She placed a light kiss upon his cheek, before leading him to her bed.

Edison and Selah spent much of their final day of travel in their cabin. They discovered one another in a new light, seeing what they realised had likely existed between them for many years. They left the cabin long enough for a fleeting breakfast. As the light streaming through the windows changed as morning moved into afternoon, and now onwards to late afternoon, Selah and Edison noticed a marked change in scenery as they lay blissfully beneath the bed sheet together. Her head lying upon his chest, Selah sighed contentedly.

"How different the world looks now. Do you think we have crossed into the Free States yet?"

Crow held her as he pondered her question. "If we haven't yet, we will shortly. Copper Lakes feels like a world away now. I've never seen land like this before."

A world of hilly spaces and dense pine forests, vast lakes and soaring mountains had given way to flatlands and dusty plains, rivers and streams and rocky outcrops. Now, though, the vista had changed again. Muddy, grassy ground dotted with bushes and vibrant coloured flowers, towering trees with vast trunks and roots twisting through stagnant swamp water, long beards of moss hanging from their high branches. And the weather had changed too. Even in the comfort of their luxury sleeper cabin, the oppressive heat from outside found a way in. There was a slight hint of the heavy humidity outside as well, something neither of them had experienced before.

"I think we are going to need a change of wardrobe," Selah murmured. "All my clothes are far too hot and heavy if this is a mere flavour of what to expect."

"Mmmm. I think you are right, my dear. I don't normally need to dress light. That shall have to change now."

Selah stirred, and propped herself up on an elbow, smiling slightly at Crow. "Come on, we should go and shower before dinner." She rolled out of bed and took his hand as she headed to the bathroom.

Crow and Selah enjoyed a leisurely dinner as it was their last night of luxury aboard the train. They even ordered the most expensive wine available. Something that didn't go unnoticed by their crewmates seated about the carriage. The couple showed no inhibitions in hiding their new status; the relief in escaping the crumbling United Republic of the High Commission had given them a new outlook on things. They enjoyed the band playing music common to the area as they sipped their wine and indulged in the most incredible seafood feast they had ever encountered. As the vibrant orange sky darkened towards rich purples, they finished their meal and returned to their carriage. The pair reclined in overstuffed chairs, watching the world pass them by through the windows of the shared lounge space.

They both enjoyed the quiet for a while, enjoyed one another's company in a different light. Before long, Eliza, Fi, Abel and Booker trickled their way into the lounge.

"Captain. Selah. Are we ready for tomorrow?" Fi wasted no time in getting straight to business.

"Straight to the point as ever, Fi, don't ever change."

Crow chuckled. "We need to maintain the pretence that we don't know each other once we arrive. I genuinely think we will be fine at this stage, but I am never one to get complacent."

Abel chimed in. "Makes sense Cap. But what are we looking for? Like, what's the mission?"

"Get the lay of the land. I need to know what the city feels like. I want to know everything we can. Is it stable, safe, politically sound? The works. I am certain everything is fine, but it's a must. Don't draw any attention to yourselves. You're tourists, exploring and experiencing the city. Watch and listen. If you can, avoid asking questions. If you can't, be careful. Reuben seems to think Arcos won't be ready for another three or four days. I need to get hold of him by then. Once we are sure, we will get the rest of the crew down here to join up with us."

"Okay, but how do we stay in touch? Relay what we've found?"

"This will be the tricky part. We need to be careful. We can't stay at the same accommodation, not yet at least. If there is even the slightest of chances that anyone has spotted us together back in Pike River and sees us all leaving the same train carriage on arrival, or sees us together in any capacity beyond casual greetings in passing, we may have a problem. Selah might well have this one solved for us, mind you."

"In the middle of the city, there's a vast square. It covers around twelve blocks. It's littered with seating, pockets of green space, two large boating lakes and an enormous bandstand at its heart. Looks like little cafes and bars reside in small shack buildings all over, and around its perimeter. I would bet it's the heart of the city. Likely full of people as darkness falls. Dinners outside, drinks, live music and shows. I suggest we aim to cross paths at the large fountain to the north of the bandstand here." She opened out a city map and tapped the area she had in mind.

"Sounds good. Tomorrow's Thursday, so people will be unwindin' for the weekend, I'd reckon. Say ten thirty each night? Keep it simple. If it's busy, so much the better. Brush past and drop a note in a pocket or palm it." Booker made it sound incredibly easy.

Crow pondered this a while. "Okay, but we still need to be careful. Drop a note, and that could be it. Do not identify yourselves in anything. Not even initials. I don't want or need to know who wrote them. Find a way to sneak a room number in the first note, and the hotel switchboard number. If anything needs to change, I will call your hotels."

A murmur of agreement rippled through his crew.

Eliza looked like she had something she wanted to say, but Crow waited for her to broach it.

"Sir? I get that we needed to get out of Dodge as quickly as we did, best we not get caught hanging around. But why La Ville de Cuivre? Strikes me as an oddly specific place to choose when there are plenty of places over the border much closer."

Crow stayed quiet for a moment. He hadn't planned on revealing everything to his crew so soon. Selah placed her hand over his gently as she looked at him.

"It's only right they know what is going on, Crow. Best

not to leave them in the dark to find out later on."

He reluctantly agreed. She was right, of course she was. He had hoped he could delay a little longer, though. Edison wanted to understand what they were looking at before drawing anyone else into things. He relayed the events that transpired when he met with Atticus Rigby in the undercroft back in Copper Lakes. As he finished, the crew around him fell silent. Crow pulled the now-heavily crumpled piece of paper out of his inside pocket and laid it upon the table between everyone, smoothing it out. The other four crowded around it as Crow sat back in his seat, taking Selah's hand.

"What's this supposed to mean, Captain?"

"I wish I knew, Fi. I am as in the dark as you are. That is, in part, why I wasn't going to say anything. I wanted to work it out, or at least start to puzzle this one out before making any decisions."

"What do you want us to look into on that front?"

"Nothing yet, Eliza. I want the crew back together before we start galivanting around town on hare-brained errands with no logical conclusion in sight. Let's focus on getting settled and go from there."

Agreement rippled around the group. As they stood to retire to their cabins, Fi paused as she reached the door first. "It's good to see you more relaxed. You too, Selah. We're dead happy for you. Everyone else will be too. It took you long enough!"

Crow and Selah stood in shocked silence as their small crew left, smirking jovially. They thought they had been so careful, and neither had realised the crew had been wondering about them for so long. They laughed, walking back to their cabin to enjoy their final night aboard the train.

The deep red behemoth of a locomotive screeched to a halt in the vast station on the edge of La Ville de Cuivre. The station was spectacular. High-arched glass roofs and ornate iron supports formed an open, airy canopied concourse. Metalwork was painted in rich green, deep red and gold, a riot of colour compared to the more practical stations in Copper Lakes and Pike River. People bustled around jovially, the sound of music surrounding them from a bandstand in the centre of the station. Crow stepped down from the carriage following the porter with their baggage. The humidity struck him, snatching his breath as he helped Selah down from the train. The air was thick and moist, oppressive. He had already foregone the coat and hat but had to remove his cufflinks and roll up his sleeves. They both followed the porter as he carved a path with their luggage trolley through the crowds and out to the bustling street in front of the station.

As the porter hailed a taxi, Crow and Selah stopped in their tracks, stunned by the sights around them. The streets of Copper Lakes seemed lively, filled with bustling, happy people going about their day. Men dressed in freshly-pressed suits, top hats and tails, women in long flowing dresses, dainty hats and parasols strolling along the avenues and streets. People were dining in restaurants, sitting outside on cafe terraces, enjoying the wine bars and theatres. Only now in the Free States could they see how wrong life under the High Commission was. All of the people enjoying the city were of a higher status. The factories, warehouses and working classes were kept out of sight. They had their own districts of the city, on the outskirts. Grubby restaurants, dingy dive bars and tenement buildings crammed to the walls with more residents than there was comfortable space for.

In La Ville de Cuivre the crowds were made up of a smorgasbord of society. Well-dressed businessmen conversed and mingled with shop workers, dock workers and grimy-faced factory workers. Farmers and fishermen chatted with high society families. In the Free States, it seemed every person to a man and woman were truly free. It was noticeable that nobody seemed to be living on the streets, no sign of homelessness. Wealth was definitely on a sliding scale, but it seemed everyone was treated with care.

The technology was a cut above anywhere within the United Republic as well. Horses and carts were nowhere to be seen. People had their personal vehicles. Each a mechanical marvel. White steam plumed skywards from valves and pipes as eight-jointed legs scuttled these contraptions around the streets like gleaming metallic spiders. Neither Selah nor Crow had ever seen anything like it. Following a piercing whistle from the porter, a gleaming silver mechanised crab scurried over on delicate feet. It hissed steam and water vapour as its segmented legs lowered to the street, the cabin dropping down to permit them access. The door dropped downwards and a set of four steps unfolded to the ground before them. Inside, Crow and Selah settled themselves on the plush, polished leather bench as their luggage was loaded in the back. The driver took his seat and began to work a mind-blowing number of levers and switches in the front cab. Steam briefly clouded the windows as the vehicle rose on its seemingly fragile legs. As it began to build speed down the street, the pair stared out of the window, marvelling at the technology.

"Edison, I've never seen anything like this. I thought the Republic was progressive and advanced. Well, that's what they'd spout all day long anyway. This is something else, though. No street dwellers anywhere I can see. In the Republic, they'd be everywhere, especially near the station. The streetlamps don't look like they're oil either. And these carriages, they are incredible!"

"This place is a world away from that which we are used to, that much is true." Crow could not tear his eyes away from the window. The city moving by in a steady, rhythmic rise and fall of the carriage. "And do you know what else I'm noticing? Everyone, and I mean everyone, seems to be happy. Not to be complacent, Selah, but I think we've found our new home."

"For the time being, anyway. Where are we heading?"

"There's a large hotel right on the square. I thought it might be a good spot. Plenty of rooms there too. If all pans out as we hope it will, this could be the place we reunite the crew."

"Best not to get ahead of yourself, Edison. Let's take this slowly and make sure everything is as it seems."

"Very true, Selah, we still have a job to do here."

"And don't forget Rigby's mysterious note."

Crow grew gloomy thinking about it. He was hoping to put it off a while but knew it would have to be investigated soon.

"Quite right. But better to worry about one thing at a time."

The pair sat quietly in contemplation as the carriage transported them through this mysterious new city.

Crow and his advance party worked far more thoroughly than they needed to in scouting out the city. They spent over two weeks getting to know the ebb and flow of the city, how the people lived, how everything worked. They were supposed to have made contact with Reuben four days after their arrival. Though Eliza wanted them to update him that it may be a bit longer before the rest of the crew could join them, Selah talked her down. This was easier said than done with brief notes exchanged once a night. Their second weekend in La Ville de Cuivre was an eye-opener for them. Word of the fall of the High Commission had reached the Free States by this point.

Singing and dancing filled the streets. A carnival atmosphere spread throughout the population. The sprawling square in the heart of the city was full of life and celebration. The crew relaxed a little, though not fully, not until they were ready to contact Reuben. Republic flags were burned without fear. Papers spoke of the attack on the

High Commission as a day to be remembered. People were talking openly about what had happened. Their actions were being celebrated, unknown heroes who had taken down the tyrannical United Republic of the High Commission.

"I think it's time."

"I think you're right, Selah." Crow pulled out a tarnished silver pocket watch and snapped the clasp on the cover open, checking the time. "I am not sure how easy it will be for us to get a hold of Reuben now, though. I will work that out tomorrow."

"The ship fitter back in Pike River. If we can get hold of him, he may be able to track him down and have him return a call?"

"A ship fitter won't have a telephone, but you may be on to something. We can try the inn where they are all staying if they have a phone."

"If you try early enough, you might get Reuben before he goes anywhere, though I wouldn't bet on it."

"On that score, you are completely right." Crow chuckled. "Reuben rises before the witching hour is done!"

"We'll be meeting the rest soon, we best be off. How do you mean to play things tonight?"

"No need for a clandestine handoff tonight, my love. I believe we are safe. Let us all meet as friends and celebrate tonight!" Crow stood, and playfully twirled Selah to the music. She hit him lightly, laughing at his sudden bravado. The city seemed to agree with him. If truth be told, the city agreed with her too. A weight had lifted as soon as she stepped off the train. Her constant anxiety had ebbed away, and now she was keen to reunite with the rest of their crew.

⚙⚙⚙

Crow had not risen early enough to catch Reuben before he headed out. He had not slumped into bed until the first pink tinges of sunlight kissed the horizon. He and Selah had met with the other four and embraced their newfound freedom. They celebrated, and danced, and sang and drank with wild abandon. They enjoyed their first night not pretending to be different people. Crow was paying for it now, though. He had forgotten just how many years had passed since he was able to drink without a care and not suffer for it the next day.

Selah was already up. He could hear her in the shower. Edison rolled over, swung his legs out, feet on the cool floor. He sat himself up, as upright as possible, with an almighty groan as a searing pain dug in behind his eyes. He stumbled over to the dresser where a jug of water stood, slick with condensation. His hand shook as he tried to pour himself a glass of water to quench his dry, thick tongue. He threw his head back, downing the water in one big gulp, then refilled the glass as he heard the shower stop. He caught sight of himself in the mirror. He looked a mess. Hair dishevelled, sticking up all over. A course stubble shadowing his face. Deep, dark circles enshrouded bloodshot eyes. And his head, the pain was almost too much to take.

Selah left the bathroom, drying her hair as she headed to the closet in their room. She smiled at him.

"I like the stubble. Maybe you should grow a beard."

"Right now, I'll settle for getting rid of this blasted headache. I need a shower. And breakfast. Fuck that grains

306

and fruit bullshit. I need a greasy, fatty, meaty breakfast. I feel like I played poker with the devil and lost."

Selah laughed heartily. It was a sound that echoed inside his skull, though he would probably have liked it if not for possibly the single worst hangover of his life.

"Come on. Get in that shower, it may help. It may not. But you have a call to make. Get going."

Crow stood up unsteadily, knowing better than to argue. He shuffled into the bathroom and turned on the shower, running the water as cold as he could. It took his breath away with a gasp as he stepped under it.

Edison Crow sat in the small office of the hotel. The elderly couple who owned it had taken quite a shine to Selah and him, affording them little extras at meals, cutting their bill to the bare bones. He had been sitting in the office for hours, waiting for the phone to ring. Crow had called to speak with Reuben once he had feasted on the biggest plate of greasy breakfast and three steaming mugs of strong black coffee. By then, he was too late to catch him. He was slumped over the little desk, dozing. The shadows grew longer as the day grew later. The phone rang, waking him.

"Captain Crow?" A deep voice crackled down the line, the distance obvious.

"Reuben. It's time for you all to join us. Leave as soon as you can."

Acknowledgements

I started out on my journey to write this book back in November 2019. I had no idea where it was heading and whether I would reach the end of the process. But I had the seed of an idea. Some loose threads of the plot and a glimpse of a few of the characters were all I started out with. Around a year after I had started, my first draft was complete, and what a journey it's been. A journey I would never have finished without the support and encouragement I have had along the way.

To my wife Vanessa – thank you for always pushing me to sit down and write, for encouraging me and for putting up with me bouncing random ideas about all the time. Thanks also to my parents for the support and encouragement to actually put the finished work out there. Through my book reviewing, I have had the pleasure of meeting and getting to know many authors. Two of those have become good friends and have given me endless encouragement, support and unlimited advice. Without that, I would have struggled, so a massive thanks to A.K. Alliss and Richard Dee. Dean, thanks for the coffee and motivational chats that have spurred me on. And last but by no means least, a huge thank you to Jen at Fuzzy

Flamingo. Thanks for all the conversations, advice and the incredible design and editing work that helped make this book a reality!

Printed in Great Britain
by Amazon